Stanly Community College Library
141 College Drive
Albemarle, NC 28001
Phone: (704) 991-0259
www.stanly.edu

D1781795

# Running Out

a novel

## Dave Essinger

Mint Hill Books
Main Street Rag Publishing Company
Charlotte, North Carolina

Copyright © 2017 Dave Essinger
Cover art by Dave Essinger
Author photo by Alice Essinger

See more of Dave Essinger's work or contact him at
www.dave-essinger.com

Library of Congress Control Number: 2017932476

ISBN: 978-1-59948-629-1

Produced in the United States of America

Main Street Rag
PO Box 690100
Charlotte, NC 28227
**www.MainStreetRag.com**

*For June and Levin, for whom I'd go farther.*

# One

A mile, two miles below, the landscape scrolled serenely by, an irregular patchwork of conifers and bare deciduous forest where the snow showed through. Occasional lakes and rivers flashed like mirrors. Dan let the vibration of the small aircraft's engine move up his legs through his feet on the floor. His elbow buzzed where it touched the window.

"Down there on the left," the pilot called. "Last paved road in this part of Québec. Mandatory registration, to drive it. There's more moose down there than people."

Dan pulled the valve on his water bottle, drank a single swallow and snapped it closed with the palm of his hand.

"New gear?" Deb asked idly.

Dan turned his wrist, still not sure if he liked the fit of the bottle's strap over the back of his hand. "Just a race giveaway," he said. "It's not as nice as yours," he added, without thinking.

She looked away: every little thing was a reminder. Over the last year, she'd fought her way back onto the elite circuit alone, while he trained in the opposite direction, running meaningless trail races.

Her distraction now was justifiable, though, with her father's ashes in a quart-sized Ziploc bag under her seat. Dan reached to put his hand on hers. She gazed out the window, immune to consolation.

Between them, Susy slept peacefully in her carseat. Half an hour passed, the roar of the engine hypnotic, and Dan marveled at the emptiness below them. Its vastness was calming, remote and removed, when seen safely from this altitude.

"Textbook undisturbed taiga," the pilot narrated. "Bog and muskeg. Scrub pine forest. Birch, alder. Further north you go, the more it thins into tundra."

"Are you looking, now and then?" he asked Deb. "It's beautiful."

"Mm-hmm," she answered, her eyes on their daughter.

After a while, his eyes perceived a straight line in the landscape, and at first he doubted himself, thought he was habitually imposing signs of humanity where there were none.

The pilot turned and yelled back, "We'll be to your river pretty soon. I'll come in pretty low." He smirked. "The small cargo door slides. Stay buckled in."

Dan caught Deb's eye and nodded at her bag, under her seat. "It'll be time here."

She looked back at him, impatient, and he held her gaze: no, he wasn't going to do this for her. Finally she reached beneath her and withdrew the freezer bag of ashes. They looked like fine gray oatmeal, with a few calcified shards of bone. Deb nodded questioningly at Susy. Neither of them had explained to her what they were doing, or what was in the bag.

"She's sleeping," Dan murmured, and turned back to the window. "It won't even take you a minute."

They were descending, and the line below them had grown more apparent. It disappeared in rare open snowy ground, but became clearer as a paler, partly cleared stripe when it passed through dense growth. Then he saw light flashing off parallel filaments, and what looked like regular metal structures. "Are those powerlines, do you think?" he asked Deb. "What could they be powering out here?" Leaning forward, he asked the pilot the same thing. He was curious, only making conversation, really. The man turned his head, cocked an expectant ear and asked him to say it again.

And just then, past the pilot's listening profile, Dan saw a pair of geese suddenly rising. They were huge, so close he could have counted their beating wing feathers, and he flinched involuntarily just before the prolonged rattling thud that could have been one goose or both of them striking the plane.

The pilot spun around as the plane slewed sideways hard. It felt like they lost a lot of altitude fast as he cursed and fought the stick. Then, just as they leveled out, a spindly top-heavy treetop appeared out Dan's window, and the impact that immediately followed was like running over a curb in a car at fifty miles an hour. The plane lurched sickeningly. "Motherfucker FUCK!" the pilot yelled into the instrument panel. An alarm began buzzing, the engine over-revved, and behind it all rose the horrible roar of wind.

"Hold onto something," the pilot said, and Dan twisted toward the carseat, but Deb was already covering it with her body. His vision focused on her fingertips against the plastic, red under the nail and the surrounding skin white with pressure, and Susy's bright blue eyes open in orbs of surprise.

Then everything turned upside down and up and then down again, time and sound neatly disconnecting, and a splintering impact was followed by a rush of debris rattling off the fuselage. Something like a single frame of black on a filmstrip passed, and then all was bright, and motionless, and silent. And for a moment he did not think or process further what had happened and what it meant. The last sound echoing in his ears was Susy's wavering, rising cry, abruptly cut off before its peak. He lay still waiting for her second bawl, waiting through her superhuman ability to draw breath and marshal power for a true yell, remembering all the times he'd thought that she had stopped crying when incomprehensibly she'd only been still inhaling, still building up.

He'd brought his child to a plane crash. *There it is*, he thought: *I've failed as a father*. His head felt too full of blood and his joints all wrong. He understood he was upside down.

Finally, Deb drew a shuddering breath, and when he heard Susy make a small complaining noise in her throat too, his priorities reasserted themselves, reels of a slot machine snapping mechanically into position. *Out of the plane*, he thought, and *flares*, and *radio*. Upside down, it was maddeningly difficult to even find the release to his lap belt, and then he had to hook his forearm under the armrest and flex to create a little slack. As soon as the buckle let go he tumbled, barely tucking his head in time to take the fall across his shoulders.

Deb was already kneeling beside him on the plane's ceiling, pulling at the straps to Susy's seat. One more latch, and Susy fell into her mother's arms like a movie soldier shot off a parapet.

In front, the pilot was still harnessed in, surprisingly fine hair hanging down from his head. As Dan moved toward him, the man jerked his arms spastically.

"Where are we," Dan demanded. "How far is it to—" Then he saw the extent of it, the smashed disarray of the cockpit. The plane had skidded forward, upside down. The plastic of the windshield was crazed and fractured. Rocks and brown grasses and chunks of frozen mud spilled through the side windows. The instrument panel and the firewall behind had given like French doors against the bulk of the engine as the nose of the plane had crumpled.

The whole front of the pilot's shirt was sticky with blood where a lichened branch, flashed up one side with new wood, protruded from his chest just beside the sternum. A thick rivulet of blood streaked upward from the man's collar, along the jugular toward his ear.

Dan told him he was going to live, he was going to be all right. It was a lie, but he could think of nothing else to say. "There's a, a, an emergency beacon, or something, right?"

"We're flipped over," he said. "The antenna's on the—it can't—"

"A search party, then," Dan said. "They'll come for us. We'll get you to a hospital. You're going to live through this."

The pilot shook his head. "You really don't—out here, nothing's—" It sounded like he croaked the word, "Saffron," and Dan thought he was delirious, already gone. Then he said it again and Dan understood: "Sat phone." He coughed and waved weakly at his chest, tapping at what looked like a bulky regular cell phone. "Help me get."

Gingerly but quickly, Dan reached past the man's trembling hand into the mess of blood and withdrew the satellite phone from his vest pocket. Its plastic surface was slick with blood, and as Dan turned it over, sparkling shards of plastic fell into his hand. Green and gold circuitry was visible, and he held the phone dumbly.

After a second or more of silence, the pilot spoke first. "I'm so sorry," he said. "Your daughter. How old?"

Dan stiffened, registering the pity, the forgone conclusion.

Blood bubbled from the pilot's lips. *So sorry*, he mouthed again silently, shaking his head. *Fuck you*, Dan wanted to tell him, but then he understood that the man was dying, not in minutes but right now, as he watched. His anger dissolved and all he felt was relief, at being useless. The dying man's eyes searched his, and Dan remained blank, offering neither forgiveness nor accusation. Dan sifted his emotions carefully for anything he was supposed to feel, any omitted duty that would rear up as guilt later, but he truly didn't know this man. He was not responsible for his misfortune.

The pilot's chest convulsed then, and a gout of blood burst from his mouth. Dan thought it had missed him at first, but on looking closer, fine red specks of the man's last breath had delicately sprayed both of his upturned hands.

Behind him, Deb clutched Susy to her with one arm, her other hand floating palm-down over her knee, each finger flexed so straight he could see the tendons in the back of her hand. She was exhaling in the tiny fast breaths they had practiced in childbirth class. Her face was pale, her lips pressed together and bloodless. Her closed eyes twitched beneath their lids.

"We have to get out," he said and tugged once at Deb's arm. She was half-standing until the weight hit her other leg, and her face twisted in pain.

Outside, the plane had cut a ragged two hundred yard swath through the trees and undergrowth before the wings had sheared off, only one of which was visible, hanging ten feet above the ground like a toy thrown by a tornado. The cabin and fuselage had plowed a further dirty stripe through uneven snow that looked knee-deep in some places and wasn't even a ground covering in others.

The surrounding trees were all too scraggly and thin to provide real shelter. Deb held Susy in one arm and steadied herself against Dan's shoulder with the other, and they trudged back along the path of the crash to a hump of raised and relatively dry ground. Dan cast repeated wary glances back at the plane. No sounds arose but the sighs of bent underbrush, rearranging.

Susy's crying eased to a queasy whine when Deb sat down, and Dan said, "Let me see her. Let me hold her over here a minute."

Deb's elbow described small circles as she rocked Susy in a tight arc, close to her body. She said, "She's fine. Not yet."

"I just," he started calmly. "I want to check for—can you see her pupils?"

"Her pupils are just fine," Deb whispered, her own eyes closed. "She's OK." Twin spots of livid red burned under Deb's cheekbones, the rest of her face chalk pale. She stopped her rocking motion, and Susy whimpered querulously.

"What about you," Dan said. She did not answer.

They had first met over an injury, when Dan was in his first year of grad school, logging hours in the sports med clinic. When he entered her examination room, Deb jumped up. Her first question was, "I won't have to rest it, will I?" Something about her skittish gaze, along with her long limbs sheathed in smooth perceptibly twitching muscle, made him think of a deer, poised for flight, uncertain whether she'd been seen. She must have come without telling her coaches, who would have made her a direct appointment and clear-taped a giant pack of ice to the front of her leg.

"I'm not the doctor," Dan said, handing her the clipboard that asked patients to rate their pain on a scale from one to ten. "I wouldn't know about that."

"But come on," she said, leaning back on her strong leg. "You have an idea." She tilted her head at him, then said, "Dan. It's Dan, isn't it? You ran cross country, like two years ago?"

"Yeah," he admitted, blinking. He did remember her. At practices, though, doing different workouts, passing in opposite directions, there'd been few opportunities to talk. And then his own season had ended so abruptly.

"You still run with the guys," she said, "but you never finish with them."

He acknowledged this, still hoping to shrug off the subject without looking evasive.

She persisted, "Yeah, my sophomore year, it was big gossip. When you walked off the team, before Nationals. It was like, a couple guys knew the story. But no one would say." She studied him a moment. "So what happened? Why'd you quit?"

Dan stopped. "Well I didn't quit," he said. "It wasn't… like that."

"So what was it like?" She watched him, obviously waiting.

"So it's which leg?" he demanded. "Your right? Not both?"

After a second, she nodded, lifting her right leg toward him, letting the foot turn out. "I ran with shin splints all last summer," she said. "I don't care about those. If it only hurts. I'm worried about—you know." He understood that 'stress fracture' held a special superstition she dared not name. She'd be terrified of losing the rest of her season.

Dan said, "The doctor will want x-rays. But those won't show anything unless it's been weeks already."

She nodded along with him, letting him finish, then asked what he could tell her now.

He opened both palms, helpless. She persisted until he finally, after a glance out the half-open exam room door and listening the whole time for footsteps in the hall, consented to lean over her and tap gently along the length of her limb in question.

She jumped at his touch to the belly of her calf. "Your hands are cold," she said, but he hadn't thought they were, really.

And now at the crash site, they were reenacting that first pose: her bare foot raised, his fingertips along her bone. He felt gently around the swelling ugly knot in the middle of her shin, and without inflection, pronounced it a clean break through the tibia.

A latent mistrust rose in her eyes, and he recognized the calculation of diagnosis against desire, and against her own experience of what she could endure. He watched as she leaned forward and pressed weight through the broken bone, compelled to test what she already knew, her expression cycling between intense focused attention and pain.

They were amazingly lucky to be alive. He knew that. Still, for what it meant to all of their continued survival, the flash of force that had broken Deb's leg might as well have been a judgment from God himself—random, terrible, immutable.

Ten yards from the wrecked fuselage, the kerosene-stink of av-gas enveloped him. Dan breathed shallowly through his mouth and knelt to peer up into the inverted cockpit. Among the dials and cracked gauges, a radio seemed intact, but its face was unlit. Reaching past the dead pilot, hanging now with his arms above his head in an absurd hallelujah, Dan snagged the dangling headset, then pinched the radio's power dial. A single spark could immolate the entire wreck; after two heartbeats he twisted the switch.

A burst of static rose in the headphones, then vanished like a fleeting wind. He turned the radio off and then on again twice more, and got nothing but silence. Like an idiot, he barked "Hello? Hello? SOS," into the dead mic. In a burst of rage he roared, "Work, goddamn you!" and twisted the dial savagely one more time. The part came off delicately in his hand, lighter than a bird's bone.

He held the dial a second more, feeling its plastic roundness and ridiculous lack of weight as the high reek of gasoline filled his sinuses. All around him was the intermittent plinking of liquid on metal. The fumes were making his head ache. He scanned the cockpit for anything worth salvaging, maps or charts, though it had been a mess to begin with before being turned upside down and shaken. A red cross on a white tin caught his eye, and he picked up the small, entirely inadequate first aid kit. He scooped a sheaf of printed and handwritten papers from the ceiling.

A long khaki bag was jammed under the seat beside the pilot's, level with Dan's head now. He felt tent poles through the fabric and wrenched the bag loose. Behind it was a bright blue backpack, the kind a kid would wear to grade school, and when Dan tugged at it a gallon jug of water fell at him like a poorly laid booby trap. The plastic jug didn't break, and Dan gathered everything up in his arms and scuttled backwards out of the plane.

He went back to retrieve their own luggage, their heavy duffels and Susy's diaper bag, all of which had been unsecured and somehow not taken any of their heads off in the crash. Hustling all the weight made him breathe hard, and he tasted the acrid fuel-filled air on the back of his tongue.

"Do you see anywhere better for the tent?" he asked when he got back to Deb. He began assembling the collapsible poles and set everything up as quickly as he could, keeping in motion. The backpack revealed two thin thermal blankets, matches, a cheap knife, a box of nutrition bars, and odds and ends like iodine tablets and a pocket mirror. A flashlight, which he clicked on to verify a feeble beam. There was also a flare gun, which he handed to Deb. "Looks good for one shot," he said, to which she had no comment. He shook a bottle of ibuprofen, popped the cap, and held four out until Deb opened her palm.

Reviewing the campsite, he said, "It'll get cold tonight. But you and Susy should be OK."

Deb smiled humorlessly. "Me and Susy?"

Dan didn't answer, instead turning to his bag and pulling out first his shoes, then his camelback hydration pack. His hands shook less when he had something in them, and now he wanted to get his shoes laced while his fine motor skills were still there. Tiny goals, he thought, single steps.

"What are you looking for," Deb said.

Above, the sky was a ringing blue against the jagged scape of pines. "Those powerlines," he said. "I remember which way they were. I'll follow them out. And, maybe even be back yet tonight. Who knows."

"You heard what the pilot said," Deb said. "There's nothing up here. Literally nothing at all."

"Now you trust him?" Dan said.

Deb blinked, and he didn't mention the hurried stop in Matagami, the glossed-over business with the flight plan. She shook her head adamantly, though. "That's still the first thing," she said. "The first absolute rule: stay put. Wait for help."

"If someone's looking for you, sure, yes," he said. "Then you should stay put."

Deb spoke past him. "There has to be," she said, her voice taut with concentration, "there has to be a beacon, or something. There has to be."

"No," Dan said quietly. He saw the dying man's face again. "It was damaged in the crash, it wasn't transmitting. He told me so."

"When he doesn't come back," Deb said. "Someone will come looking."

"Eventually," he said. "Maybe. But when would that be? Tomorrow? The next day? Longer, before they notice and start looking?" He nodded at Susy. "How long are you willing to wait?"

Susy was flying the tip of a pine branch back and forth in the air and making swooshing noises. Was this his child, so unnaturally calm amidst chaos? He wanted to check her for shock again, and keep checking, until he found a diagnosis he could fix.

"A day," Deb proposed. "Overnight. Until tomorrow, to give a search a chance. They don't have to *find* us. The flare gun—we'll fire it, as soon as we hear a plane. Or—we could light the wreck on fire."

For a second he hated her calm reason, then he collected himself and responded. "The first day," he said. "Everyone survives the first day. It's the next twenty-four hours. Exposure sets in, food and water get low."

"All right. You know what? All right. If I can't talk any sense into you," Deb said. She tugged up at the right leg of her jeans. "If you won't stay here. The second part is still, stay together. Don't scatter." She nodded at his trail bag. "What have you got in there? Your ankle brace? Roll of tape?"

She knew he did, along with everything else he never cleaned out of it. "What for?" he asked.

"A splint?" she said. "I don't know. Something so I can walk. You're the, the sports med already."

"You can't be serious," Dan said. "You won't get half a mile."

"If you're so sure we're going out of here," she said. She was rotating her ankle and grimacing, and held her shoe in one hand.

"You'll break it worse," he said. "You won't be able to walk at all. Not to mention, ever race again. And Susy," he went on. "Carrying her would slow us down. Here, she's got water, a little food. Shelter. Sort of."

Deb glared up then, her face shaking. "I will carry her out of here on my fucking back if I have to," she said. "I will shatter my tibia into a hundred pieces." Her eyes burned. "I'll crawl. You know I will."

Her ferocity unnerved him, but Dan flattened his lips to a line. "You need to stay put," he said, "and off your feet. Don't stress the break any more than you have to. You're stable now, and I'm not worried about shock, but—" He stopped, then went on more gently. "Look, when the adrenaline wears off. It's going to hurt worse. You could feel a lot weaker." He apologized that the ibuprofen was all they had for pain. "You could pack snow around it, around the front of your shin, if you have to. It would help the swelling. But I'm more worried about you keeping warm." He felt like he was talking to himself, mumbling into the recorder he carried to clinic appointments. He looked at Deb, then the tent. "Let me help you lie down," he said. "We can at least keep your leg elevated."

"What if you die," she stated, her voice breaking. "We could—never see you again."

He looked at his hands for a whole breath, then another. If there were a hundred tender things he never knew how to say, nothing about this crisis was giving him the right words now. "You stay with Susy," he said. "I'll go. You know that maximizes her odds." He turned on his watch. The little bar on its screen inched up interminably as it acquired its satellites. Its GPS coordinates, when he reached help, would direct rescuers back exactly to here. "I'll follow the powerlines to open ground. Higher up. I'll try my phone every hour." He swallowed. "It will work."

When he held out his hand, she took it, and he pulled her up carefully and slid her arm over his shoulders. Even as he guided her the short steps toward the tent, his free hand above her hip, she only put a part of her weight on him, hopping on her good leg. The tent barely let her lie down stretched from corner to corner, and when he placed Susy's diaper bag under her heel, her foot pressed the fabric wall. "That hurt?" he asked, and she shook her head.

"I don't need so much room," she said. "We can all of us fit."

He touched two fingers to the first ray of her foot, and followed it up her metatarsal through her thin sock. "Right there, is your dorsal pedal pulse," he said. "As long as you can feel that, it means you're getting blood flow." She should rotate her ankle a bit every hour or so, he said, to keep blood clots from forming. He wanted to ask her to repeat what he'd told her; he wanted to take her hand, make her feel her own pulse, so she'd know where it was.

Susy, quieter in the back corner of the tent, watched the shadow of a pine bough blur and sharpen as it brushed the fabric outside. Dan thought of the day barely two weeks ago when Deb had left for Vancouver. It was her first major race in years, and the first night she'd spent away from home without Susy. "Just go already," he'd snapped, "please. If you don't make a big deal, Susy will be fine." He could get through dinner and bathtime and bedtime perfectly. What he'd not prepared for, what he was hoping to avoid, was explaining why Mommy was crying when she drove away. "Well you know I'm right," he'd said, when she looked at him reproachfully then. "It's just going to freak her out."

Now Susy looked on suspiciously. She was being unusually quiet and attentive, waiting to see what her parents would do. Here was the most important reason to keep calm.

"OK then," he said, on his knees on the vinyl floor beside Deb, speaking down at his hands, "I should get going."

Snow crunched under Deb's elbow as she shifted her posture, grimacing as the movement reached her leg. "I know," she said. Her acquiescence was too easy.

"I can't just, sit here," he protested. She knew, he'd told her, how it always was for him, how he got about problems he couldn't fix. It might be his central failing as a person, as a man, as a runner, as a father, but naming it did no one any good now. "There's nothing I can do for you here."

"We'll be fine," she said.

"Hm," he said once, the way he cleared his throat before lectures, then turned to Susy. "OK, sweetie," he said, reaching to brush her hair lightly with his fingertips, his thumb along her smooth cheek. "I'm going for a run now. You stay here with Mommy, and I'll be back as soon as I can. I love you, OK?"

Susy looked skeptical, but replied, "Have fun."

Outside, he made his preparations quickly. The trail bag he never emptied kept yielding useful items as if by magic: spare socks, a fistful of carbohydrate gels, a baggie of electrolyte capsules. Gloves, a knit stocking cap that was warmer than he needed right now. A headlamp with fairly fresh batteries, that he hated zipping into his pack: it felt defeatist, like giving up on rescue before dark.

He made himself take his shoes off again and apply petroleum jelly between his toes and everywhere that ever rubbed; he looped a tiny roll of duct tape through one shoulder strap as further backup against blisters. Of the eight nutrition bars from the pilot's stash, he took four: every calorie he carried increased his range. He unscrewed his hand bottle and scooped it full of wet crunchy snow from the drift beneath their pine tree. From the plastic jug, he poured about a quart of water into his camelback, leaving the rest for Deb and Susy. Finally, he changed into shorts and a moisture-wicking tech shirt. Wearing any more would make him sweat, inviting hypothermia. A breath of cold air moved against his face, and he shivered standing still.

When he ducked to reenter the tent with the remaining supplies, Deb's eyes looked rounder, the tiny muscles that narrowed them so much of the time relaxed. For a second he feared shock, even this late, or another injury he had missed. Then he realized it was a trusting look, almost dependent; anyway, without wariness. He couldn't remember the last time he'd seen her so vulnerable. "Be careful," she murmured.

He let his coat drop to the ground beside her. "Extra blanket," he said. These could be his last minutes with his wife and his daughter, and all he had for them was the coat he couldn't carry. Somewhere a pine cone dropped, and there were tiny chuckling sounds of water, snowpack busily melting beneath them. He slipped off his bottle's hand strap, and held it out too. "Easier to drink out of," he said, "than the gallon one." Deb blinked up at him, making no move to take it. His coat, both arms splayed beside her, looked like an invisible man embracing the ground. He tossed the bottle at its empty shoulders, where it landed with the softest of blows, almost inaudible.

## Two

Say there's a girl, a young woman—smart, ambitious, contemplative, in all the ways a parent hopes their kid will grow up to be. Say she's perched somewhere high up, with a view of the surrounding country. A bird blind, maybe. It's cold in the elevated blind, and no matter how the girl flexes her fingers and blows on her hands, the wet gets in, stiffening her joints and making it hard to write. What is she writing? The molecular formulae in her notebook bend toward the blunt and illegible, some of the structural diagrams clumsy in their connections, but the notes are only for her anyway, and will not need to be reread. It's in the act of writing them that she commits the principles to memory, data flowing from her fingertips and as quickly passing into obscurity.

It's an unlikely study spot, the small town metropark effectively deserted in the season of wet and mud, but that's what attracts her: it's quiet, with near zero chance of being disturbed. Below her, a mated pair of avocets patrols the strip of reedy shore, racing back and forth and poking their beaks in the sand. She's volunteered here for the Parks Service before, during migratory surveys and the annual count over her winter break from school, though there's not much action here now.

Although the avocets should be elsewhere this time of year, other than that they're unnotable, absolutely un-rare. The girl likes that they're here, ignoring the magnetic pull and turn of the seasonal light. Some facts about avocets: they roust their chicks from the nest within twenty-four hours of hatching, which could look like cold parenting, but she's seen the birds fearlessly drive hawks much larger than themselves away. The avocet will modulate the pitch of its call when attacking the larger birds, mimicking a Doppler effect to distort their rate of approach. The little bird is far and far and still far and not a threat and then *wham*.

The girl is annoyed to see a runner on her beach, the same path she came in on, though the wetland area is technically open to the public. The runner is alone, maybe in her forties, in tights and ear-warmers and a windproof shell. She doesn't stop, her pace metronomic, her eyes to the muddy strand, emitting puffs of breath that hang in the wet air behind her. As she passes, subconsciously, the girl holds her breath, hunched low in her blind.

Wheep wheep wheep, calls the female avocet below, trailing the runner territorially. Why's the little bird running headlong over the wet sand, the girl wonders, when she could as easily fly; why is she exhibiting nesting behavior so much too early in the season? But birds don't ask those kinds of questions; only people paralyze every decision with meaning, obsessively picking apart motives and events.

The penciled chemical diagrams blurring from the girl's notebook bleed things down even further. At the cellular level, life itself becomes transactional, diagrammable, even if the terminology describing it is obtuse. *One molecule oxidizes, accepting electrons from another,* she writes, *becoming, as it gains, "reduced." Another sheds electrons, and this is called "gain." An equation that describes this correctly is "balanced."*

Say there's a girl, somewhere high up. Alone, somewhere with a long perspective.

# Three

The day his father-in-law died in Windsor, Dan had been in Ohio, pacing back and forth at the front of a lecture hall and reviewing his Intro Physiology class for their final exam. He'd tried standing behind a podium, but always felt a mild panic at the stagnant seconds piling up against him. Now he ventured up the aisle, breaking the fourth wall. Maybe half the students were paying attention, and those turned their heads as he walked by, spectators at a slow and dreamy tennis match. "At least some of this," he said, "you already know. Because you've personally experienced it."

These students were mostly pre-med and health sciences majors, with a scattering of his own physical therapy advisees thrown in. Memorization, he said, would only take them so far, and any way of making the body's esoteric mysteries more relatable would be a lifesaver for those taking O-Chem in the fall. When he reached Clyde, the horse skeleton at the back of the room, he said, "The body burns through its reserves systematically and efficiently. You've all, at some point, sprinted before." He cast Ann, his grad assistant, a complicit glance, gave Clyde a tap to the femur, and turned back up the aisle.

A few athletes exchanged grim looks. A boy slouched in an aisle seat shook his hair from his eyes. "I don't run unless I'm being chased," he said proudly, and a murmur of laughter rippled over the rows.

"Fair enough," Dan said. "Long as you know what you're avoiding." He should congratulate Ann: she'd be graduating in a week, and at least two of the fairly prestigious internships for which he'd recommended her had come through. "Moving ahead. Sprints," he said, "burn ATP. Adenosine triphosphate. Great stuff, for a few seconds. Then—who's raced a slightly longer distance? Say, a mile, or a 5k?" The two track guys, bored, half-raised their hands, as did a handful of students who looked more uncertain. "OK, well, now we're talking $VO_2$ max as the limiter, or the total volume of oxygen delivery to working muscles. Anybody run farther than that, say, a 10k, or ten miles?" Half as many hands. "This slows maximum pace further, partly based on lactate threshold, or the ability to hold a steady-state pace without accumulating too much lactic acid. So, how about longer than that? Anybody go twenty miles, maybe a marathon?" A lean guy in back, TJ, raised his arm, and Dan nodded, focusing on him. "OK, great. I'm guessing after, what, 16, 18 miles—it got harder, right?"

TJ smiled and looked at his shoes. "Yeah. The um. The wall."

"The wall, exactly," Dan said. "This is when the body changes from its preferred form of energy, glycogen, over to body fat. TJ, how'd that feel? Did you notice when that switch-over happened?"

"It blew," TJ said. He rolled his eyes and shrugged, half embarrassed and half enjoying the attention. "I'm not fast or anything, to start with. And after that? It was like, working twice as hard. And going slower."

"True," Dan said. "Hard work hurts. Still, each of us in this room carries enough energy in the form of body fat to cover 300 miles, minimum." A girl in the third row curled her lip. "Oh, fat's miraculous for long-term energy storage, Lana," he said to her. "It just doesn't re-convert efficiently. Metabolizing fat devours more oxygen, more water, and eventually requires amino acids from somewhere—from your own muscle tissue, if necessary." He told the class to imagine an internal combustion engine, deprived of gasoline. It was one of his favorite metaphors. "Feed the engine vodka, or mouthwash, or paint thinner: things that will burn, but will eventually destroy the machine." The body functioned predictably, he told them, exercising its options from the most sustainable down to the least. It was a beautiful thing, really.

"Well what happens after that?" Del asked. Del looked sleepy, and had no notebook or pen. His text was closed on his desk. Del always asked exactly one question per class, as if this constituted participation.

"After what, Del?"

"What happens after marathon distance?" Del demanded. "You just keep burning body fat to go slow until that runs out, or what?"

"In theory, sure. If something else doesn't stop you—dehydration, inadequate nutrients to metabolize the bodyfat, kidney failure from muscle breakdown—you could literally cover hundreds of miles." Dan smiled placidly. "In practice, it gets complicated, but—to put it simply—the body that resists death at the cellular level the longest, can go the farthest. You know, it's all about dying slowest. But then. We're all dying right now anyway. Every minute of our lives. Aren't we, Del? Biologically?"

"What do you mean 'in practice?'" Lana interrupted, letting Del off the hook. "Hundreds of miles. Why would anyone do that?"

One of the football players chimed in. "Hey, I heard Mr. C ran for twenty-four hours one time. That true, Mr. C?"

"Where'd you hear that, Ty?"

"I heard you were a big-time track star too," Ty persisted. "Like, All-American, or some shit."

Dan blinked. "Someone's gotten their facts confused. And anyway." Here he let himself smile at Lana, almost subconsciously, angling with his eyes, prying just a little bit, teasing it out of her until he got a polite smile back. "Like Lana said: hundreds of miles. Why would anyone ever do that?"

His eyes skipped involuntarily to Ann again, which felt illicit now across the public distance of the lecture hall. He pulled up his first slide, a cartoon of the Cori Cycle, and half his front row leaned forward, pens poised.

In his office, Dan hit "Send and Receive" once and then again. His inbox held nothing new, and he had no reply for Craig, the only one of his old teammates who'd gone competitive. Craig had picked up enough international 5k wins to make a name he then milked into rabbitting on the track circuit, setting a clockwork first lap pace for the milers before discreetly peeling off the outside lane. He'd written ostensibly to congratulate Deb on her podium finish a week ago, but asked tactfully what Dan was doing too, if he had any races on his calendar or was "getting back into it at all."

Dan didn't have anything to tell him. The long slow stupidity of ultramarathons on trails held no respect in Craig's circles. From a pro perspective, Dan might as well be another jogger, beat and out of shape and lucky to fend off the college kids at his local Turkey Trot 5k every year. A national championship race for the hundred-mile trail distance would be held practically in his back yard in the coming summer, and Dan had entertained the thought of running it, but even if the biggest stars dropped out or stayed home, it wasn't like he'd win the thing. Dan wasn't sure what a victory there would prove, and he was done caring about championships, anyway. If anything, those memories seemed someone else's, those of a naïve youth, training hard for all the wrong reasons.

Now he just enjoyed the distance, without putting anything else on it. He'd hardly done a lick of speedwork in years, building instead a deep, deep mileage base, which fit his life now. He could cruise half a dozen low-key 50ks in a summer, and he loved nothing more than showing up on race morning at whatever nature preserve or metropark, plunking down twenty bucks for his entry, and then just running how he felt, for hours. As long as it took. Sometimes he did win, but it didn't matter when he didn't. And sometimes just finishing had been a transformative experience.

He'd tunneled off into these thoughts again, staring through his computer screen, when Ann tapped at his door. He must have appeared unsettled, because she hesitated in his doorway, her pretty face clouded with concern. "Those journals I borrowed," she said. "I wanted to—"

"Of course," he said. "Sure, come in."

A convergence of factors affected what happened next. For one thing, his office was oddly laid out—long, and rather narrow. The bookshelves on both walls made it tighter. When students came to see him, it worked as long as one appointment exited before the next tried to come in, but there really wasn't room for two people to pass. If he hadn't risen like a doorman as Ann slid by him, and then if she hadn't taken the two steps to leave the borrowed journals on his desk and turned to meet him as he came back, they wouldn't have been suddenly facing each other, the layer of space between them so thin it could have been a junior high dance. He hadn't stepped sideways and she hadn't sat down, for a least one second and then at least a couple more. He was aware of a clean dry scent, maybe her facial soap, and some kind of citrusy bodywash, and under that, whatever dryer sheets or fabric softener she used. It was like unexpectedly being inside a bubble with her, sounds from outside coming as if from underwater.

Joe's knock at his door didn't fully register. Joe had been on the faculty since before Dan was a student, and now he stood in Dan's door, which had never been closed but only cracked. Joe looked down at the sheaf of papers in his hand, review sheets Dan had left in the copier, and turned away.

Ann stood frozen another second, her face turned toward the door and away from him. Then he moved, shuffling back a half step until he felt the bookcase's shelf behind him, under the points of each shoulder blade. Ann nodded awkwardly at the journals she'd put on the nearest corner of his desk, then left, without saying a word. Dan's heart thudded three times hard and he felt a numbness in his face. He blinked, letting the purple subside from his vision and listening to the click of her shoes down the hall.

When he looked out, the hallway was empty. He wouldn't go after Ann; addressing or even acknowledging the awkwardness would only make it worse. Anyway, it was almost summer. He'd be back in the fall, and Ann would not, gone to Cleveland or St. Louis or Nashville for good.

He'd like to catch Joe in his office, so he could make the obligatory joke at Dan's expense, and Dan could shake his head and look embarrassed, putting this all behind them right away. Not that Joe would really think anything untoward. It was just—he'd advised Dan's thesis. And chaired the committee that hired him.

Dan glanced at the clock, too aware of the time he was wasting. He'd planned to be already running by now, and he needed to learn to leave some things unresolved, and quit obsessing over what he couldn't fix. The long summer break would blur or erase a lot, and he could still, if he hurried, get a couple road miles in; he could call Deb, tell her he'd pick up Susy from daycare on his way home. Or—it had been raining all week. His favorite route through the state park would be at its muddy best.

Dan shut his office door, reflexively holding the knob to lessen its click against the latch. He slipped off his dress shoes, peeled off one sock then the other. The nubbly industrial gray carpet felt rough, dry, and delicious to his bare feet. He pulled the window shade down and hurriedly changed into his shorts and trail shoes.

Twenty minutes later, he was tearing down a narrow trail, and thinking blessedly of absolutely nothing else. At this speed, anything less than his full attention would send him crashing to the ground. He leaned around switchbacks, gulped huge lungfuls of air and concentrated on reaching and pulling with his forefoot through every stride. Rocks and stumps forced creative, split-second choices, but he never failed to be amazed by the biomechanical miracle of his every footstrike, and the infinite adjustment of weight and balance over roots and sharp rocks and mud. On good days, he loved his body, not in any kind of vain way, but in appreciation, a gratitude for its continued faithful functioning. On the best days, he had only to make the decision and then hang on while his body carried it out, devouring each mile of trail faster than the last.

Some days, he perceived a lingering, cumulative effect, the tiny muscles that stabilized him on uneven terrain still strong, his slow-twitch fiber recruitment nearly maximized, the microscopic capillaries that ferried oxygen to his cells proliferating. At the vascular level, even his shins were visibly roped with veins after a run. After this long, he was forever tuned not to speed so much as efficiency, the glycogen streaming to his muscles supplemented with steady low-grade bodyfat burn, his muscles themselves accustomed to cellular starvation. Running still felt like his natural state, and he was most at ease in motion. His metabolism slipped into the familiar groove, all his systems settling down and just doing their jobs. Even if all the rest of the day his limbs felt twitchy and his mind conflicted, for that segment of time, all his purposes were aligned, and all his goals coincided.

The last twenty yards of trail shot him down a terrifying short hill, turning his legs over as fast as he could just to keep his feet underneath him. At the bottom, he shattered a slow stream with two spectacular splashes and let the bank on the other side absorb his momentum before he emerged in the parking lot. His soaked trail shoes slapped loudly on the pavement and threw tread-shaped nuggets of mud as he came to a stop, lungs aching, legs numb with biochemical byproducts, adrenaline crackling through his veins. He was plastered with mud from the knees down. His arms were splashed with black water, and a crosshatching of blood-dark scratches blossomed under the mud drying white onto his calves.

He was overdue, no doubt expected home an hour ago, but that was nothing new. If Deb wondered where he was off to lately, she wasn't asking. She'd been in a heavy training phase, and he wanted to give her that space; it was an understanding they'd always granted each other, even before she had attempted this jump to the elite level. He remembered the 'taper madness' of forced rest before a target race, and understood the kind of pressure she'd been under for the last month.

And then in Vancouver a week ago, the lead pack had evaporated in front of Deb with two miles to go. It was a completely unexpected chance, in what was only supposed to be a tune-up race—but who couldn't have opened up then? With a taste of the lead, and what looked like a real shot at winning, suddenly right there inhaling the exhaust from the camera van, the rest of the field fading, all except for the one African girl, achingly thin, hovering off her left shoulder? The other woman's too-visible bone structure really did made her look birdlike, fragile, and she seemed to hang at that pace effortlessly until the final four hundred meters. Then Deb had been simply outkicked, her hands clawing at the air, her shoulders bunching, form disintegrating. The camera caught her choking back tears in the finish chute. At home, Susy hadn't recognized her mother's face on live TV, but perked at a scrap of her voice before they cut away to interview the winner.

Before his heart rate settled too much, Dan restarted his watch and set out down the park blacktop that led to the main road and town. He leaned forward into a wind he hadn't felt in the forest, weighting his body against the air. Back home, he used the garden hose to powerwash his shoes and legs. Patches of mud had dried and tightened onto his skin, and he aimed the stream to chisel those away. The water started warm where the hose had lain in the sun all day, but in no time it got shockingly cold.

When he shoved open the back door, sweat immediately beaded all over his body from the close inside air. It took a moment for his eyes to adjust. "Daddy," Susy observed, and raised her arms.

"Daddy's too yucky to pick you up, sweetie," he said. "Did you have a good day?" Some days he felt like he hardly knew his daughter, that pushing her in the running stroller while she snoozed was something less than parenting.

Susy repeated, "Way too yucky," and returned to guiding a wooden car around a curve in the carpet's design.

Deb sat at the table with one hand shielding her eyes. Still in her workout gear, one trainer unlaced, she must have picked Susy up straight after her run.

"Everything OK?" he asked, and she stiffened.

"I got some news," she said.

He held his hand an inch above her shoulder. Susy contentedly swiped the car back and forth before garaging it in one of Deb's old Nikes turned on its side. Dan felt his posture leaning away, his shoulders rising.

"My brother has a new cell," Deb continued. "I didn't recognize the ID."

"Your brother." His hand hovered, even as Deb remained rigid, the muscles all down her spine tense. "What—?"

She waved in the air, dismissing, but her voice stayed tight. "My father went in the hospital last night," she said. "He died this afternoon."

"Oh," he said, touching her shoulder now. "I'm sorry." After a moment, three easy breaths that he counted, he asked when the service would be.

"I'm not going." She twitched her head once, as if a fly had lit on her hair. "I have nothing to say to anyone there, alive or dead."

"Your brother called you."

"Notification. Not invitation."

"He could have waited, in that case." Dan wondered if she could be in denial. "Maybe you're not thinking clearly," he offered. "It's not a decision you have to make this minute." Vancouver had rattled her, there was that too.

"It's decided. All right?" she said, shutting her eyes and touching both hands to her head.

A pop psychology thing, some survey Deb had pulled out of a magazine when they were dating, had rated their relationship potential "poor," as an oldest child and an only child of a single parent. In retrospect, Dan had been his father's caretaker more than he'd realized, and this made him and Deb both leaders psychologically, two personalities most comfortable in charge. They'd laughed about the survey, read into it the wishful thinking of some frustrated middle-child grad student, but it did explain the one personality trait they had most in common, had once shared—that overpowering competitive streak, the naked physical ambition so few understood. Was this another way it manifested, he wondered, in a banal compulsion to run each other's lives?

She put her hand on top of his for a moment, and let it lie lifeless then drop. "Bradley didn't say when the service was. I didn't ask." She shook her head, then looked up, past their framed wedding picture on the wall. Their wedding party had all been teammates, and now the groomsmen looked unhealthily lean and startled to him, the bridesmaids coltish and drawn.

"Do me a favor, OK?" she said. Her eyes hardened, and she tightened her lips and rolled them together once, as if spreading lipstick. "Don't answer our phone for the next few days. Just, check the caller ID first. I want it to go to voice-mail."

Although he knew it was the wrong response, he couldn't help being impatient. "You are not even being serious," he said, and when she got up and shouldered stiffly by him into the kitchen, he followed. "The man is dead. Whatever you want to feel about your family, this is not the time to act like a—"

She turned swiftly, hands on her hips. "What? Act like a what?"

Dan took a breath and rotated the corner of his jaw, hoping to look exasperated. *Childish*, he'd wanted to say, *like a child*. Susy was in the other room, but still within earshot. He lowered his tone. "Look. All I'm saying is, don't make any hasty decisions. OK? And, handle it in a way you'll want to live with later." He added, "It was unexpected. I know. You're, you're surprised now, and—"

"Surprised," she repeated. "It's not like he ever did a healthy thing in his life. By all fairness, the man should've dropped dead a decade ago."

"It's your family, all right?" he burst.

"We're out of propane," she said. "I want to grill chicken tonight. I need more lean protein." She plucked her keys from the hook by the fridge, leaned around the corner and jingled them once. "Susy? Want to go for a ride? See horses?" She said Dan could come with them, or not.

Dan swung his arm to snatch her dangled keys. "I'll drive."

Outside the college town, the landscape opened up immediately. Dan knew its flatness, through all the seasons, a dozen times over. Once a part of the Great Black Swamp, the whole area had been filled in and drained a hundred years ago. Deep ditches lined every county road, perfectly straight except for the parallel jogs on the map that were some long-dead chain surveyor's compensation for the curvature of the earth, effects of a geography so immense it could only be comprehended in segments.

Years ago, he'd pitched it to Deb as a distance runner's dream: flat as a tabletop, roads all in regular one-mile squares. The real hopefuls, the established men and women picking up subsidies and endorsement deals, were training in Mammoth Lakes or Flagstaff, and she'd had interest her senior year from that project in Michigan. Dan's postdoctoral fellowship had only been expected to keep them here a year, but then it turned tenure-track; he had proposed, and they were newly engaged. There had been so many unknowns then, uncertain and conflicting goals. Dan glanced from the road to the mirror: in back, Susy was watching the flat land slide by, kicking her feet and humming.

When he brought up her father yet again, Deb wondered aloud if he was projecting. He slammed the heels of both hands hard against the wheel. "I am not!" he said. "God damn it, will you stop coming back to that?" Dan felt the blood pounding in his palms, maybe bruises rising down near the bone, and registered the unwarranted violence of his reaction. Deb sat in unimpressed silence. In the back seat, Susy made a small perturbed noise. Soon she would be old enough to form conscious memories of them fighting.

After a moment, he went on, quieter but obstinate. "You need to accept that he's dead," he said. "As in, gone. You had chances, you knew it was coming, and now it's, it's, irrevocable."

"If you want to talk about something," Deb said lightly, "call it what it is. Is all I'm saying."

"I'm talking about your only father. And absolutely, the man had his faults," Dan said. "We all know that. But really? Was he—completely unforgivable?"

"There was the cheating on my mother," she said, and made a noncommittal motion with one shoulder. "Long-term, and multiple times. There was that." There it was again, the new level that had crept into her voice of late.

"Your mother, then," he said. "Shouldn't you go then for her? To support her?"

Deb snorted. "My mother was her own victim," she said. "She knew everything that was going on. She let it happen. I just, couldn't even—" She broke off, fired a look out the window, and turned back to him. "I have no respect for her at all."

"You didn't love either of them, then," he said. "Even before. When you were younger."

"Maybe love," she said, suddenly tired, "maybe it's like a muscle. The more you don't use it—it atrophies."

They were about to overtake a lone bicyclist, and Dan drifted left of center to pass. "I don't think it is," he said, wanting to challenge her subtext outright, but unwilling to be drawn off subject.

"C'mon," she said. "You know all about that—how the body works, I mean. Whatever doesn't get exercised." In the corner of his vision she made a scattering, vanishing gesture with her fingers in the air.

He turned fully to face her, unable to phrase what he wanted to ask: whether emotions you counted on to be permanent could be turned off, some neural pathway in the brain rerouted, if you tried. Or, worse, if you didn't concentrate on keeping them on. And if this were true, whether she thought it was a one-time switch, or ever a reversible thing. It seemed important, this one metaphor that should not be so reductively biological. "You only get one chance at this," he said, teeth gritted, staring at her.

She returned his stare and said nothing, and he considered possible meanings of what he had just said, no longer sure which he had intended.

"Is Mommy sad?" Susy asked, just before bed. Dan's hand was on her Tigger lamp, ready to turn it out. After bathtime, Deb had admitted she was at least distracted about her father, and Dan offered to read Susy's bedtime stories by himself; it surprised him when Susy accepted this. Now she fixed him with a pointed look, as if she had been waiting to get him alone. "Is she sad because Grandpa died?"

Dan withdrew his hand from the lamp. "Well of course she is, sweetie." How much, he thought, had Susy picked up, or Deb told her? "He was her daddy, you know." How much more was he going to be called on to explain here—why people died, and didn't come back? If he, her own daddy, was going to die? Or why Dan didn't have a daddy or mom? "She's sad because she'll miss him," he said quietly. "Will you miss him too?"

"OK," Susy responded, and lay down on her pillow, tugging her favorite Sleeping Beauty blanket over her shoulder.

"Want me to turn out the light now?" he asked. When she nodded, her eyes already shut, he clicked off the lamp. Sometimes a goodnight hug annoyed her, but he knelt down to press his cheek to the top of her head tonight anyway. She sighed. Her wavy dark hair, still damp, smelled like lavender shampoo and felt like a smooth cool pillow against his own face.

In bed, much later, he rested his hand on Deb's ribcage, feeling the floating of her breath, her pulse tapping under his fingertips in its impossibly slow and distant rhythm, a full second and a half passing between beats. Though she seemed asleep, he murmured anyway, "Just please." She'd been right about everything in the car, he admitted it. But after all of it with his own father. A series of mistakes that shamed him, there was no other way to put it, and watching her in the same situation now, even with every understandable reason in the world to— "Please let's just go for the service," he said. "For me then. If not you." *And Susy*, he thought, *she needs to understand it*, but he didn't say this out loud, reluctant to invoke his daughter in that way.

He imagined the oxygen barely moving through Deb's lungs, such was her stillness, but then she drew the deepest and slowest of breaths, pulling all the air in she could before letting it back out. "OK," she said. "OK. We'll go."

The next day, Dan knew he was being too solicitous, asking Deb if she was OK in the gentle voice she hated, ignoring it when she predictably snapped back. "This'll destroy my training week," she muttered, folding laundry. The pile was more than half Susy's stuff, the rest mostly socks and running shorts. Dan reached in the basket for the slacks he'd worn the day before, handing back the sports bra that came out with them.

"Aren't there still all those great trails? Back behind your parents' place?" Deb was sorting laundry into an extra pile for suitcases. "Bring trail shoes," he said. "Maybe we can both get out. One of your sisters could watch Susy. We never do that anymore."

Deb scowled into the laundry basket, holding one of Dan's mud-stained socks and searching for its mate. "Not really quality mileage."

"Recovery," Dan maintained. "Soft surface. Pine needles, all that. Best thing for you right now."

She shook her head. "We won't have the time, to make it worthwhile."

"We'll go early," he said. "Or late. I'll bring my headlamp." He bumped his hip against hers. "I might even share the water from my very stylish backpack," he said.

She did smile dimly at this. "It makes you look like a third grader."

"But a flashlight on my forehead redeems that. Right?"

"So I'll get to listen to you slosh for two hours, then be blinded every time you look at me? Tempting."

"Psychologically," Dan said. "It'll be good to get away." He would go into her closet later on, he thought. Toss a pair of her old shoes in his own bag.

She frowned again. "Can I tell you?" she said. "Honestly I just resent him, I think. For interrupting my life right now. I think that's the single only thing I feel." She went on. "I mean, you're right, I should go, I'm going. Whatever. But if not feeling anything about it makes me a bad person..." She shrugged.

Dan sighed then, and almost told her she knew she'd feel different about it later. Then he realized: she didn't know how it would get later. She wouldn't. Both of his own parents were gone, had been gone. He knew what to expect and how to expect. He had gotten proficient at the expecting.

Deb had never lost anyone, though. Even her grandparents, the ones she was close to anyway, were still alive. She'd probably thought she was prepared, but just had no frame of reference, no real experience with loss, of any kind: nothing substantial had been denied her, no possession or attribute prematurely taken. Even the races she hadn't won had been, at worst, postponements, losses only of time and not potential. As for relationships, Dan was pretty sure she'd never even been in a breakup she'd cared about. She had no idea what real loss entailed.

He didn't want to do that to her, to make her feel that. She'd just sleepwalk through, though, repress the whole thing, if everyone let her. She would fixate on her training; Dan knew how well that worked.

Before the afternoon service, they went to brunch with Deb's sisters and brother. There was a breakfast buffet that Dan circled, eyeing the foods architecturally. Two each flapjacks and waffles made a supportive, slightly concave base, allowing him to mound scrambled eggs and hash browns against each other in the center. He chose sausage patties rather than links, for stability.

Deb's sister Sarah was visibly appalled when he lowered the plate to the table, and her husband looked like his manhood might have been insulted. Deb ignored her modest plate of crepes, craning her neck to look around the restaurant every few minutes and avoid eye contact with her siblings.

No one wanted to scatter the ashes. "It'd take like a week to even drive there and back," Marie said, tapping at her iPhone.

"That's the thing," Sarah said. "It doesn't take anyone else into account. Typical of him. Isn't it."

"What's this river called? I can't find it," Marie said. "Do you think he's been there? Or did he just pick, like, the remotest possible place he could find?"

"Don't say that," Deb's brother Bradley said. He held his tailored cuff an inch above the surface of the table, his coffee mug trembling in the air. "He wouldn't just pick someplace off a map."

"That's exactly what he probably did," Deb snapped. She turned sharply away in her chair, arms folded over her chest, and an uncomfortable silence followed.

"I can fly you there," Bradley interjected. "Whoever wants to do it. I can have an itinerary in an hour." Bradley had somehow, as Dan understood it, saved a left-for-dead air-expedited courier company from bankruptcy before the ink was dry on his MBA, ascended via corporate power vacuum to CFO, and possibly not slept more than three hours a night since. "Private flights. No, you know, airport security shit."

"I'll pay to FedEx it," Sarah quipped. Her eyes flicked past Deb, but got no acknowledgment.

"And we'd get to ride along with what, Bradley," Marie said. "Teeny vials of uranium? Kidneys on ice for transplant?"

"It should be one of us," Bradley said. "I can't. But one of us should." He looked around the table, and no one met his gaze.

Marie's husband threw a commiserating look across the table that Dan was too slow to answer.

Bradley glared venomously between his sisters. "I know I'm the only one who cares," he said. "I fucking get that." A waitress passing with a plate of waffles didn't look up. His face quaking like a furious toddler's, Bradley slapped a credit card down on the table, half in a smudge of dark jam. "But I'm asking you, please."

Sarah folded her arms. Her husband looked ill.

"We'll do it," Dan said. Deb looked at him uncomprehendingly for a moment.

He never had been able to stand a silence if he had its answer, he told himself — that was it. He'd always been that way.

Outside the restaurant, he told Deb, "I'm sorry, all right? I can't help it. Sometimes I feel like, I don't know, like the complete opposite of the guy in Hamlet, you know?"

"Hamlet," Deb repeated.

"Yeah," he said, leaning forward, looking for her eyes. Since before they'd left, she kept detaching, just closing off. "You know, the play? Shakespeare? Where the guy's paralyzed by indecision, and because of him everybody ends up dead?"

"Yes," she said, blinking, as if snapping out of something. "'The guy'? In Hamlet? I'm pretty sure his name is Hamlet."

"Right," Dan said. "Him. I've got his exact opposite thing here. Sometimes it's like I can't not say anything. I'm just, just completely incapable of inaction. You know that about me. All right?"

"I want to get back to Susy," she said, searching the parking lot. Bradley was pulling his town car around, to drive them back to Marie's house and the kids.

"Well we haven't committed to anything," he said. "We can still pull the plug on this. Say it's my fault, that I have to get back or something, make me the asshole, I don't mind."

She fixed him with an almost pitying look.

"What?" he said.

She watched him for a moment more. Behind her, a black, newly-washed sedan nosed out from the rows of parked cars. "You can just say it, you know," she said softly. "Doing this means something to you."

"No," he said reflexively, then stopped. There were times when she surprised him, when she understood what drove him more than he did himself.

"It's OK," she said. "Really. We're already here. It doesn't make any difference to me."

Then Bradley was there, solicitous and grateful, opening their doors.

Bradley arranged, in less than twenty-four hours, their itinerary of successively smaller and more turbulent flights north into Québec. When the penultimate one landed at the Rouyn-Noranda Regional Airport, a copilot advised, "Ask in the office. Guy you want's in and out of here."

Dan deplaned, ducking his head and maneuvering Susy in her carseat. Their bags were waiting on the tarmac, and Deb lost no time in hefting hers and heading straight for the nearest building. Dan followed, disoriented after the day's travel, Susy's seat banging against his hip no matter how he held her. Deb disappeared into a large Quonset building with corrugated metal walls.

Entering the hangar was like plunging from wakefulness into dream, with no buffer of sleep in between. Part of it must have been the high ceiling and exposed girders, the sense of being inside an enclosed but depressurized space. There were several light aircraft in various states of disassembly or repair, but no one working on any of them. Two men in coveralls leaned against a wall by a Coke machine.

"We could turn around," Dan said. "Find our own flight back."

"We've come this far," she said. "We need to rest anyway. Susy needs to rest." Susy, cooped up in her carseat for a sizeable part of the day, fairly vibrated with pent-up energy. Deb looked between them, nodded curtly, then strode toward the mechanics. "Bonjour," he heard her call out, and then the rest of the conversation was unintelligible. She spoke animatedly though, and her tone sounded natural, even confident.

She returned and said their pilot was due in the next morning, and that they would take a taxi to a hotel.

"You speak French," Dan said.

"When in Rome," she said. "Les Québécois ne parlent pas Anglais."

"No," he said. "I mean, *you* speak French."

She looked at him, smiled. "You knew that."

He had known in theory, but now realized he had never heard her speak it comfortably, in real conversation. "I'd forgotten." He knew she'd spent long stretches of time with her grandparents in Montreal, long enough to have attended part of grade school there, but she never talked about it much, and Dan had a sense she'd been sent there to avoid some unpleasantness at home. "I never knew you kept it, I guess. You sounded good. I'm impressed."

"Thanks," she said, the delicate lines in her forehead visibly relaxing. She slipped her arm through his and leaned toward him so their shoulders were overlapping. Her foreign voice, the accent in her words, echoed in his ears. It was like discovering some huge new island that had been there all along, just off the continent of her personality that he knew.

Deb did the talking when the taxi came, and Dan sat mute holding Susy. The airport highway rounded quickly toward a fair-sized city, late afternoon sun angling off coffee shops and gas stations. As they neared the city center, a clear space opened off to the right, and it took Dan a moment to recognize the empty white expanse as a lake, still frozen and snowed over. The air temperature was balmy, not that different from home. "Where even are we?" he asked, and

Deb answered, "Québec." From her tone, he couldn't tell if she knew more than this herself.

The girl who checked them into the hotel looked up in interest when Deb gave their address in Ohio. As soon as they were in the room, Deb was changing clothes and lacing up her running shoes. "I'll be back in an hour," she said. "There's a path, around the lake."

"Be careful," he said. Dan could only think that they were a very long way from home.

The room, though, was like any budget room anywhere. A small kitchenette with microwave and fridge fit a more long-haul clientele, but the wallpaper and seascape print above the bed were no different than in any chain. The air smelled blank, deionized or disinfected or whatever they did. There were no inscrutable toiletries or fixtures, and the outlets were the kind he was used to. Dan wasn't sure what he had been expecting.

He sat Susy to play on the bed while he unpacked. A collapsible crib stood inside the door, and Dan assembled it, conscious of Susy watching him. He loved the kid, he was sure of it, but alone with her, he never knew what to do. It was like spending time with a distant relative: sure, there was that bond, but no topic of comfortable conversation, no established mode of behavior. The guilt and uncertainty just made him itchy to lace up his own shoes and disappear, tag off for an hour of his own when Deb got back, which he knew was exactly wrong. He worried there was some emotional confidence or skill as a father he lacked and didn't know how to convincingly fake; though she never voiced it, Deb seemed surprised at his ineptitude sometimes. He could only imagine how helpless his own father must have been, single parenthood thrust upon him so suddenly.

Presently Deb returned, cheeks bright from the cold air. She held a small square of cardboard, a postcard. "It's a poem," she said when he asked. Her lips moved just a little as she held it, reading.

"You have a good run?" He moved closer, to see over her shoulder. The card was in French. He asked, "What's it say?"

After a quick glance up, almost shyly, as if checking she still had his attention, she read, "'I am the space of the wind, the clock where stops…where the time you know stops."

"Huh," he said, but she went on.

"'I am immensity,'" she added, though he got the idea it carried more meaning than that.

Susy wandered into the bathroom then, trailing her fingertips along the wall, and Dan got up, walked after her, and turned on the light. As she looked around, he idly lifted a paper-wrapped bar of soap from the sink. The same brand name was repeated twice, apparently the same in French as in English.

Deb slipped by him and collected Susy in one arm, offering a juicebox. "You're thirstier than you know, hon," she said, carrying her back out. "From being on the airplanes all day."

Dan turned the bathroom light off, but stood a moment looking out from the dark into the larger room. He wanted to mention the soap, but thought it would just seem ignorant. He had the idea they could be having an adventure and weren't, or at least it could still be a more enjoyable time. He wished he'd remembered she spoke French.

In the morning, Deb was conflicted all over again about the ashes. "I do feel weird about it," she admitted. "Is—is 'insincere' a thing? Like, a way I should worry about feeling here?"

He wanted to answer quickly, with something certain, but he stopped and thought about it instead. "Maybe," he said. "Possibly. Yeah?"

"We're here," she continued. "We could have a day here. Get something to eat, let Susy hear another language. And then go back?" She looked at him hopefully.

He turned up his hands, at a loss. "You get one chance at this," he offered. It was all he knew. "Look," he said. "One more plane. And, not even landing. Fly there. Open the bag. Throw out the bag, if you want." He sat on the bed. "And that's it. I can wait here with Susy."

She frowned, displeased at the prospect of loosing the ashes herself. He imagined a propwash twisting around the fuselage, blowing ashes back in on her; he saw Deb, horrified, covered in the powder that had been her father.

"Or, we can come along," he said, aware that he was framing her choice: she could go alone, or it would be all of them.

"You don't think Susy will—?"

"We'll take her in her carseat again," Dan said. "One last plane. We'll all be together, and then it's direct flights home. She'll be fine."

This time the cab took them right onto the airport grounds, the tires bumping rhythmically over seams in the concrete. It sounded like someone repeatedly chewing and swallowing, and Dan couldn't help thinking, wasn't there a metaphor about that he'd heard once, an old myth about some kind of seeds, and Hell? It was on the tip of his tongue.

Their last pilot was a lanky, loose-limbed man, with brown hair that shaded into red through sideburns that stopped in a clean line a half-inch below his earlobes. He had a grease smudge on his cheekbone and did not step out from the shadow of his Cessna's wing.

"Salut," Deb began, and he immediately answered her in English.

"You fly for TriAx, right?" Dan asked. "You're our guy?"

The pilot looked skeptically over the three of them, Susy in Deb's arms, their bulging duffels on the tarmac, the empty carseat on Dan's elbow. Leaving any of their luggage in Windsor would have required going back to get it instead of flying directly home, and leaving Susy with either of Deb's sisters—Dan hadn't even suggested that.

"I'm sorry," Deb said, turning away, her hand on Dan's elbow.

The pilot stopped her. "No, you're right," he said with a glance at Dan. "I'm your guy." He turned and opened two double doors on the side of the aircraft. Inside were two pairs of passenger seats. "Climb in. You can tell me your deal on the way."

"See?" Dan murmured. "Everything's going to be fine."

While they were taxiing, Deb leaned forward and launched into the details: the ashes, the name of the river. "Any point on the river," she said. "And, not even landing. Just there, turn around, come back."

"It was her father's last request," Dan added, and Deb glared at him.

"My flight plan's filed. Straight-up milk run, Matagami and back."

"But you can take us there," Dan asked.

"Oh," the pilot said, "Yeah," and then "yeah," again.

"What," Deb asked, leaning forward. "Is that a problem?"

"No. No. It can be done." Then he shrugged, shook his head and smiled. "It's fine. I'll deal with it in Matagami."

It was sunstruck noon by the time they put down on a tiny airstrip surrounded by pines and spruce. "Welcome to the North," the pilot said. He grabbed a satchel, suggested they stretch their legs, and got out.

Deb would have had to edge past Susy asleep in her carseat to get out, and shook her head to Dan's questioning glance. He climbed down and shut the door softly behind him. It was maybe fifty degrees, but felt warmer in the sun, and the snow piled like cake frosting all around the runway was incongruous. From the ground, the trees in every direction were gangly, tall and thin with little balls of branches balanced at their very tops. If he squinted,

Dan could imagine them as spindly palms, and the snow as white coral sand, the whole scene a picture from some wartime outpost in the South Seas.

The pilot returned, walking fast. He looked irritated.

"Everything good?" Dan asked.

"We're fine," he answered, climbing back in the plane. "Don't worry about it. And, anyway: this way, I can take you straight back to Rouyn."

Deb nodded, pleased, and, unexpectedly, reached over to quickly squeeze his hand. Dan looked up, and she smiled at him quickly. "Thank you," she murmured, "for being here." He blinked and smiled back, nodding *of course*. He knew how hard it was for her, though, this conscious effort, when she tended usually to close off under this kind of stress. They were working on it, though, weren't they? They were.

Looking back, Dan wondered if he'd just been pleasantly distracted then, at the moment when he should have had the premonition. The pilot turning the engine over in Matagami, Dan squeezing Deb's hand back and buckling himself in, saying nothing—this was the last time he'd had any control. After this, their options had entirely vanished; he thought of the screen of an old TV when you pull its plug, the picture distorting to a white pinprick of light, twinkling once and then snapping to black.

## Four

One of Dan's earliest clear memories was of bare trees and a washed-out sky, like the one above him now. He'd been with his father, and the air smelled wet and cold. A low-flying shape had passed over them: a single Canada goose, not even honking but just giving a tight, audible gasp with each wingbeat, straining desperately forward with every reaching muscle. High Vs of geese had been flying over all day, and though the low one seemed to rocket past overhead, Dan knew it was a trick of perspective, that the lone goose never stood a chance of catching the high flocks.

The feeling it gave him then was not sad exactly, or quite empty, but compelling in its simplicity: of course the goose was being left behind, and would die; and of course there was nothing for it to do but try its hardest anyway.

Looking up now, outside the tent, he saw nothing, not a single hawk or vulture circling. And then it was the old familiar one foot in front of the other, into the woods, not looking back. Very quickly, the way before him consumed his attention. From their clearing, the forest had looked impenetrable, and it only opened for him grudgingly. Then it was eerie how quickly it swallowed him up, closing like heavy stage curtains behind him. He thought of stories and calculations, equations and stories. In his mind, the numbers and narratives unspooled like kite string on a windy day, the same themes repeating.

He imagined how it would be when he arrived, when he reached inevitable civilization. He saw himself giving the coordinates, helicopters being immediately dispatched. And then, waiting to be reunited with Deb and Susy, once sure they were safe, he would tell his story, hands wrapped around a hot coffee and cheeks full of doughnut, chewing as he talked. No one, none of the Mounties or hunters or whoever it turned out to be, would believe how much wild ground he had traversed on foot, and how quickly.

The progress he was actually making, though, was terrible. Though the snow was only a few inches deep in most places, everywhere the ground below it was shoe-sucking, semi-freezing mud, and even lifting his feet through it was heavy effort. A fifteen-minute mile pace quickly had him breathing his hardest, sweating dangerously in the chill air, and he had to back off, slow down even more. After half an hour, his GPS registered barely a mile covered. He'd exhaust himself before twenty miles of this brutal bushwhacking. The gravity of the situation washed over him again. If he'd miscalculated, if he missed the powerlines or the going never got easier or if there were really just nowhere to run to out here, a Did-Not-Finish for him in this race would mean, literally, death. For Deb and Susy too. If he hadn't realized it in a coherent, inescapable way before now, there it was: he had to do this, or they'd all die.

And he was no elite runner, really. Others could go farther, travel faster, and would be better prepared for this kind of trek, and he was not even at the peak of his own abilities. Still, he thought. He had to do it, and it was humanly possible. It could be done. People ran staged races across the Sahara, over the Himalayas. Transcontinental runs, speed records on the Appalachian Trail. The first

Western States run. Barkley. People persevered and finished those, even when they had the option of quitting.

And humans throughout history, far less prepared than Dan, had covered astonishing distances on foot. The German soldier who walked to his freedom out of a Siberian work camp. Pheidippides. The nomads who'd crossed the Bering landbridge. The Aztec couriers who ran for days on a handful of seeds. Ancient persistence hunters on the savannah, chasing antelopes to exhaustion. Like all of them, Dan had no choice of dropping out, and if there had ever been one thing he did well, covering broken ground on foot, negotiating maximally efficient output through each stage of biological breakdown—this was it. Walking would extend his range, but time was a factor: once the sun went down, the tent would be pitiful shelter.

And so he made time. He felt the familiar early exhaustion, the low-grade cell death, settling already into his legs. He focused on steps, taking it tree by tree. Every time he had a choice, he went up and toward dryer ground, and soon, if it still wasn't runnable, at least he found himself on more stable terrain. And then he was able to achieve a sort of rhythm, shouldering past one bare trunk or pine branch at a time.

Finally, after 4.3 miles if his GPS was to be believed, he began to glimpse knife-edges of light between the trees ahead of him. At first he feared it was wishful thinking, and he kept losing those slivers of open sky. He stopped, canting his head and peering as if to bend his gaze around trunks by his will. The forest was utterly quiet. Then he heard a distant barely audible chuckling of meltwater from beneath and all around him, and the single tap of one branch against another. The cold wet air was a muffling blanket, and only when it was about to drive him mad did he realize he was holding his breath; he exhaled and it roared in his ears, clouded before his face.

He started moving again, and after a few more minutes, he saw through the tangle a low bright spot. Preparing himself for a promontory or ridge that just dropped off into more impenetrable forest, trying not to get his hopes up, nevertheless he found himself crashing toward it too quickly, expending too much effort, his heart thudding in his ears over the racket of his steps.

The bright openings flickered and multiplied and he did not stop again until, shouldering through a thicket of dead brush, he reached an end to this part of the forest. Beyond a shallow dropoff, the land below him was littered with trunks and muck. His first thought was of half-drained swampland, but the scattered remaining trees were scorched, like the supports of some vast burned building, and he knew what he had reached was the aftermath of a great and uncontrolled fire.

A month ago, in line at the bank, Dan thought he heard a man on his cell phone say the words "underwater marriage." Dan's first mental picture was of a bride and groom in scuba gear, maybe doing sign language for the vows and I-dos.

The man had short black hair, crispy on the ends with gel or some kind of styling product. The ear he wasn't pressing the phone to had hair in it. He was talking about "equity, and all this investment lost, if we get out now." He paused, then continued, too casually, too loud, as if he were not in public at all. "At the same time, we've still got the payments every month. Cash we'll never see again."

It was then that Dan made the connection, understood he was talking about mortgage, not marriage, that the man's house was worth less than he owed on it. Still, though: his misinterpretation made a sense of its own. Time spent paying against a mortgage, like years put into a relationship, is supposed to build equity, and Dan wondered how many people these days, due to market or other fluctuations or lack of physical or emotional upkeep, were finding themselves upside-down, owing more on a commitment than any sane buyer would offer. And there were investments that could not be recouped or liquidated, children and innocent parties and credit ratings that one could not walk away from. Meanwhile, however dysfunctional, it was a roof over one's head, still a place to live. The analogy kept unfurling.

When he got back to campus, cars were parked in fire zones and over curbs with trunks open and flashers blinking, as students loaded suitcases and baskets of laundry. It was the Friday before the spring break, and gray lumps of snow, heavy with rock salt, sulked where they'd been plowed, but the air smelled like spring and moist dark earth. Attendance at his afternoon lecture was predictably thin, and he let them go early. With the serendipitous unscheduled half hour this left them, Ann suggested coffee.

In the café on the edge of the campus, Dan thought the server smiled a bit indulgently when she brought out their drinks, Ann's chai tea and his house blend. "Three bucks," she said with a look that was almost dreamy.

"For both?" Dan asked. "My coffee too?" He dug with his left hand for his wallet.

"Date day Fridays," she explained. "It's a new thing we're trying. Second drink free for couples."

Across the table, Ann's lips twisted with a smirk. The woman turned her back on them and walked away humming.

"She thought," Dan mumbled. He felt his cheeks flushing, which was itself awkward.

The fact that Ann was visibly blushing too didn't simplify anything. "Should we," she asked, nodding at the woman's receding back.

He said, "You know what they say, about deception. It, um. It snowballs."

Ann nodded. "The time to mention it," she said, "would have been."

"And now there's money riding on it."

"I know," she said. "Your coffee was, what, a dollar fifty? Two dollars? I think we've got to play it off now." Her eyes shone with conspiracy. "'Date Day.'"

"Dating," he said, looking up at the ceiling's exposed rafters and wiring. "Do people even still do that?" He shifted his feet beneath the table, which bumped his knees against hers.

"Hmm," she said. She lifted her chai to her lips, breathed deeply from it before drinking, and smiled. "Misunderstandings. So funny."

Dan started to tell her what he'd misheard in the bank line, got halfway into it, then stopped before the punchline. "So what are you doing over the break?" he asked instead.

Ann blinked, her expression polite but puzzled.

He apologized for his non sequitur, adding, "The rest of that story. It wouldn't have made sense."

When Dan got home, Deb was just getting back with Susy, and he followed her down the hall. "So I overheard some guy this morning," he said.

Deb was a body in motion, striding from room to room turning up the thermostat, drawing the shades in front; Susy rode her hip like a tourist looking out a bus window. "It's 60 degrees in here," Deb said. As always, arriving anywhere, she set immediately to work, adjusting the environment around her.

He told her the whole bank story, maybe because it involved a witty observation, the kind of play on words he usually never noticed. His mind rarely worked that way.

"That didn't happen," she told him. "If you want to make a point, just say it."

"It did happen," he said. "And—I'm not. What are you—?"

"There's groceries in the car," Deb said, passing him on her way to the back door with Susy. "And, never mind. Forget I said anything."

"That's not us, though. You think we're, what—underwater?"

"I don't know. It's your story. We have," she said, shouldering open the back door, "things in common, all that. Right?" Susy regarded him tranquilly.

"Look," Dan said, stepping his bare feet into his street shoes. "It can't have been—it was never—just the one big thing for you. Was it?"

They passed in the doorway, Dan heading out and Deb coming back from the open trunk with Susy still in one arm and groceries in the other, and like a choreographed move they both turned their shoulders to fit through cleanly, without bumping elbows. He collected all the remaining bags on one arm and shut the trunk behind him.

In the kitchen, Deb let Susy finally down to the floor, and began unloading juice and vegetables and bottles of barbecue sauce and salad dressing onto the counter, separating items for the refrigerator or the cabinet. Dan waited, holding his bags and feeling the gravity through his shoulder, watching Deb move. As she rotated her torso between the counter and the shelf, her arms moved like quiet automation, hands floating in both directions at once, fingertips brushing the can she wasn't looking at and lifting perfectly, passing it into her other hand, which placed it soundlessly in the cabinet without a millimeter of wasted height. "I never lied to you," he said. "Things change. It was never going to, the whole pro thing—for me anyway—"

He could see the musculature of her back and shoulders moving through her clothes; it was like watching tai chi. She said something he did not catch as he lifted his bags to the counter, the crinkling plastic drowning out all but the clipped high end of her voice.

"What?"

"I said," she said, "all right. It's fine. We've been over it, I'm not still—there's lots else between us. As much as there ever was."

He opened the first of his own bags and began unloading. Bread off the top, eggs, a head of lettuce, and the rest below that was loaded like ballast, big bags of brown rice and pasta and dry beans. "Sure," he said. "Yeah. There is. I know there is." He slapped down packs of rice like sandbags, making a low wall across the counter.

She touched his shoulder then, and he turned, not sure expecting exactly what, but she was only stopping the motion of his arm, holding him aside while she reached past to open another cabinet. He felt the pressure of her fingertips against his arm again, light but insistent. She held the cabinet door an inch open, and looked at him a moment and then past him. He knew she was impatient, just wanting to finish the putting away, but she paused and said, "You know it was never just that for me, right? Don't you?"

"I do," he said, taking a can of soup from her fingers.

The big thing, the one they'd always had in common, was built of the same stubbornness and time and solitary hard work. Few other spouses would tolerate the hours their running took away: some weeks, it equaled a part-time job. Still, their shared obsession was the most solitary of sports. None of their lonely miles prepared them in any way for other people. He wondered if they'd come together by default, mutually unfit for other relationships.

If years married equaled equity, he thought, there were dozens of ways to spend unwisely against it. Everything was a decision. Whenever he and Deb laced up and headed out the door alone, in opposite directions, he toward the park and country roads, she unerringly toward campus and the track—that was a decision. Cumulatively, those decisions added up to a kind of negligence, a lack of maintenance, as surely as not repainting the siding, or letting the lawn revert to prairie, or not lifting the carpet when the basement flooded to check for black mold.

*On* average, men are faster runners than women, over every distance, up to the threshold of glycogen depletion. Then, when fuel stores run dry after two to three hours of sustained intense effort, biological rules change. At the cellular level, starvation sets in, and continued functioning becomes predicated upon efficiency. Greater muscle mass becomes a liability, and the relative attributes of slow-twitch and fast-twitch muscle fibers become more relevant.

Slow-twitch fibers do not produce explosive power, but burn resources sparingly to generate sustained drive. Loaded with mitochondria, slow-twitch fibers predominate in effective distance runners, and create a denser, visibly darker tissue—in a chicken or turkey, these muscles make up the dark meat.

Men, due to higher testosterone levels, have more and larger fast-twitch fibers than women do, allowing for greater muscular power output—assuming ready supplies of glycogen and glucose. With limited energy for input, though, output diminishes, and powering this larger cargo costs more in resources.

Women's smaller fast-twitch fibers tend to operate closer to peak efficiency under glucose-poor conditions. They also represent less weight that must be driven, a significant advantage under starvation conditions. Post- glycogen depletion, a woman may therefore slow down less than a man would, and be able to carry on longer before succumbing to exhaustion.

Also, even the fittest female athletes carry proportionally more body fat than their male counterparts, a "dead weight" liability in shorter distances, but a fuel source under suboptimal conditions. Differences in pain tolerance, or receptivity to endorphin and the body's natural opioids, may also play a role. Whatever the reason, across broad samples of men and women at analogous levels of training and fitness, the gap in performance narrows significantly as the distance gets longer. Beyond this, studies are sparse, data inconclusive.

Beyond the forest, Dan encountered an open scrubland that could not have burned as recently as he'd first thought. The terrain was pocked with hummocks of brown dead grass, and here and there scrawny saplings, alder and ash and birch, sparked up to man-height. This paltry recovery probably represented a few years' growth in the sandy, nutrient-poor soil and short growing season.

None of the trees bore the slightest shadow of green, and he hadn't quite comprehended until now how far north they had come. Packing only for Windsor, none of them had brought winter gear. It was April. At home, the bloom was over, and nature was gearing up for full summer.

Here, a hardened scrim of snow clung to the ground and filled in shallow depressions. When his feet punched through, the icy crust gnashed his ankles. Gradually the land began to lower, and he began stepping into icemelt more often, a cold shock that wicked instantly through his shoe. As long as he kept moving, his feet would get wet but they wouldn't get cold. His trail shoes and synthetic-fiber socks would dry themselves, designed to drain water out almost as efficiently as it soaked in.

As he chugged through this half-thawed bog, his exhaled breath plumed before him. His strides kept splitting knots of low undergrowth like a comb pulled through tangled hair. His shins burned bright and cold in a thin wind, and when he looked down, they shone with a wash of clean blood, staining the tops of his socks crimson. Already his lower legs were lashed with dozens of horizontal thin cuts, none deep but all bleeding.

Cresting a small rise, he turned to survey his progress. The navigation screen on his watch showed a surprisingly straight line. Though he saw no powerlines on the horizon, his course would have to transect them.

Ahead, the land got soggier, laced with fingers of standing water, rust-brown with tannins. Keeping his line straight meant crossing the marsh, and with no clear route around, Dan started through. The acidic water made the cuts on his legs sing.

Up and down he went, over the land as it lay, crossing spits of greasy mud and sloshing again through miniature ponds and channels. Every time he put a foot into opaque water, he expected to meet resistance and firm ground quickly beneath, but on some steps he sank to mid-calf or his knee, flailing and reconfiguring his balance all the way down.

It was a strange sensation, the sustained shock of ice water around his ankles and numbness ringing into his lower extremities while, at the same time, his upper body was sweating, his heart pounding at top capacity. After ten or so yards of churning through mud, a drier route would present itself, and for maybe a minute or more he'd squish over that firmer mud, the blood just pumping down to thaw his toes before he'd have to splash back into cold water again.

Once, for just a second, he stopped and stood, stupidly, calf-deep, turning to plot direction. He felt body heat radiating off his chest and arms, cool air moving past his face like poured milk, even as his feet throbbed down below with cold. Here he was, he thought, underdressed for the long haul, half his body already soaked, prepped for motion more than survival. If he stopped moving for long, he would die.

It wasn't that Deb blamed him for the derailment of her own career and her long improbable climb back. That was more just a confluence of events, and timing. If Dan had not felt compelled to take the full-time teaching position, or it had never been offered—If he hadn't asked her to marry him when he did. If Susy had not followed quite so quickly.

If any of those events had been otherwise, their history together would not have been for Deb such a wrenching series of delays, culminating in the morning of the pregnancy test, Dan sent to buy it and just nodding and not breathing a word, and then Deb's unhidden despair that didn't make it easier. Not, first, the joy or hope or relief you saw on happy couples' faces in the easytest ads. She'd been ramping up mileage aggressively, and her bodyfat percentage had fallen into single digits, and she hadn't had a period for months anyway. They'd been sloppy about protection, worried whether they'd even be able to have children, and now what if this were a chance they would not get again?

These had not been the only conjunctions of timing. Dan had felt adrift after his father died, dropping quality workouts and openly rethinking his supposed aspirations, although he'd also blamed the increased time demanded by a full-time teaching load—which, with its medical benefits, became suddenly a necessity. So many things meant to be temporary had solidified around them that year, driven by forces beyond their control. Still, he knew Deb saw him as complicit with those forces, or complacent to them at least, all too ready to throw away everything she could no longer have. So it was never as simple as her blaming him for a particular thing. Certainly not for Susy herself.

"You're different than you were," she pointed out one morning, when she was five months pregnant. Her belly under the covers looked like she was cradling a Christmas turkey. A gray light seeped in the window.

"No I'm not," he said, still in that half-liminal space before shaking the sleep from his limbs, willing them into wakeful motion. "I'm how I've always been."

"Get back in race shape with me," she said, "after the baby's born."

"Race shape," he repeated. "What kind of race?" Every day he'd been feeling the high-mileage starvation, the inability to get enough calories, though he'd only been doing junk miles—aimless trail runs, or plodding road runs with no goal but filling time.

"You remember. Fast marathon. Your base is insane," she pointed out. By then she'd been relegated to pool running, and zero-impact elliptical sessions. "Look, you've always trained stupid anyway," she said. "So why not layer some speed work back in? And some tempo sessions, on top of what you're doing now? You know you could handle the load."

"I'm tired of those workouts," he said simply. "I quit doing them because I don't like them." He went on, "You can come back, there's no reason why not. You should absolutely try it. I know you can run an awesome marathon. Just." He paused, reconsidered, said it anyway. "At the same time? Everybody's doing marathons. There would always be, no matter what, literally dozens of guys faster than me. Hundreds."

"You don't know that. How can you know that? You don't know that you can't still, still—"

"I do know it," he said. He held his breath a beat. "I know it and I'm fine with it. I've known it for a long time now. I just—don't want to do it anymore."

She sat up, inching herself awkwardly backward on her elbows, balancing her unfamiliar bulk on the bedsprings. "OK," she said quietly. She nodded, looking at nothing, her eyes on some empty middle distance. "Huh. I've never heard you say that, I guess."

"What is it," he said, fully awake now, "about this random magical distance? Twenty-six miles, three hundred eighty five yards? Absolutely nothing begins or ends there."

"Don't blame me," she said. "It's just the only race people care about."

"Who?" he demanded petulantly. "Which people? Why do they care?"

She folded her arms over her belly. "Why don't you ask—?" she started. In profile, her jaw appeared not to move at all as she spoke. Dan didn't answer, said nothing, watched her waiting for him until finally she continued.

"Well your dad was right though. You do have a talent. And it's hard to watch you waste it." He saw her triceps tighten as she clenched her arms around herself, hugging her elbows. "You could achieve a thing. I'm not saying, world records, no, but you could—" She exhaled in frustration. "I thought we agreed. That this was important to you."

"I don't know," he said quietly. Looking directly at her now, genuinely asking, he said, "What's it like—to care so much? Can you tell me?"

She deliberately twisted the question. "I care that you're giving up on something, all right? Something that mattered to you. And was important to both of us." She waited, but he had no response for that. Presently her expression changed, from concern, through pity and disappointment, settling finally on something more closed off.

Was it quite the same as lying, Dan wondered, what he had been doing? Or as bad? Letting people believe something that, as long as he didn't examine it too closely, he'd more or less bought into himself? If he'd duped himself too, it was hardly a conscious deception.

Deb never brought up the subject directly again. Instead he watched her patience first grow brittle, then settle more substantially into skepticism, and finally ossify as disappointment.

Dan found it impossible to stay in the moment, evaluating the ground in front of him. This would have been the worst, most novice, trail runner's mistake, if there had been anything to see. Most of the rocks or bumps or decomposing parts of old tree were concealed by slush or mud or ankle-deep snow, though, and dead grasses obscured the bumps of higher ground. With every step he never knew what he was getting except by touch, when his foot met something solid.

Zátopec, the great Czech distance runner, had trained

by running in place in a washtub full of laundry, the story went. Supposedly, it provided resistance, and made bad form impossible. Who did that anymore, Dan thought, who conditioned themselves through that kind of adversity? Not the Africans, not the elite marathoners. Where would they be now, in these conditions? Picking their way slowly and carefully, taking time Dan didn't have? Halted by a broken ankle a few miles back and waiting to die of exposure, or just as useless waiting with the plane? Living and training at altitude made for great cardio, but did little for strength, and road racing only practiced the same biomechanical set of motions, over and over.

Dan's progress now was entirely unbeautiful, a flailing, stomping, splashing scramble. It was what he had practiced though, in epic mud all summer, over rocky trails covered by soft snow in winter, and through thick leaves in fall. This was core strength, this was proprioception, this was all of the tiny stabilizing muscles in his body working in concert for balance and momentum. Maybe it was too late for him to ever be graceful or purely fast again, but damn it, this, this right here—it was what he did.

A short smooth stretch of unbroken white snow opened before him, and he confidently charged over the shift line of the terrain. Mentally, he knew the snow might conceal anything, but those were the uncertainties he dealt in. Hope and conviction drove his right leg forward even as implications roiled in his half-focused mind, his attention trailing a few steps behind; all these misgivings arose even as his foot plunged deep deep down, the step already made.

## Five

Imagine the girl in the bird blind again: this is nineteen, twenty, years in the future. The girl's become a runner herself, which has surprised no one. Her legs are young, and she still has the days when it's hard not to feel full of all the impossible miles. Only a few women at the NCAA level are running faster 5ks than she is; on the other hand, if she signs on for the summer research trip, she could count on funding through much of a graduate degree, possibly even a postdoctoral year. Paths are open in her life—none chosen yet, none sealed off or passed over. She wonders if life always happens like this, ages of waiting and waiting punctuated by too many opportunities at once. The two conflicting options have arisen in the past week, and she feels overwhelmed, compelled to review the entire trajectory of her life so far before making a decision.

    The bird blind is at the far end of her running route, where she'll be left alone. Her parents will have been ambivalent almost to the point of paralysis, each for their own reasons, terrified of swaying her toward choosing either the mind or the body. The girl presumes it's because they know about both of these lives, and don't want to be blamed for any inevitable shade of regret that comes up later. Put another way, it's her father desperately resisting taking a hasty side, and her mother refusing to risk liability. Susan can understand both of these positions. She thinks often in terms of cause and effect.

She has finished diagramming molecules, and is now reviewing facts and relationships. *All known cellular life,* she writes in her notebook, *processes sugars for fuel. Sugars are partially-oxidized carbon compounds already, and oxidize completely to carbon dioxide in aerobic respiration, producing energy. Nearly all cells use the biochemical process known as glycolysis to split single molecules of glucose into two molecules of ATP and two molecules of a more oxidized carbon compound, known as pyruvate. Pyruvate is central to biosynthetic schemes, and a molecule of $CO_2$ (later exhaled) can be snapped off pyruvate to produce another molecule, acetyl-CoA. Acetyl-CoA is the foundation for energy produced in cells. Acetyl-CoA migrates to the mitochondria, where it is completely oxidized to $CO_2$ through a chemical process called The Citric Acid Cycle or Krebs Cycle. Chemicals reduced by this cycle are used in The Electron Transport Chain to generate ATP. About fifteen ATP molecules are produced from each molecule of acetyl-CoA.*

*Acetyl-CoA can be freely converted into fat and vice versa. The amount of energy produced here explains why fats are so good for energy storage. Individual fat molecules can be oxidized to make many molecules of acetyl-CoA, which can then produce ATP molecules by the hundreds. This takes time, though. Multiple molecules must be transported into and from mitochondria, and oxygen must be constantly supplied, converting one molecule of $O_2$ into two $H_2O$ molecules. The amount of oxygen in cells is a limiting factor. The upper rate limit of energy production depends on total numbers of mitochondria and the oxygen available to them.*

*Acetyl-CoA, once formed from pyruvate, cannot be converted back. While fat can synthesize in the body after ingesting sugar, sugar can never be made from fat.*

*Some reactions are irreversible.*

She wonders who she is, exactly, and what all has made her this way, reaching as far back as she can. For years, she never asked about Canada, although she remembers more than anyone suspects. She knows, for example, that her parents had their differences before then, but Canada was a turning point. Not that it fixed everything between them, what happened on that trip and its aftermath, but it was like it laid some kind of groundwork for slow change, a coming back to each other. It did; it was like that.

## Six

His leg plunged into the snowbank and kept going. And that quickly, he was hip-deep and trapped, before he could comprehend how it had happened. A mistake, he kept thinking: surely he was panicking, overreacting. He was not really stuck.

The heavy wet snow was locked around his leg. His foot had wedged between something, ice or rocks, so tightly he could not even turn his ankle.

Above, the sky was white. He felt his heart rate dropping, his core temperature beginning to decline, all his precious body heat bleeding off into space. Death in this nameless burned marsh on the tundra would not take long.

With nothing about to change itself in his favor, Dan began quickly assessing. He scanned for anything, any rock or hard place or broken stick he could use for leverage to pull himself out, but none lay within arm's reach. He tried reaching out into the snow, then combing down into it with locked fingers, but this only soaked his gloves.

Then, forcing himself to work methodically, he took off his pack and placed it before him on the snow. Like a snowshoe, he hoped it would disperse his weight over a wider area, and he pushed it downward with both splayed palms as hard as he could. It was no use. The wet snow growled and squeaked and supported much of his pressure before compacting, but his foot wouldn't budge. The exertion generated a little muscular heat that didn't last.

Trying the next thing, he curled and pointed his fingers together like a bird's beak and began digging. This was slow going, removing the snow from around his leg, and he worried his hands would be too frozen to use once he got down to the problem. He stopped once to warm the fingers of one hand in his mouth and the other under his arm.

Before he reached his knee, the problem compounded: dark ice water. He threw a few wet handfuls of snow in frustration. He shouted out loud, and instantly shut up, hating how helpless the sound made him feel.

His problem was intractable, and deeper than he could get at to work on. In a burst of anger he jammed his free leg down blindly, half expecting the devilish maw of the ice below him to trap it too. He met no resistance, though, and repeated the maneuver half a dozen times, a dozen, churning himself one-legged into an icy, slushy pit.

And then, finally, saved by something he would never know—a rock, some branch, or even just a slightly harder pocket of snow—he found a place beneath that pushed back. Tentatively, terrified of breaking or pushing through it, he placed his flat pack again on the lip of the pit he'd dug, and pushed down on it with his elbows while kicking his free leg. With a reluctant groan that sounded almost human, whatever had been holding him wrenched free. He flailed out with a swimmer's stroke, as if escaping quicksand, and hauled himself onto dirt.

His right foot was so numb for a second he was afraid he'd lost his shoe. If he had, what could he do? Fish for it hopelessly in this icy hole? Hobble half-barefoot back to the plane? Looking back down his legs, though, he still had everything: two shoes, two feet that, though they felt like someone else's, turned and flexed when he told them to.

Sobered, he thought: no more risks. By reflex, he checked his watch, expecting it to be waterlogged and useless. Miraculously, there its seconds were, still digitally spinning away. Three minutes, maybe five he'd been trapped, and he'd almost died.

He flexed one leg then the other, testing they'd still hold him, then started moving forward again. He must not squander his resources stupidly. If a mistake killed him, that would be one thing, but his responsibility was greater than that. After this he'd be back with Susy. He had to, it was ordained, the weight and pendulum swing of all the memories not yet lived was too overwhelming to be otherwise.

His task was simply to cover as much distance as it took. His whole life had been practice for this, conditioning really: teaching his body to die more slowly. His first steps were shuffling ones, until the motion pumped more warm blood through his legs and his muscles began to loosen.

In high school, Dan was never a heroic miler, and he couldn't compete as a sprinter. What he was, apparently, was a fair-enough distance guy with a preternatural kick. It took a real oddball event, a 4x1600 at a relay-exclusive novelty meet, for him to figure this out. Dan was surprised when his father named him anchor, over two senior milers of proven consistency. His father had been coaching the track team for years, and had never done anything to embarrass Dan like this before.

The day was shockingly windy, the kind of gale that tore across the back stretch of track with sustained force, unbroken for miles of flat farm landscape. Dan was a tall kid, and tended to fold forward in a headwind and fall apart; worse, the last leg put him up against a squat, aerodynamic little bastard who'd gone 4:30 the year before at State. Dan watched from the band shelter as his teammates piled on a lead he knew he'd waste.

A gelatin-legged feeling came as he ambled out to the exchange zone and his teammate tore around the final curve, fists and knees furiously pumping and spray flying from his lips in the last meters. The baton slapped into Dan's hand was a relief, a release from standing still, and as always, he exploded forward too fast, his legs pinwheeling ahead of him until he rounded the turn into the wind.

He gave up huge chunks of ground on the back straightaway, and his competitor drew up on him midway through the third windward lap. Dan hadn't had to look back, as the commotion from the stands told him everything he needed to know, wind-torn scraps of "He's catching you!" and "Kick it in, Collins, dammit!" and "You better not blow this!"

And the exhortations doubled in volume when Dan's adversary passed him with a lap to go. Dan could do nothing but hang on, his throat burning and his stride loosening, two yards, then three yards behind. Then he shamelessly ducked in to draft on the back stretch, gasping for his air in the fast guy's wake; if he let up there, the wind would tear him out of the race like a flying leaf, a crumpled bit of trash whipped across the track.

He hung on through the turn, concentrating on lifting his knees, stretching out, and not quite spiking the flashing heels in front of him. And only in the last hundred, with the gale of a wind now blessedly at his back, did he swing out a lane, negotiate the last bit of turn, and go. It was the first time of many in his racing career that his vision pixilated, just like through a bad videocamera, and then purple smudges began pulsing at the edges and center, expanding, his legs turning over twice as fast as they were built to go.

And then he was finished, finished in first, and only gulping for oxygen then did he realize he hadn't been breathing at all the last hundred yards.

On the way home, as always leaving only after all his teammates had been duly picked up and accounted for, his father said, as proud as if he'd done it himself, "You know, that was chemistry in action. Right, Danny? Your finish there?"

"OK," he said noncommittally. Did he think Dan was being too proud, letting it go to his head or something? He'd kept his mouth shut after the race, really, not bragging at all.

"Theoretically," his father elaborated, "anyone should have thirty seconds or more of anaerobic burst—where the muscles just purge and burn everything they have left, until hypoxia or lactate buildup forces a shutdown."

"OK," Dan said again. "That's good to know, I guess."

He'd restrained himself from showing outward interest, but the idea appealed to him, that all the bullshit that stupid people called "heart" or "guts" or "wanting it more" could be explained objectively. This was his first dawning fascination with the human body as machine, and what it could be cajoled to perform.

So it had started for him like any unremarkable seed, no more likely to blossom in him than in any other kid. After all, legions of gangly teenagers' lives progressed unaffected by a good race or two in high school track. Why him? Later, Dan would come to compare it to one rogue mutation, an anomaly that could lie latent for years, among the thousands of cell divisions that took place in a healthy body every day.

*When a great deal of energy is required quickly, the skeletal muscles generate it through glycolysis. Though each molecule of glucose individually supplies very little energy, the speed of the reaction pathway in the cytoplasm can increase dramatically, by up to two thousand times during strenuous physical labor. This produces pyruvate too rapidly to metabolize, so cells reduce it to lactate, which diffuses out into the blood. The liver then selectively converts that lactate back to pyruvate, from which it generates glucose through gluconeogenesis. That glucose returns to skeletal muscles through the blood. This process, in which glucose is converted to pyruvate, then to lactate, and then* back to glucose is called The Cori Cycle. The top speed of this cycle determines one's lactate threshold.

The body would ideally store its fuel as glucose, but linking these molecules in long chains produces a starch, which complexes with water, making the chains very heavy. Therefore the most chemical energy is stored as triglyceride fat. Fats can aggregate closely in droplets of triglyceride oil, without complexing with water, within adipose tissue cells. However, this energy burns far less efficiently than that of glucose.

Lactate is seen as an enemy by some athletes, as a limiter. Really, though, its production assists the muscles, shifting metabolic burden to the liver, and prolonging glucose reserves.

His senior year, Dan had multiple partial scholarship offers, and might have chosen either a bigger school with more support than Flat Marsh, or a smaller program in which he could have shone as a brighter star. His campus visit pretty much decided it, though.

At Ohio State and IU, he'd been met by an intern, given a stack of pamphlets and catalogs and passed off to Admissions for the standard tour. In Columbus, an assistant coach had repeated everything Dan already knew about their program and outlined the scholarship details reluctantly, as if Dan had been trying to haggle them; in Bloomington, his sit-down with the head coach had been a recitation of the stars who'd achieved greatness under this man's personal tutelage, culminating with the pronouncement that he could make a decent runner out of Dan too, maybe. The man's athletic dept. UnderArmor tech shirt stretched to contain his gut, and Dan would have bet he hadn't done a ten-minute mile in ten years.

At Flat Marsh, the distance coach's office was the only address he had. Coach Longabarger was sun-bronzed with bushy gray hair long enough to tie back, and wore running shorts, flip-flops and a "Pre Lives" T-shirt that might have been hand-lettered. "Come in, come in," he said, swiveling in his chair and lifting his feet off the windowsill. Cardboard moving boxes, variously half-unpacked and sealed with packing tape, were piled against one wall, behind the door, and beside the desk. He gestured Dan and his father toward two duct-taped chairs and said, "You've been laying down strong times."

The office smelled of Icy-Hot and shoes. Longabarger shrugged and said, "It's a growing team. You want to be a part of it, all my job is, is to help you get fast." He glanced at Dan's father. "Am I right?" Peering back at Dan with concern he asked, "You bring your shoes? The guys'll be going in a half hour or so. What do you wear, a ten, nine-and-a-half?"

As soon as the visit was over Dan's father burst, "You know who that was, right?"

Dan thought about it. "Who?"

"I mean, you recognized his name, right, Hal Longabarger? World-class marathoner, back when the US had fast marathoners? Somehow I hadn't connected it, I didn't think it would be him."

"Him?" Dan said. "Wait." He couldn't connect the ex-hippie in flip-flops with—well, with the fastest guy who'd had the worst luck. "That guy? Like, the best American marathoner to never win a major race, that was him?" He went on, "Burned down by Kenyans in London, and again in Berlin, destroyed by Ethiopians in Boston—totally blew up in New York in 1980-something? Him?"

"Imagine that," his father said. "The chance to run, train with, a legend." It was so like his father, seeing what he wanted to in spite of the facts. His dad straightened then and pulled a self-mocking smile that showed all his teeth on one side, none on the other. "If that's what you're looking for of course, Danny," he said, and pushed his knuckles into Dan's shoulder. It was a gesture he never used, at all, stupid and jockish. Embarrassed, Dan asked again where they'd parked the car.

That August, Dan reported for the preseason retreat in the hilly southern tip of the state, mentally prepared to be the smallest fish in a bigger pond. When the road turned to dirt he stopped, consulted his directions, and kept going, finally turning a corner onto a little circle of cabins. Two lean and sunburned guys slouched against a station wagon. The taller of them cradled a super-soaker, beads of condensation glistening on its tank. Dan killed his engine and stepped out, asking around his open door, "This the cross country camp?"

The taller one gave Dan a half nod as if in apology, raised his barrel, and blasted him in the forehead with ice-cold water.

His whole body shivered as he wiped his eyes. "Very nice," he said. "What was that, like an initiation?"

The gunman looked blank, then said, "Oh sure. Yeah. That's it. You're in, man."

"Like a gang thing then," Dan said, deadpan. "Soak in, soak out, huh?"

"Oh, he just likes squirting people, is what it is."

The tall one shifted the squirt gun to his other hand and pulled a disgusted, wronged expression. "And he," he said, jerking his thumb at his companion, "just likes making everything sound pornographic and wrong."

The other shrugged and said, "I have a gift." He stepped forward and extended his hand. "I'm Hughes," he said. "This is Lightner. Your trigger-happy pal."

"Nice to meet you," Dan mumbled, flicking water from his fingertips and shaking his hand.

Lightner flung open the wagon's tailgate and opened an Igloo cooler full of jiggling water balloons and plastic water pistols. "Might as well pick a weapon," he said. "Guess you're on our team now."

That evening, Grolewicz, a returning sophomore, explained, "Longer lets us choose our own mileage goals."

"Oh," Dan said, figuring out he meant Longabarger, the coach. "How'd he get that nickname?"

"No one knows," Hughes chimed. "He might've made it up himself."

"You've got no history yet," Lightner said speculatively to Dan. "Maybe go easy this first week. If you start strong and then fall off, he'll ride your ass all season."

The mileage loads Lightner and Hughes assigned themselves were stunning, and Dan should have had no trouble "going easy."

All that September, Dan felt like a zombie, dead and reanimated, at least from the waist down. Because the others sweated and puked and stumbled through it, though, he found a way to keep going, mile to mile or on some days minute by minute. They all wore T-shirts that said 'My Sport Is Your Sport's Punishment.' They stayed unimpressed when other athletes moaned about 800s in the heat or two-a-days, and shared a barely unspoken contempt for the pale overweight students plodding across the quad. For all the suffering there was a honing, a feeling of being strong and fast and getting faster, an idea that everyone else secretly, possibly subconsciously, wanted to be them.

Once, professing a concern that they weren't getting the full college experience, Dan convinced another freshman runner named Nate to hit a midweek party, off campus. When they got there, a boy with curly black bangs looked up from a hanging swing on the porch. "You here with someone?" he demanded.

A pretty girl elbowed his ribs and said, "Be sociable, Raymond."

Raymond shook his head and stalked off. After stabilizing herself in the now-unbalanced swing, the girl apologized and pointed a small metal pipe at Dan, a lighter flat across its bowl.

Dan only hesitated a second before taking it and, trying to look like he knew what he was doing, clicked the lighter and circled the flame over the bowl once while inhaling. Though trying to take air in through his nose, it still burned hot in his throat, and a ribbon of smoke escaped when he breathed out, suppressing a cough. He pointed the pipe at Nate until he took it.

The girl waved at the empty half of the porch swing, and Dan sat. "I'm Megan," she said. "You been here before?"

Dan shook his head. Nate gave her the pipe, stared at his hands for a moment, then stuffed them in his pockets. "We don't get out that much," Dan explained.

She nodded.

The porch was strung with white and blue Christmas lights, and in their soft glow, Dan suddenly thought the skin along Megan's neck was the smoothest thing he'd ever seen, like the inside of a seashell. He wanted to feel its texture with a fingertip. Instead, he asked if she lived here.

"I know the guys who do," she said.

There was a tattoo above her wrist bone of two flying birds, done in shades of blue. When he asked about it, she turned her head partly away and, in a gesture he found inexplicably intimate, lifted her hair to expose two sets of blue lines below her ear. It took him a second to recognize another tattoo, in simple curves, like minimalist seagulls. "Two birds," she said. "It's kind of my thing."

"Bluebirds," he repeated, knowing that wasn't quite what she had said.

"Well, birds," she said. "And, mine are blue. So far. But not all blue birds are—you know. Bluebirds."

"OK," Dan said, reminding himself to smile. He wanted her to keep talking. "Blue jays," he said.

Her smile warmed. "Right," she said. "Kingfishers. Nuthatches. The indigo bunting." She said she was studying botany.

"Not majoring in…birds?" he asked, feeling stupid. What would that be called? Zoology? Did their school even have that? She asked what program he was in, and he sighed and said, "Track." It was where he spent all his time anyway, he explained.

Megan nodded sympathetically. "Don't you like it? You could quit. If you don't like it."

He nodded, opening his mouth to reply, then saying nothing, simply conceding her point.

"Your friend's wandered off," she observed.

Dan looked thoughtfully at the space where Nate had been. "He does that," he said.

And after a while, Megan saw people she knew, and Dan didn't know what more he'd expected to happen anyway. It was a large party, maybe a hundred people.

Next morning, their workout was hellish. Dan and Nate dogged out a good four miles, alone at a pathetic pace, before the walls of his headache began to recede. "Is there a self-denial thing?" Dan asked abruptly. "To what we're doing here?"

"Depends," Nate said. "I guess. On what you think you're missing."

Dan mulled that.

"And whether," Nate added presently, "the other thing—that you imagine you're missing—is really real."

"You're saying this is real," Dan countered. "Out here. Right now."

"Right now is work," Nate said. "Sometimes I think—that that's a rare thing."

"Calories," Dan said. "Joules. Kilowatts. Energy, work. What's your point?"

"I don't know," Nate said, then, "If your work is real—I guess—what else do you need?"

"You'd make," Dan said, "an excellent monk."

"Ha."

"No really," Dan said. "A running, isolated, celibate, hermit. Monk."

"We're already," Nate observed, "all of those things."

Dan shut up then and concentrated on his headache, and on exhaling. Nate was right. They were monks: they'd taken vows, entered an order. It was a choice, and he could quit. But the dozen other men on the team had made the same choice, and theirs validated his. Maybe that was how monastic orders worked, he thought, all the others propping each other up. Maybe that was how whole religions worked.

"At least a monk," Nate said, "has purpose." He sounded defensive, as if Dan had insulted something he actually believed in.

He and Nate fell out of touch after graduation. Since then, Dan sometimes imagined him with a shaven head and beatific smile, living in some Buddhist retreat in California or Nepal, sneaking out the gate every morning at dawn, running shoes concealed in the folds of his orange robe.

Dan's first race of college cross country was an open meet on the home course, a pancake-flat mowed grass 8k that cut through the state park's woods and meadow. Dan ran unattached, with no school logos showing, "Just to preserve your options," Longabarger said.

Dan didn't mind. He and Nate lined up in the open box with the leftovers from a dozen other teams. Farther down, Longabarger paced in front of their team in its starting box, more visibly nervous than any of the men on the line stretching or retying their spikes or bouncing lightly in place. Then, just before the last call to the line, he hurried down toward Dan and Nate. "I know," he told Dan, "you're going to want to take off. But try for control, OK? Don't even think of it as a race. Feel what it's like, you know the course, you won't get boxed out." Nate got no such speech: Longabarger looked him up and down and said, "I know you'll run smart."

When the starting gun went off, everything exploded into pounding hooves and flashing spikes. Dan hurtled to the front like a surfer riding a wave, and after a half mile he tucked in behind a knot of five or six runners in the lead, knowing he was going too fast but afraid to let go.

"Dial it back, Collins!" he heard Longabarger yell at the one-mile. "Strategy, strategy!" At halfway, the lead and chase packs began to blend and Dan was relieved to see Flat Marsh's purple jerseys alongside. Longabarger's first words at three miles were for the varsity frontrunners, but as Dan tore past he called out, "Collins, you still have time!"

With a mile to go, Dan felt the last month of high volume in his legs with a pervasive ache, and every stride felt shorter and heavier than the last. The leaders were out of his sight before the finish got close, and he had no kick left anyway. He staggered in, formless and wheezing, as other schools' runners thundered by, more than he could count passing him in the last minute.

If he'd been running in team colors, after leading the first mile he wouldn't even have scored. Milling with the others through the finish, though, before he'd even gotten his breath back, he wasn't angry or even disappointed. He thought instead, this was good. This was difficult. There was a challenge, a strategy he could train up to. Next time, he thought, he would ride the brakes, not get caught up. He would save himself, spend shrewdly, and finish strong.

And for a while, for days and weeks and consecutive months all in a row, everything moved forward harmoniously. Through Regionals, and indoor then outdoor track, and over the summer, Dan ran his miles religiously, happiest during the heavy weeks and restless during the lulls, but only rarely did he feel the urge to do more—and less would have been incomprehensible to him. His times came down. He felt himself getting stronger.

Mostly his days were too full for worry, and his academics dovetailed in. Craig and Hughes and half the track squad were majoring in Physical Therapy, and Dan found the program comfortable, filled with like-minded individuals. And the pre-PT course content itself all supported his passion, explaining on a mechanical level, a chemical and biological perspective, the strange marvel of why his body worked the way it did. When he decided to stay on campus over the summer, to train on his own and knock off a couple required courses, his father wrote the checks. Dan ran and went to classes and ran some more, in satisfying and productive routine.

By the time his sophomore year began, Dan was really hitting his workouts. Running with the team again, he had trouble holding back, and pushed pace hard on intervals or tried to hang onto the faster seniors through threshold workouts. It was after one of these days that Dan sat hardly able to keep still as Longabarger paced in front of them. As much as his legs thrummed with tiredness, his one heel or the other kept tapping; it was weird, he thought, how he only felt awake anymore when he was totally drained.

"I might as well tell you," Longabarger said, with an indifferent tone implying he held little by such predictions, "we're favored to win conference this year." He smiled at the air, focusing on nothing. "Don't let that change the way you race, or practice, or tie your one shoelace before the other. Let other people talk. You run."

"Well conferences," Dan spoke up. He felt effervescent, a little goofy. "Sure, conferences. How about after that?"

Longabarger blinked at him; Dan just grinned. "How far do you want to go?"

"How far is there?" Dan said. "Nationals? Let's do that."

"OK," Longabarger said, deadpan. "What about the rest of you guys? Nationals, you in?" After a few noncommittal grunts of assent, a snicker or two and a muttered "Why not?", Longabarger nodded at Dan and said, "You meant to run there, right? Not to go watch? As a spectator?"

"Nope. No sir. Let's run it."

"We could," Lightner pronounced, then looked around as if startled, surprised he'd said this out loud. "Well I mean it," he said. "I mean why not? We're fast. We're stronger than we've ever been, every one of us in this room. We have as good a shot as anyone." He glanced around quickly, worried, searching for support; Dan nodded. "Right?"

Longabarger stayed still for so long it was as if he was frozen, or had forgotten where he was. His gaze floated over Lightner's head with a kind of bemused sadness, a detachment. Dan recalled Longabarger's old write-up in *Runners' World*, the Boston Marathon report and the one from Berlin he'd dug out of the library's microfiche catalog. "Hope Denied," the headline from the Boston recap read, and in the others, Longer was barely mentioned, an also-ran. After what must have been a full agonizing minute of silence, Dan started to wonder if the man had suffered some sort of aneurism in front of them, if he was going to creak forward slowly like a tilted statue and fall dead at their feet.

He finally spoke, only his mouth moving. "Why not," he said drily. "You ask why not. Because you're pretty fast, you ask, why not. Like just being good, being fast, even being fastest is enough to—" It took this long before his eyes awoke, and like someone startled awake, he smiled at them quickly, almost shyly. "All right. I'll tell you. You get there one race at a time. Training one day at a time. One god damn stride at a time." After a long speculative moment, as if explaining it to an imbecile, he continued, "You, all of you: run. It isn't rocket science. Train harder, equals, run faster. Harder almost every day than the day before. Harder than all the other guys on all the other teams. Then: go and run faster than them. And even then, understand you may not win. You can do all the work, and get nothing."

"Wull." Hughes spoke, and everyone looked. "We know we won't win by not doing it. So. You know."

Longabarger surveyed them all quietly for another minute, then asked, "So, really? All of you? Did you all suffer some kind of, I don't know, group heatstroke today?"

"Apparently," Dan said soberly.

"OK," Longabarger said. "Fine. I usually wait a couple weeks for this, but what the hell. All of you, think about how far you want to go—this season, next year, through your college career. Write it down." He held up one finger. "Be realistic. I'll tell you if you can't do it. But tell me what you want to do. Then," he said, and shrugged again. "I'll write you the workouts. You, do them how you want."

And the thing was, they made it, as a team, to Nationals. In a correlation that never quite computed or seemed real to Dan, as if it were some dream where all it took was willing a thing for it to happen, no single step along the path seemed individually unbelievable, but the cumulative result strained probability. They had never been a team headed by a single star, and once the season progressed to larger meets, none of the men won a race outright again. They didn't even finish in consistent order, Lightner and Hughes trading off fastest times, and then at the conference meet Dan had an unexpectedly strong day and came in twenty seconds ahead of both of them. Even their top seven runners were not a given through the regular season; Longer might decide any of the men looked tired, even at the hotel the night before the race, and give his starting spot to Wes or Latham in reserve. So while other teams' singular stars stole the spotlight and chased course records at meet after meet, Flat Marsh quietly kept packing the top twenty finishes, and racking up team wins all fall.

Over that season, the tone of Longer's speeches changed, right up to the night before Nationals. "Every one of you," he told them quietly, "has become something this season. You all know it, sure, but now I'm saying it, is all. You've each become something stronger than you were before, individually." He recited as solemnly as if reading a eulogy. "You've also become a team. A collection of individuals who weren't one before.

"There's a difference between your sport and everyone else's," he went on. "Hey. There's a fundamental personality difference between you as distance runners and just about everybody else on this planet. That difference is, you know pain really well, and even though you know how much it's going to hurt, you choose that pain, again and again every day. I mean, a football player knows, every play, he might get hit so hard he'll end up in a wheelchair. Hockey players know they're maybe not finishing the season with all their same teeth in the same places. Firefighters know they could get burned alive, soldiers expect to get shot at. But all of them, they all hope it won't happen today.

"You guys, you know what's gonna happen, and every day for the last ninety days, you chose the pain anyway. I want you to remember that tomorrow morning, when you're in total oxygen debt and your legs feel like sand and by god it just hurts—I want you to remember: Wait. I chose this. I want this. I love this.

"It's what you were working for, all of it. It's a choice you have to make every second all over again, a commitment you've got to constantly reaffirm. You're here, you each of you got here, because you know what happens any time, if even one time you take the easier choice." His pointing finger bobbed vaguely above their heads, in threat as much as benediction. "Be proud of what you've done. And the choice you're going to make tomorrow."

Overall, by National standards, their team performance was mediocre the next day, but Dan and Nate and Hughes and Lightner hit their marks and ran their best races of the season. Post-race, Longer pulled out all the positives, pointing out not just how they had all improved individually, but how many of them would be returning next year. "Some of you, it's not impossible, could make it back here individually. But if you all stay healthy, you can come back a very strong team." He fanned a handful of envelopes like a poker hand, dealt them out flat with names facing up, sailed Nate in the back his like a Frisbee. "Assuming that's what you still want to do. If it is, here's your summer homework."

The guys exchanged glances. "Why you giving us this now? What about spring? You're doing track again, right?"

He tapped the last envelope twice on his knee, then handed it to Dan without looking at him. "You don't need me. Just log these summers. Do that. Then come back and run Nationals again."

Dan searched online that night for the thirty-year-old video clip, and watched Longer's lapse in London, when he broke at the twenty-third mile. He played it half a dozen times, transfixed, watching a man at a critical moment reaching, and finding himself inadequate.

As spun as he was by Longer's resignation, Dan hardly had time to take it in before the call came about his father. And then he was transported to a whole new dimension of disorientation and confusion.

His father's method should have been foolproof, except for the lengths he had gone to to avoid endangering anyone else: yellow and black biohazard signs in every window of the car, along with detailed instructions for disposing of the car itself. If he hadn't printed "Danger, Chemical Suicide" in such large letters, the old farmer from across the road might not have looked closer, might have left the basket of corn and zucchini on the doorstep when no one answered his knock and gotten back in his truck and driven off down the lane, instead of smashing out the rear driver's side window with a rock.

"I had the cap off the cleaner bottle, Danny," he said. "I almost poured it anyway. But, you see, hydrogen sulfide works so fast. And, and it's so deadly. Just a breath or two, through the broken window, and Mr. Goodwin would have—well." He smiled. "He's been good to us, since your mother," he said.

They sat on the porch of the old farmhouse, wrapped in sweaters in separate chairs. In spite of full sun, it was December, and therefore, cold. Across the road, old pumpkins in Goodwin's field sagged like deflating balloons, holding frost to their north sides. Every October weekend,

Goodwin sold cider and tractored haywagons full of families through the field. He charged three bucks per pumpkin, or two a head for just the hayride.

"Did you clean it up already?" Dan asked. "The car? Is it—I don't know—toxic?"

"The car," his father said, his mind not registering for a moment. "Oh. Of course. It just, it'll need a new window. I never poured the chemicals. There's no other damage."

The car had been old when Dan learned to drive in it. He could imagine his father taking it in to school on Monday, a plastic bag cover flapping and thundering over the broken window.

"So had you been planning this?" Dan asked numbly, then wished he hadn't.

"That's just it, Danny," his father answered with nervous enthusiasm. "That's what was so sloppy about it, I mean it's funny to say I'm embarrassed about that, but—" He stopped and started again. "If I'd planned it, I would have done everything differently. It came over me too fast, I can't explain, I just didn't feel there was time to think it through any more, before I lost my nerve, you know. All I had on hand was, was, that sulfur spray for the apple trees, and the cleanser from the back bathroom. And, sure, hydrogen sulfide stinks, and that's not a way anyone would want to go, you might think, but it works so quickly, and the ingredients were right there, and—" He shook his head. "I'm sorry. I don't mean to put all this on you. If I said, at the time, there was just a rightness to it. That's more than I can explain. But, whatever it was that felt—necessary? That passed. It won't—I don't think I'll—don't worry, is what I'm trying to say. It wasn't an accident or a mistake. Obviously. But it won't happen again."

"So I...don't have to worry?" Dan repeated, tasting the craziness of those words like its own bitter flavor on his lips. The air was unaccountably still, and between the sun and his body heat he felt a small boundary layer of warmth accumulating around him. Whenever he moved, or even shifted his weight and allowed his chair to rock underneath him, the air pocket dispersed, and he felt cold new fingers brushing against him.

What he wanted to ask and could not find words for, was what had happened while he was gone. If he had come home for the summer, Dan thought, if he had been here, he would have sensed that kind of sea change. Instead he'd left his dad alone in the big old house, with no daily routine to occupy him over the summer break, and all kinds of thoughts Dan could only guess at rattling around and building up, unattended, inside of his head.

His father shook his head, contrite, like a chastised child. "No, no. You don't have to worry. It just…got bad, is all." He admitted it was selfish of him. "And you. You're on a really good track. You know that, right?" He smirked. "But don't get the idea I'm done working on you yet. I just…took my eye off the ball, for a minute."

"A lapse of focus," Dan said. "Huh."

The next morning at breakfast, Dan blurted, "Longer says we could go back to Nationals. Maybe do better next year."

His father looked up from his bowl of Fruit Loops and milk. He was still buying himself the name-brand cereal with the toucan on the box, when practically everything else in the house was generic or store-brand, when even the local grocery stocked the same artificially colored chemically obscene cereal by the three-pound plastic sack. "That's good, Danny," he replied. "That's good. You do that."

# Seven

The sun that had shone brightly in his eyes when he got out of the thick forest was now warming the backs of his shoulders, and still he had not sighted his powerlines. At least he had gained a shallow spine of drier, rocky ground, and he deviated from his straight course to follow it and make better speed.

It made him anxious to have covered so little distance by now. He'd lose the daylight in a matter of hours. He opened the valve to his pack, lifted the tube to his mouth, and took a quick pull of water, then another. Although this spot looked no higher than the last time he'd tried, and no manmade feature broke his horizon, he slid his arms from the straps, getting one hand tangled and cursing before pulling it free. Working too fast and fumbling the zipper, he pulled his cellphone from the pack, unsealed its Ziploc bag, and turned it on.

He then followed the same ritual as the other times he'd tried, holding the phone aloft as if an arm's height made a difference, counting under his breath to thirty and, when not even the shortest bar of reception flickered, turning to the next cardinal direction and repeating. It felt prayerlike, and if he had the idea there was anything out here to pray to, he might have tried that as well.

It seemed impossible, for anywhere to be this remote. Intellectually, he understood he might be the only living human in a hundred square miles, or even much farther, but his mind resisted that kind of enormity.

Above him, the thinnest wisps of cloud streaked the sky. One line seemed straighter than the others and, squinting, Dan recognized it as something that made him feel paradoxically even more isolated: was it a jet contrail? As he watched, the end of the trail blinked—perhaps a signal light, perhaps a metallic part of the aircraft catching the sun, miles above. The thin white line pierced like a needle into the deepening blue to the east, a turquoise that seemed to darken and rise as Dan watched. Where was that flight bound? A transcontinental, heading for LaGuardia out of SeaTac? Or even a transatlantic out of O'Hare, arcing out over Nova Scotia? He imagined passengers drowsing in window seats, legs asleep, in-flight magazines sliding down their laps. By proximity they were the closest people to him, unreachable, utterly oblivious, and transient, racing away from him down here, alone, on one spot on the surface of a huge spinning indifferent planet.

And all the time the GPS on his wrist was tracking and cataloging his exact location on that planet, accurate to within twenty feet, even better on open ground. Such precision, in perfect sync with an invisible satellite that was inaccessible and inscrutable as God. His fragile life seemed suddenly full of ridiculous one-way miracles, like the stupid GPS watch: fantastic at receiving data, but useless when it came to communication.

Dan stayed home with his father for a week. His dad was irritatingly meek and apologetic—chastened and embarrassed, Dan thought—but he seemed stable, and Dan couldn't wait to escape back to campus.

When he returned, his teammates were still indignant over Longer's departure. "Abandonment," Craig went as far as to call it, three miles out on the covered bridge route. "I mean, was I wrong, was there not a sense of commitment? Like he didn't use that word and expect it out of us pretty much daily?" The emotion seemed so trivial, Dan had no response.

"He's right, though," Nate pointed out serenely. Dan felt a vague desire to break the rhythm of his stride and straighten his arm into Nate's ear. "It's a trajectory. We don't need him to complete it."

Longabarger had told none of them any more than Dan had heard. His phone went unanswered, and e-mail bounced back undelivered. His office had been cleared out, and if administration or the athletic director's office knew anything more, they weren't saying. One rumor had it that he'd returned the envelope with his contract extension unopened. "You don't think he was sick, do you?" it was speculated. "Like, dying or something?" Or, "a family thing." Maybe it was legal troubles, gambling debts, some secret scandal or addiction.

Dan pushed pace and faked being too out of breath for conversation. He'd seen people choke before, fail to execute when it counted. All the time, in races, stronger runners who should have left him behind had lost their form and fallen off pace, and Dan blew by them without analysis. He saw no point in it. When the gazelle falters, the lion doesn't ask existential questions.

His mind replayed the clip of Longer disintegrating three decades ago, before mile twenty-four in the marathon. He had simply made a desperate gamble that failed, pushing too soon, urging the cooler rest of the lead pack to a pace he could not himself sustain. The video captured the look on his face as he first realized what he had done, then felt his mistake unfold, and finally, Dan imagined, consciously gave up. It was a stricken look, but also a tragic acceptance, a drowning man no longer fighting for air. In that instance, Longer had miscalculated, but in the larger picture Dan read a repeating character flaw, a congenital weakness of will.

This confirmed something for Dan. Weakness, settling for second, was pervasive. Giving up once could consume your whole life, if you let it. Any seed of failure, once sown, would bloom ferociously.

Longer's replacement, as it turned out, was a proponent of "structure" when it came to training. Some of the team members adjusted to this philosophy more readily than others. Nate, for example, pacifically coasted through every workout, and seemed just as happy to have his mileage assigned each day for the coming month. Dan especially chafed under the rigid and prescribed training plans, and though he never intended it as organized insurrection, couldn't help complaining. Hughes and Craig usually chimed in bitching as well, and though Lightner kept silent, Dan always imagined he was on their side.

The new coach, Parkins, ran them all in a disorganized series of distances through the indoor track season and outdoor as well, and Dan endured it, keeping the fall cross country season in mind. Then over the summer, unsupervised, he threw out Parkins' plans and ran Longer's, which incorporated far more trails. Left to his own interpretation there, too, Dan skipped most of the groomed straightaways of their school's course in favor of *trail* trails, as rocky and rooty as he could find them, with downed logs, slippery mud, and spiderwebs parting across his face and sticking to his forearms. Frequently he'd find himself no longer on a trail at all, but a quarter mile down a dry streambed or deertrack that led nowhere.

When practices resumed in August, Parkins' micromanaged workouts were immediately oppressive to Dan, and the others felt restless as well. Dan felt exerted and drained to little effect, and though they all began clocking decent times as the season took shape, none of them were racing to their potential.

One day, two weeks out from Regionals, their route took them temptingly past the park. As they approached his favorite summer trailhead, Dan found himself pacing to the front of the pack. Then he called out, "Bonus mile!" He pivoted toward the embankment and sprang off the road and onto the trail, blazing his best pace for a good minute before looking back.

He pulled up around the first curve, just out of sight, until he heard at least some of the others following him. When Hughes appeared, Dan waved and took off. The single-track was too narrow for running side by side, and unless he let them pass, no one would see him smiling. Overjoyed to hear the hoofbeat and heavy breathing of the whole team following, Dan led out as hard as he could, lungs burning.

When the path widened over a dry, rocky streambed, Dan almost boiled over in mirth to hear Lightner coming up behind: "'Scuse me…thanks…Can I get by here? On your left." This was exactly the kind of thing for which Lightner had no patience at all, and it overjoyed Dan to have made the senior commit. Lightner would pour on all the speed he had now to overtake Dan and Hughes, rolling up the narrow path behind them struggling not to sound out of breath at all.

Dan pushed just a little bit harder, his feet finding their own way over rocks and roots he knew almost by name. "If you want to know why this is stupid," Lightner spoke, still a few yards back, far enough Dan could pretend not to hear. "I mean, sure, we can handle it, without getting hurt. But the kids behind us—just out of Boy Scout camp—"

Dan stretched, pulling himself forward. If he hit this last section fast enough, he could take the short series of five small logs that lay across the trail exactly in stride. It was how he imagined a star hurdler must feel, hitting his marks in perfect sync.

Then he heard a missed step behind him, a ripple off beat in the cadence. A second later came a sharp cry and a curse.

Lightner sat in the middle of the trail, rocking from side to side. His forearm looked like it had one too many joints. Hughes hovered by his side, half-kneeling with one knee not quite touching the dirt. His face was frozen, like he wanted to help but was afraid to touch anything.

Then Nate was there too, and Dan heard the rest of the team. In a matter of seconds, they would all be clustered around, leaning in to see, stumbling and murmuring. Dan felt suffocated. "Can you walk?" he demanded of Lightner, "Can you stand up? We're almost to the road. If you can walk out that far."

Lightner squinted at his bent arm, like the pain hadn't hit yet and he couldn't make sense of what he was looking at. It did seem like an illusion at first glance, like the party tricks that make your thumb look detachable, or the way you can wrap your arms around your own back so it looks from behind like you're making out with someone. Though the skin was not broken, it stretched tent-like, plum-colored and pulsing, where Lightner's snapped humerus cantilevered out.

He could walk, though, and between Dan and Hughes and another of the men who had had some kind of training in CPR or emergency first aid or something, Dan didn't catch all of what he said, they kept him walking to the flat gravel road.

Nate stood poised, comic-book hero ready, to dash off for help. "Should we call an ambulance?" he asked. "I mean, and tell them to come here, or what?"

It took Dan a moment to realize they were looking at him. "My car," he said. "It's the brown—you know which one. It's in the stadium lot, it's the closest thing. I left my keys on top of the tire, front driver's side. Just, go get my car." Nate looked uncertain, so Dan repeated, "Get my car. And bring it back here. We'll drive to the emergency room."

When still no one moved, Lightner straightened and scanned them all with a look of unmasked, incredulous contempt. "Will someone just go somewhere already?"

And Nate wheeled and was gone, the white soles of his shoes flashing.

Dan remembered later, as they waited and shuffled Lightner in a small circle in the gravel, he and Hughes at opposite shoulders like guards escorting a prisoner, noticing a scrim of dried leaves caught under roadside brush, and smelling a tinge of woodsmoke on the air, and for just a minute not remembering quite what season it was, surprised to find fall upon him already. Somehow the days and weeks had led already to October. The sudden periods of coolness, when everyone felt suddenly faster and split times started to plummet, and the trails grew dry and packed hard and covered with a shifting carpet of leaves that hid the rocks and roots beneath—those were nearly here.

When Nate pulled up in Dan's brown Toyota minutes later, even though it was what he had asked, Dan felt a petty ire at how calmly he stopped before them, without a squeal of brakes or spray of gravel. As if in compensation, Dan found himself moving too fast, making jittery mistakes. Buckling Lightner into his passenger seat, his hands shook, and then behind the wheel, he floored the gas once before remembering to shift into drive.

"Sorry," he mumbled, and attempted to cast his passenger a reassuring glance. "I know it hurts. I'll get you there as fast as I can."

"Actually," Lightner said, "if you can believe it, it's really not so bad. Yet." He stared at his arm, fascinated, unable to look away.

"You know," Dan said. They were speeding down the straight country road now, the forest already a low fringe in the rear-view's horizon. The outline of the stadium and, to its left, the spire of the campus belltower rose slowly ahead, like stately ships across a calm sea. "You know, if the details, of how this happened exactly, don't all get told. That we were out on that trail, and it was my idea. I don't know, who needs to know that. Is all. You know?"

Lightner shook his head in exasperation. "Sure, yeah. Say I just what? Slipped off the pavement? You like that? Because, I am that believably clumsy."

"You were right, OK? I mean, entirely right. I, I, shouldn't be, I don't know, shaking shit up myself, and certainly not, not, dragging anyone else with me, it's just, I just—"

"Relax, OK?" Lightner cut him off. "Look, I won't 'rat you out,' OK?" He paused. "Anyway, it's not me you need to worry about. Is it?"

"What?"

"I mean. If you're all, getting a story straight. Don't you think, the other guys, the freshman merit badge crew, who didn't see a thing that happened from the back, but were just following along when we diverted the whole train into deep dark forest? Who are probably just getting back in from workout—aren't they the ones you should be debriefing here?"

Dan pondered this. After a moment, Lightner hissed sharply, a sudden intake of breath. "Are you all right?" Dan asked.

"It's starting to hurt more." His eyes were slits.

"Is there anything I can do?" Dan could see the seatbelt pulling against his arm, and reached to loosen it.

Lightner looked up then, and said, "You could keep your eyes on the fucking road!"

Exactly as he said this, Dan's front tire bumped roughly off the road on the left. He overcorrected, causing the car to neatly switch fields, skip completely over the road, and swerve into the ditch on the right. Now the wheel wrenched itself from Dan's hand, and when he twisted it back, it responded too smoothly, steering nothing but air: the car continued on its path, the oblique-angled front wheels plowing through weeds and loose gravel that pinged against the undercarriage. Touching the gas pedal made the tachometer surge and stirred a whoosh of debris below, but did nothing to change their direction. The car glided as if on rails, listing more and more to the right. He held his foot over the gas, waiting to feel any bit of traction take.

For just a moment, Lightner stared at him in disbelief. The vehicle hung, balanced; Dan saw the tendons in his good arm as he gripped the seat. It occurred to Dan in a detached way that he could straighten the wheel and throw the car in reverse.

Then something gave, a resigned groan rose from the suspension, and the passenger side of the car dropped. A loose pen skittered across the dash, and they were no longer balanced but sliding.

Even in its acceleration, the slide down seemed to last gracefully forever, like a leaf through the air. The collision, the crumpling metal, when it came, was almost delicate.

Lightner held his arm like the body of some broken dead bird. For a long moment, he said nothing. Then he laughed, a braying laughter, shaking his head at the stupidity of it. Dan saw tears squeeze from the corners of his eyes, but still he laughed, shaking his head and cradling his bad arm in his good one, and laughing and laughing.

So many times, over all the years since, Dan wondered when he'd crash his own life again. It seemed a thing he might do just because he could, the only power he had. Otherwise, he was a dumb body in a trajectory, a bullet already fired. An electron in its orbit. There was something of a manly tradition to this fatalism: chosen or not, it was the path taken by all the fathers he'd known.

The next day, when Parkins said, "This shakes up the roster for Regionals," Dan blinked. It was just Lightner's arm, and Regionals weren't for two weeks, and it had even been pronounced a relatively simple fracture in the emergency room, despite its gruesome look, and the prognosis was optimistic—surely Lightner would be able to race.

"I've put a lot of thought into this," Parkins went on, watching his hands as if he held something important in them. They were empty as far as Dan could see. "You're going to have to trust me, to make a long term call." He nodded to Lightner, sullen in his plastic cast, watching the floor. "I'll leave it up to you. Do what you can this week. If the arm's not a problem, and you think you can race, you'll come with us."

Lightner nodded, as if this were not news, and he and Parkins had already discussed the matter.

"Collins," Parkins said then, only now looking up, right at him, with a look Dan understood to communicate he got no joy out of what he was about to pronounce. "Collins. You're staying home."

"But I," Dan heard himself protest, incredulous. "If I don't run Regionals." No Regional finish meant no Nationals, with the team or alone. "You can't," he blurted. But Parkins could. And he had.

"Are there any questions?" Parkins asked gently. "I want to know now if there are." He looked around the rest of them, avoiding Dan. Nate's expression was drawn in, pensive, and Hughes, visibly agitated, opened his mouth, wet his lips, then stayed silent. Lightner stayed blank. "OK then," Parkins said. "Easy day today, guys. Keep it under control out there."

Dan stood as the rest filed out, but he didn't follow. After the room emptied, Parkins recited some bullshit about still having next year, and needing to know what to expect out of every runner at every start, and teams needing to trust each other, that Dan let roll over him and all run together.

He nodded once and walked out. The guys, he knew, had taken the short west loop; he started jogging east, picking up pace fast, pulling short, fierce breaths and dropping five-minute miles into the dimming sky with the sunset at his back. Ten miles later, counting by the country roads, he wanted water and his legs ached, and he did turn back, but held the hammer down on pace all the way back to his apartment.

Standing in the shower, his throat burned and his hamstrings rang with dull pain. His calves twitched visibly, threatening to charley horse when he flexed them the least bit, but his only clear thought was not knowing why he had stopped. He felt irrationally disgusted with himself for not just burning pace east all night.

He didn't go to practice the next day, and by the end of the week, when the others departed for Regionals, he knew he was never going back at all, for cross the next fall or winter track or spring. His scholarship could go to hell, he thought: he had a 3.97, and his advisor needed an assistant anyway. Work-study and departmental aid would pick up a lot of slack.

He kept in touch with the team members, and followed their performances. No one mentioned to him their disappointment at Nationals. After final exams, as the college town emptied out and the first real snow dampened and insulated everything, he started meeting Hughes and Nate and a couple of the others for runs again. Some days it was almost like before.

"A runner can go two directions from here, you know," Nate said one afternoon, apropos of nothing, as they changed out of their clammy gear. The weather had turned from sunny to snow to sleet while they'd been out. Nate peeled off one cold sock and slapped it on the cement floor.

"Two directions from where?" Dan asked.

They were in the public section of the facility, the larger locker room for students and everyone. Four days before

Christmas, the field house was staffed by a skeleton crew, the indoor track silent, and all the treadmills and elliptical machines on the glassed cardio deck above it were still. "Well, from where you are now," Nate said. "After college racing. I mean—you're done, right? You're not coming back to the team. After this."

"I've been wondering," Dan admitted, "if I've done what I can do at this distance. You know?"

Nate nodded, not sympathetically, just acknowledging.

"But yeah," Dan said. "So what does that leave? Is the question."

"Well. There's going farther. Right? Moving up. Half, or full marathon. Or, theoretically, there's the other—"

Dan cut him off, barking a manufactured laugh that echoed off the cold metal and tile around them. "A sprinter, you know I'm not," he said. "Track racing can entirely go and fuck itself." He added, "With all due respect."

Nate smiled calmly, and Dan wondered where he was getting this older and wiser routine, how he imagined himself to have seen so much more, or be such a veteran. "I meant," he said, "no one ever gets faster. After a point. Or jumps down in distance. Guys either move up, to extend their careers—or quit altogether. To, I guess, dominate local 5ks. Be a civilian."

Dan was quiet. He had never thought about running competitively beyond college. He'd always viewed the elites, those who raced professionally and for whom training was their only job, as part of a fairy-tale universe, a reality removed. It felt irresponsible, partly, like something society had no room for. And when he knew so many people were struggling and working terrible jobs just to stay in school, Dan had even been embarrassed about his own scholarship—money, practically, they gave him to play. Was it possible the world would really keep paying him to do the same thing, after graduation, as a grown-up? And now that Nate had said it out loud, he was waylaid by the choice: go pro or go home. "I guess Longer'd know about that," Dan said. "I mean. How to make it happen. Huh?"

Nate just gave the slightest of shrugs, the patronizing way Dan imagined a psychiatrist might, answering his question with another question.

"Huh," Dan said. The long-sleeve tech shirt that had been just right on their run stuck cold to his skin now, mostly in front where the sleet had blown into them. He fought one arm out of the shirt and then the other, then reached through and pulled it over his head, a creature sliding out of its old slick skin. Flinging the shirt from his fingers, the wet fabric hit the bench beside him with a startling slap, and stuck. A second later, a little embarrassed at the unintentional drama of his gesture, Dan picked up the shirt, walked to the shower drain, and wrung it out. Then he shook out a plastic grocery sack, wadded the tech in it, and threw it in the bottom of his gym bag to take home.

# Eight

*Hypoxia, most simply, is a radical depletion of oxygen in the blood. In extreme physical exertion, the skeletal muscles desperately demand oxygen; they cannot convert pyruvate by glycolysis into $CO_2$ for energy without it. The problem is that the greedy muscles aren't the only system drawing on a finite supply of blood oxygen. The liver, for example, needs it to convert body fat into ATP.*

Susan is comfortable with the science; it's a thing she understands. What makes animals move, and people, the practical and mechanical—the parts that can be quantified. It's a trait she comes by honestly, as they say, inheriting it along with others: like, a certain stubbornness. Or a devotion to particular ideas, refusing to let go of a thing long past its rational best-by date. And possibly, clinical depression.

She's been accused of a fixation on tragedy, a relentless search for causation: some event or fixed star to blame it all on. A need to manufacture conflict, or a hardship to have lived through. The person who accused her of this is no longer in the picture, because (as he's said) what relationship wouldn't collapse under that kind of pressure and scrutiny?

*The brain needs constant oxygen and glucose to survive. When the brain runs low on oxygen, it overrules all other systems. It shuts down the whole show, and you hit the ground. Unconscious, your muscles relax, and you breathe deeply. This switch flips instantly when oxygen stops reaching the brain.*

*The effects of prolonged, less drastic, oxygen deprivation are not as clear. Many neurological systems are affected, but data on precisely how and when are less conclusive. One hypothesis equates the oxygen-starved brain to the proverbial frog in a pot of gradually heated water, oblivious until the pot's boiling and the frog's half-cooked. Another model posits mild, increasing perturbations to the brain's perceptions, throwing flashes of interference and drifting toward static.*

Like a radio station fading out of range, Susan imagines.

# Nine

The spine of drier raised ground did not last forever, and soon Dan's path had to dip back down. He did not allow himself to disbelieve in the powerlines; he would certainly come to them soon. Then he would make better time. Then, he would have a path to follow, a direction. Then, the thin blood that burned across his shins would dry; then all the mud weighting his shoes would fall off as he ran over firmer ground. Now, though, as he slogged and galloped across marshy taiga, he thought of all the ways he should have taken more time back at the crash site, before leaving Susy and Deb. What would have constituted a proper goodbye? Would anything have been enough?

He thought of them braving the night in the shitty little tent. He should have talked over more what they would do, in that eventuality. And in case Deb's injury got worse, he should have patiently and exhaustively detailed every possible complication, and its remedy.

Really, he did not have the harder role here. Given the choice, he would always prefer to be the one running, instead of waiting. And the hard part was not even keeping himself going; if anything, it was the opposite. Already, thinking about Susy, and all the slow biological steps of exposure and how they would visit upon her in order—already with this on his mind, Dan was exerting himself stupidly, working too hard.

Pacing smart was impossible, while inside his chest something was caving. His ribs wanted to compress, pushing him into huffing oxygen-max sprint mode. When he closed his eyes to rest them from staring at the fixed distance of the ground, the black behind his lids showed Susy's toddler face, eyes rounder than he'd ever seen them in real life.

"I'll be back for you," and "I'm going to go run now;" had those really been the best he could do?

Cursing, he reined himself back again. He was being stupid, self-indulgent. He knew what the emotion did, physiologically, to his heart rate and blood pressure. He was wasting energy. He would regulate himself to calculated, judicious thoughts, and save the raw ones for when he needed the endorphin rush.

Though he'd never told this to anyone, when he used to race, and even still on some long runs alone when he was bored, he imagined his body's chemical resources lined up like a series of buttons, everything a very futuristic sci-fi control center, with alarms sounding and computerized voices intoning *purge glycogen reserve, on three,* or *initiate anaerobic protocol.* He'd envision the last mile or two of a big race, upshifting through his lactate threshold pace toward V-dot and past, as a sequence of calmly executed orders in the conning tower of a crash-diving submarine. Anything helped, to distract his mind from the pain of it.

*Bypass lactate loading alarms, push epi, push l-dopamine, purge, purge; initiate overstride. Override safety protocols. Purge ballast, all nonessential systems to standby, abortabortabort macro through cellular, we are anaerobic on three.*

It worked a bit. Psychosomatic or not, a couple times when he'd felt his reserves getting iffy, he'd thought, *gimme a little epinephrine, just a little dopamine surge*. And he'd have to rein himself back, right away: a tingling shot down his spine and the next he looked at his watch he'd be forty seconds hot on pace, and he'd think, a little scared, *easy there. Hold on to that. Save some.*

It was a mental trick he dared not even think about now. If it worked, it would be stupid and inefficient, and if it didn't—if he hit the turbo button and got nothing but a thud—it would break him.

What he needed here was control, and restraint, and patience. He had no idea how far he had to go. With nothing but time to explore it, a potentially perverse thought sparked in his mind: what he had before him was really an opportunity. Wasn't it? A test like none he had faced before, or was likely to meet again. An unknowable amount of time and distance to be bridged. And he could not be more compellingly motivated. Was it selfish, was it screwed up of him, to derive any thrill from his situation? Had he been too quick to leave the crash site, abandoning his wife and child behind?

Being honest with himself, though, he detected no guilt. There had just been no other way of doing things. There hadn't. If he hadn't struck out overland, they would be together waiting to die.

And as strangely as it fit, he was uniquely, fortuitously suited for this challenge. Sometimes life delivered itself like that. Hadn't he heard about the solo researcher, in the Antarctic or somewhere unreachable, a surgeon who by dire necessity had successfully removed his own inflamed appendix? An unthinkable task, but one his particular training had prepared him to execute. Flipping his own situation, if it seemed implausible that he, a distance runner, should be given a test precisely of distance running, what about people who had died in situations he could have survived? It became a matter of statistical inevitability, but would the universe create such a possibility only to dash it?

In any case, here he was, faced with a singular test of physical endurance that removed willpower from the equation. Whatever it required, he would do it. The lack of choice made it simple: all it left was time, and pain, and exhaustion, for as long as it took.

And so, when he rounded a little brushy hillock and saw against the darkening eastern horizon, burning like fire in the last rays of sun, the unmistakable repeating geometric arc of the powerlines less than a mile before him, sagging like any suburban telephone wires, his elation was tempered with something else. He dared not name that feeling as disappointment, but still—it was an emotion of loss. This would not be half the challenge he was prepared to take on.

He stopped and let the sight linger a moment, to imprint it in his memory. Then he leaned forward and lifted his legs back into motion, so much energy left in them really, his footsteps crackling lightly over the thawing ground.

When Dan returned home for Christmas after quitting the team for good, his father looked older. It was like Dan had been escaping in a pod at near the speed of light, becoming more alive every day at college, his father behind him growing exponentially more decrepit. Had Dan just not noticed the shake to his old man's hands, had his hair been so brittle, his complexion so rough, all along? Was it new, since he'd tried to kill himself, or had it been accruing all along? Dan should have come back for Thanksgiving; his excuse about helping with the International Club dinner felt shameful.

"So," he asked, folding himself into the one of the straight-backed dining room chairs that never had been comfortable, "how's things?"

His father shrugged, half-smiling shyly, and offered him coffee. "Sorry," he mumbled, lacing his fingers around his own steaming mug when Dan declined. "The group sessions, everyone just goes through pots and pots of the stuff. And, and chain smoking—it's like the poor saps need a break every twenty minutes."

Dan nodded. "You're still going, then?"

He swallowed from his mug, emptied it, put it down, then looked into its bottom again. "Cultivating bad habits," he joked. "But yeah. Yeah. I am." He asked about the cross country post season, why he hadn't seen Dan's name in any finishes since the Conference meet. "You didn't answer my e-mail. Was there an injury, or…?"

Dan looked evenly at him. If there were questions Dan was not permitted to ask, then there sure as hell ought to be ones he didn't have to answer. "No injury," he said. "I'm fine."

And his father looked away. "Shame about Nationals, though," he said.

Dan backpedalled a bit. "There's next year," he said, which was not technically a lie.

His father nodded, accepting the non-answer, and Dan understood how it was between them now: No Comment, and No Questions Asked. These were the courtesies they would extend each other.

On Christmas afternoon, they drove to the supermarket in town, where a take-out turkey dinner for two with trimmings awaited. Dan looked out the window, watching the scenery pass: corn stubble, gray slush and road salt lining the ditches. Somehow even the car smelled like burnt percolator coffee. At least he'd gotten the window replaced.

"I'm not running indoor this year," Dan said, apropos of nothing. He'd been thinking that he felt adrift, without any particular calendar or goal now, unsure what he was going back to after the break, and apparently this sentence was how it came out.

"Oh?" His father switched his gaze from the road once and then again. His lips trembled as if reading something with great concentration.

Dan feigned interest in a passing nativity in someone's yard. The figures, Mary and Joseph and the Wise Men, were painted on flat wooden cutouts, chips around the edges exposing the yellow-white of cheap pressboard. The facial expressions were all a little askew: Mary looked exasperated, Joseph oddly hopeful bending over a manger that might, from a passing perspective on the road, have nothing in it. One of the donkeys had blown down and was partly buried, unattended to since the last snow; Dan almost wanted to ask his father to stop the car, so he could get out and go fix it. "I've been wondering," he said, "what I could do at a longer distance."

His father lit up a little at this; Dan could tell he was suppressing a greater reaction. "I'm happy to hear that," he said cautiously. "You know—I was hoping you'd make that decision."

"Decision."

"I wasn't going to say a thing. You had to see it yourself. But look at, at everything you've done so far. This is the next step. It's made for you," he said, still a little guarded. But his restraint was crumbling. "It's the legendary distance, Danny." He lowered his voice. "The country's ready for a real marathoner."

All that spring of his junior year, while the word "marathon" never left his own lips, Dan wasn't closing any doors on it either. When he let himself think of it, the possibility was electrifying.

His tempo runs got longer, and three days a week he added a second easy run to boost his mileage volume. Most weekends, he dropped in a single longer run, stashing a bottle of Gatorade in a ditch or snowdrift and staying out two or three hours.

He let his workouts schedule themselves, and while that approach lacked the science or sequence of a concerted plan, it allowed him to train exactly how he felt like, every day. Lacing up his shoes was never once accompanied by loathing or dread, or the idea that anyone was making him do it. Outside of his manageable class load and his token hours as a student worker—which mostly doubled as homework time anyway—he was filling his days with what he liked best.

He cruised endless ribbons of country road, sometimes spacing out for literally miles until startled by a honk from a car he hadn't heard coming. As the snow melted and the trails in the state park thawed, he spent hours churning through icy mud. He had plenty of patience for the distance; it was everything else in life that took too long, that could never finish and move into the next thing quickly enough for his taste.

He still fell in with the team some afternoons. The first time, in January, was awkward: Lightner fixed his gaze straight ahead, focusing on his breathing. After Dan matched his pace for half a mile, Lightner peeled off abruptly to untie and relace both shoes. Dan slowed up for Hughes and Nate, along with two of the younger guys he'd never gotten to know as well.

Around them the bare fields glittered with crunchy, granular snow. Every exhaled breath fogged before them then blew back, or rather they passed through it, parting the cloud with their faces in the second before the dry air reclaimed the moisture. Dan did not speak the first word, and for a while no one else did either. Though the sleeves of his tech were sweaty and the outer millimeter of his skin was as cold as half-thawed meat, he felt good, impervious and warm at his core. Ahead of them a single turkey vulture hung silhouetted in the air, as motionless as if stamped against the brilliant blue sky. Lightner did not reappear.

Nate explained, "Lightner wanted to win, is all. He's not pissed so much at you."

"Understandable," Dan said.

"Sacrifices," Nate went on. "Rewards. We can't always set our own terms."

Dan processed this. Two deep breaths went by, then two more, and the moment for replying passed.

With an impatient huff, Hughes swung aside a step, creating a vacuum that usually pulled Dan involuntarily forward to lead. When he held back, Hughes caught his eye and nodded at the open slot, hopeful, goading. "You gonna roll in with us?" he asked. "Could just, blend in with the crowd."

"Better not," Dan said. "But thanks."

"Ah c'mon," Hughes said. "There's this whole batch of new chickies, out for middle distance this year. Just cruise by 'em with me. Everyone'll look."

Dan winced. Was he that infamous? New-season gossip would fade soon, though. To Hughes, he only said, "Always thinking of me, huh?"

"Sure I am," Hughes said.

Dan smiled. For a moment he felt suspended, unsure where exactly he was on this familiar route—did they really only have two miles left? If he concentrated on the rhythm through his legs, the steady pull and huff of breath through his lungs, there was nothing to worry about. No before or after, no lingering or impending unpleasantness. No approaching reason to turn off and leave the group. The cold air flowed past his face and gave the insides of his cheeks the taste of hardwater ice cubes, and again he had his favorite feeling of simultaneously moving fast and not moving at all, landmarks going nowhere, of occupying the only point there was in space and time.

Now he could taste that same mineral-laden cold as the dusk came down over the taiga and the moist air began to chill. This would have been foreboding without the mighty salvation of the powerlines before him, ready to lead him out from the wilderness. He reached them just as the orange glow of the setting sun extinguished from the wires overhead.

He need not have worried about overshooting the powerlines, passing beneath them in the dark, because the terrain change was dramatic. The ground had been both evened and treated with some sort of herbicide; he could see in the dying light that grass grew, but taller vegetation had been curbed.

The moon was already well-risen, waxing, almost full. Silhouetted and monolithic in the moonlight, an enormous steel stanchion stood twenty yards to his right. The next one to his left was quite a bit farther away. He had the sense of standing beneath some enormous insect.

But these structures were manmade. Humans had laid this path across the wilderness, and humans actively maintained it. Electricity meant civilization, at both transmitting and receiving ends. Either direction was a destination, and now even at night he would make much better time over the cleared ground. There was nothing left for him to do but pick a direction and follow it out. South lay, generally, increasing population and inhabited territory. North, though, lay the purpose of these lines, the reason for their existence, either the outpost being powered or the source of the electric power. And how much farther north could either of those things be, before distance overcame practicality? North was counterintuitive, true, in that it meant increasingly rugged landscape and climate. They had flown from the south, though, after leaving the road far behind, and he had seen nothing below him then.

No wind moved, and without the crunch of his feet on the ground and the white noise of air past his ears, he could hear the hum of the wires above him. The sense of epic adventure he'd felt before was gone, but the thought of Susy and Deb shivering in their tent, bundled against the growing cold and dark, rekindled his urgency.

He quickly slung off his pack, found his headlamp and Ziploc of batteries, and suited back up. Moonlight fell silvery and blue across the patches of snow. Then, a flick of a switch cast a brilliant pool of LED glow at his feet, eclipsing all else.

His breath clouded before him, fogging and dispersing in the beam of his light. Pivoting deliberately to the left, he set out again, and now over the sounds of his own breath and his steps, he tried to hold onto that hum from above, letting it comfort and lead him. He passed the first tower, and then about a minute later, the next. To occupy his mind, he counted them, but without any real object. After all, he was sure to arrive somewhere now. All he had to do was follow the path.

After graduation, the three-year doctoral program in Physical Therapy at Flat Marsh had seemed a natural next step while Dan weighed options. And right away, he enjoyed grad school, freed from the classes he didn't care for and with broader rein in the subjects he liked. His hours in the clinic were enlightening as well, and for the first time he began to see practical applications for all the subjects he'd only studied in theory so far. He met the athletes who came in not as names but as scared kids, their voices hushed and contrite, brash basketball players or muscle-bound wrestlers struck teary-eyed at the possible loss of a season or an entire scholarship.

The office staff speculated, often with startling accuracy, on who they would see when. "The Debennet girl, she's one," Joe had pronounced, calling her a Roman candle, overdue for burnout by her sophomore year. "North American ranked in high school, and you know she had better offers than here. And she's hitting every single workout like race day." He'd lifted his coffee cup and frowned mildly, as if surprised to find it still empty.

The day Dan met her in the clinic, he knew they were wrong about Deb. She was an anomaly, determined, neither about to burn out nor take uncalculated risks. Maybe he identified with that.

A week later, he smiled when he recognized her on campus, and gave a little half-wave.

She looked confused, then worried, and stopped. "Is something wrong?" she asked. "They told me, the X-rays—"

"What? No," he said. "I was just—saying hello."

She smiled and shifted her bag to her other shoulder, but the concern didn't leave her eyes. "Oh," she said. "Hello."

A moment passed where Dan thought he should say something and continue on his way. Instead, he said, "It was shin splints, right? The best thing? I mean—that's what you were hoping?"

"Yeah," she said, loosening.

"I'm not the doctor or anything," he added.

She cocked her head now, amused. "No," she said. "You made that clear before." Around them, though a few students hurried past, traffic on the quad had dissipated. "Listen, I have a class," she said.

"Oh yeah," he said. "Sorry. Hey, if you want though— let's talk more. Sometime."

She looked away, eyes lowered; he would come to learn this expression well, her reaction to any unexpected emotion. Then she replied, "Yeah. Sometime's good."

Over the winter, they saw each other a couple times a week—usually socially, as part of a larger group. She'd text him when people from the team went off campus for cheap pizza night or a movie, and he invited her when someone in the grad program threw a house party. Though they were often seen together, no one would have called them a couple.

There was the curly-haired tennis player he saw her with a few times in November, who disappeared after break. Dan dated a theater major for a while, who was so busy with rehearsals that it was a month before they realized that, alone, they had nothing to talk about.

Then, after a party in February, he and Deb had both walked outside at the same time, and turned to each other on the rental house's sagging front porch, the fog from their breath wreathing them both in the cold wet air. Dan had a strong sense that they were in the same place and within the same moment, and instead of saying anything he put one arm around her shoulders then the other, and she moved closer instead of farther away. She had a roommate in the dorms, so they went to his apartment.

Though after this, their friends all seemed to recognize them differently, neither of them called it anything, and Dan remained guarded.

A month or so later, came the first big home meet of the outdoor season. A dozen of them had planned to go out afterward, and when Dan's father showed up in town unannounced, Dan saw no reason not to invite him along.

He took his father to the stadium first, where they wandered the meet for a while. The smell of hot dogs waxed and waned every time they passed the concession booth, where his father stood half in line, squinted at the menu board, put one hand to his wallet and the other to his chin, then turned and walked away.

"We're going to dinner later," Dan reminded him.

"What?" His father peered at him for a second as if he hadn't heard, and then before Dan could repeat himself asked, "You're not uncomfortable are you? Here, watching?"

Dan shrugged. "I drop by a lot of home meets. It's no big deal." Two of the current distance guys passed, their spikes scratching on the concrete, and waved at Dan. He nodded back, embarrassed by the timing, as if he'd staged it. "Let's go sit," he said.

From the aluminum steps, he could see the soccer field, where loose groups in like-colored jerseys, the away teams, trotted through paces and warm-ups. There was a guy Dan swore he remembered racing—he recognized his stride more than anything. He moved his legs with a little sideways swing outward followed by a pigeon-toed reach with the forefoot, nothing obvious or that most people would see, but it was the kind of thing Dan noticed. The man was finding his last-lap pace a half dozen times and then immediately backing off it, a compulsion Dan knew well: your conditioning had been there a day ago, five minutes ago, but would the speed be there now? And now? And now? Enough left when you reached for it? It was like scratching a scab, unable to let it alone long enough to heal. Dan did love that feeling of floating just at the precipice, ready to explode; he'd never been able to keep collected when the gun went off, caught up in the rush of the start. But he'd walked away from it early, and on purpose.

A group of middle-distance girls from another school turned at the soccer goalposts and ran back, long legs flashing and reaching in the spring sun. Dan could almost smell the sweet dirt and cloverheads kicked up from their spikes.

He followed his father past a half dozen perfectly good seats to an empty row halfway up. Through the next three events, his father constantly leaned forward to watch, glanced behind him at the flags lifting halfheartedly in the breeze, and turned to shade his eyes and gaze out over the parking lot.

Dan sat very still himself, saying nothing until Deb's race was called. "So, watch this one girl go," he said, his own voice terse, speaking like a parent to a hyperactive child. He added uselessly, "Tall, with the ponytail."

"Yeah, who is she?"

"Just, a girl I've been seeing."

From the corner of his eye, Dan watched his father take this in and consider his response. "Which lane?" he asked, scanning.

"Four, probably," Dan said. "There she is." While some of the other women bounced in place or shook their legs out or circled their arms, Deb stood still in her lane, shoulders relaxed, as if mentally someplace else entirely.

"Is she fast?" his father asked.

"Just watch."

At the starter's signal, the women all set to their positions, then with the start exploded into long flashing strides, leaning left around the first curve as the staggered starts evened out and the pack converged.

"Oh," Dan's father said, after the first lap. "She's going to get boxed in." He looked over at Dan, worried, then back to the track. After a lap, a long-boned woman with a wide, almost violent arm-swing took the lead, breathing with her lips pulled back so far Dan could see her teeth.

Deb held in the middle of a crowd of bobbing shoulders and bouncing ponytails, her eyes focused serenely on the back of the woman ahead of her. After another lap, the pack started stringing out again, a pair of gasping girls falling off the back, their form degrading, heads tilting back and eyes half lidded. "She'll have to get out of that," his father pointed out. "Look how much she's giving up on that lead." Here his voice was even, collected, someone who knew what he was talking about. He gave Dan a little shrug. "I mean, it'll be a solid finish. She could fight back up. Maybe to third."

"Hold on," Dan said quietly, his gaze pinned on the far turn as the pack roiled around it in a flurry of shins and spikes, the leader nearly ten meters ahead by now. And then emerging from the turn, as if she'd practiced it exactly like that, as if oblivious to all the runners around her, Deb gave a little push off her left foot and kicked over a lane, into the straightaway in front of the stands. Her posture tilted forward just a hair, and two of the women ahead of her fell back and then a third, but she was still on the outside of the pack entering the near curve. She leaned in left, her right elbow arcing high, stuck in the outer lane, and then on the back straight she surged just enough to drop back in, now in third.

What happened was always hard to pin at this point: it wasn't that her stride lengthened so much or her turnover increased that noticeably, just that every step seemed to earn her more ground. It wasn't even a kick this early, with almost half a mile to go, as much as just a challenge, to see who'd fade. Often, rival runners let her go from here, betting she'd misjudged and couldn't hold pace. As if thinking exactly that right now, the girl in second backed off, and seemed suddenly pulled backward relative to Deb.

Deb settled in behind the leader then, not passing, just pushing. The other girl must have wanted desperately to look back, to gauge Deb's reserves or even stare her down, but dared not waste the half-stride and break her rhythm to do it. The leader's head was starting to shake from the effort, white spit flying from her teeth. Deb marked up behind her, cruising easily.

Then, when anyone else would have waited for the back straight to make her move, Deb kicked out and around into the turn, passing the other woman on the outside as if she'd been waiting only to deliver that exact insult. Clear by the back straight, five yards ahead by the last curve, she looked to neither side as she rolled through the finish line with vicious, confident strides, her face pale except for blood-red spots burning beneath her cheekbones.

Dan's father's face was lit like a kid's at Christmas. "Oh, wow," he said, and "Wow!" again. "Jesus! Did you see that?" he asked, rhetorically; Dan knew he couldn't help himself. When he finally turned to Dan, beaming, some of his awe was still there. "This girl could go places, Danny!"

Dan nodded.

"Everyone went on," Deb said that evening, when they picked her up from her dorm. "Said they were too hungry." Tiny beads of water from her shower clung to her hair where it was tied in a loose bun.

"Should we catch up with them?" Dan asked. His father looked distressed.

Deb shrugged. "It's no big deal." She nodded at his father and said, "Hi."

When he was done apologizing, his father congratulated her on her race.

She ducked her head sideways as if embarrassed, but Dan noted no accompanying blush to her complexion.

"You knew it was going to go exactly that way," his father said, "didn't you? You knew exactly when that woman was going to fade. We could tell."

"No, no," she said, her voice quieter, her eyes on the ground. Here suddenly her cheeks did redden, though she turned as if to hide it.

She had run strategically, his father added. A perfect mile. He turned to Dan. "So where are we going? Is there still that Italian place?"

"You know what a lot of people call the perfect distance," he commented over breadsticks. He looked between the two of them. "The perfect marriage of endurance and speed?"

Dan took a long swallow of his ice water.

"The marathon," his father continued, "exhausts all the body's metabolic systems, in order. And more than that"—here he nodded meaningfully—"it's psychological." He sipped the melted ice water from his glass and went on. "Running your own race, means ignoring all the rabbits. Whatever the leaders want to do, forget them, for the first twenty miles."

Deb was smiling politely, a model of patience.

"Then you have the last 10k," his father said. "The elites, you see the real elites, pick up through the last few miles."

Dan let his attention drift. In the last half mile of every distance he'd raced, he'd always felt briefly transcendent. For a few seconds, in oxygen debt and hurtling toward the finish line, it always felt like the body and mind could be swayed, an ancient flight instinct invoked as if a sabertooth tiger were on his heels, and he might cheat the limits of the biological world. Dan attributed this delusion to the really good drugs releasing: epinephrine, dopamine, floods of adrenaline. Wonderful while they lasted, they dissipated too quickly, without ever delivering quite what they'd promised.

His father had asked Dan something, and was looking at him now expectantly. "You've told her, right, Danny? About your—your training? The whole plan?"

"Dad," he said. "No. Not really, no. I haven't—advertised it." He turned to Deb. "I'm sorry," he said. "He does this. Exaggerating, making it all—"

Deb looked quickly back and forth, between them. "He's proud of you," she said with a small smile.

He'd been superstitious about the word 'marathon,' for two years not admitting it to anyone. Maybe it carried some glamour factor for Deb, though, as if he were a young soldier in wartime, newly signed up and waiting for something bigger than himself to carry him away. And there was her initial impression of him, as the rebel who'd walked off the team. His defection might have appeared assertive, independent, at the time.

This was all speculation, though, on Dan's part. Though they started seeing much more of each other that spring, there was no clear cause and effect to it, and her motivations remained a mystery to him. She seemed consistently possessed of a singular determination, in all aspects of her life, a manner of simply deciding something to be true and proceeding accordingly. When he went home with her to Windsor for Easter break, and met her family there, nothing he could learn about her upbringing enlightened him further.

Her father Bernard—the baggie of sad ashes back at the campsite, a couple ounces of gray flakes and the entire reason for their insane errand north—had been what people called an avid outdoorsman. Glass-eyed animals galleried every wall of Deb's childhood home. At dinner, the preserved heads on the facing wall, an elk flanked by two smaller antelope-like things, reminded Dan of anatomy classes and biology lab. He couldn't shake a phantom whiff of formaldehyde beneath the smells of turkey and gravy and pies; he imagined the preserving fluids leaching out into the air, the gunned-down animals having their own last laugh over the slow poisoning of Bernard's assembled family.

Deb's mother, seated under the lesser antelope, worried out loud that Deb looked thin, and tired, casting a wary eye on Dan.

"You know she's bad with money," her father said, speaking to Dan but grinning tightly over his fork at Deb. "She could've stayed in Windsor for school. It's an excellent university. I would've paid her full tuition."

"Her scholarship must help a little," her mother murmured.

"Her sisters," Bernard countered, "won't owe a dime in loans, after four years."

"She'll for sure go All-American," Dan said. "Again this year. In case she's too modest to say."

"What're you, there?" Bernard asked. "Division II?" He eyed Dan's runner's physique and asked if he ran as fast as his daughter, and if it paid for his school.

"It covers enough," Dan answered, dodging more subtexts than he could identify then.

Bernard subscribed to the particular view of manliness that required material evidence, the way the tropheyed heads on the wall asserted his dominance over nature. Dan, meanwhile, held little respect for overweight older men who paid exorbitantly to kill exotic animals with high-powered weapons, instead of putting themselves to any real physical test or hardship. And her mother was the epitome of timid, hesitant when she had to speak at all and then relieved when ignored. Dan could find no echoing personality traits from either of them in Deb. It was like hovering a piece unsuccessfully over a jigsaw puzzle.

Now, Dan wondered whether Bernard had ever been to the desolate country he was running across. Did it hold some special memory for the man, or was it only the idea of remoteness? Could he have picked a place he'd never seen, something romanticized or that he'd just liked the look of on a map, an emptiness in the middle of nowhere, the last bitter challenge in a life he'd seen as unsatisfactory, too soft? That seemed heartbreaking, but what did it mean that he'd told no one his reason for it? Here they were now, Dan jogging over the wild vastness to his bobbing headlamp in the night, while Deb and Susy shivered miles behind, and very literally, there was no knowing why.

Clearly the man had been conflicted. He'd professed to loathe the carpet-wholesaling outfit, the day-job that financed his desperate assertions of a more hearty persona. Hence the hunting trips, the cognac and single malt scotch and long rifles, his laughable assertion that a man ought to be able to live off the land. Had the guy given a shit about literature, he would have idolized Hemingway. Although if, instead of checking out with a mundane heart attack, Bernard had blown his brains out in a hunting cabin like Hemingway, Dan would have had to at least respect that kind of exit. It would been putting his money where his mouth was, so to speak.

Not that Dan was qualified to judge. What end was better than another? Heart attack in bed. Shotgun in a cabin. A devastating pharmaceutical combination, in a sad Formica kitchen that hadn't been redecorated since the 70s.

Where Bernard had bedecked the walls of his home with trophies to himself, Dan's dad had done practically the same by proxy, monuments not to his own glory but his son's. Plaques, medals, college awards and, before the end, a couple marathon trophies, along with every tacky finisher ribbon Dan had ever brought home from off-season 5ks in junior high; these had covered two walls in the TV room and been moving onto a third.

His father had pointed out the new shelf he'd nailed up and kept bare, reserving it, he said, "For the good ones, the real achievements, Danny. If you'll let me keep an eye on them for you." That last shelf stayed empty. Packing up his father's house, Dan had been embarrassed by the sheer volume of all those cheap plastic prizes. The three cardboard moving boxes sat in the attic of his own house now, unlabeled.

Dan was not sure what Deb did with hers, the medals she said she never cared about in college. She wouldn't have sent them to her parents, but Dan never saw them around their own house. Dan wondered who she'd done it all for.

That summer, when Lightner was completing his medical residency in Toledo, sometimes he would drive down, calling Dan from the interstate. "I'm forty minutes out," he'd say. "You up for a run or not?"

As it happened, Dan always was. They'd meet at the state park, and Dan would wait while Lightner hurriedly stripped out of his scrubs behind his open car door and pulled on his shorts.

Lightner always pushed pace hard on these runs, and Dan never asked directly what was going on with him, or exactly what frustration or aggression he had such sudden need to burn off. The stress and unpredictable hours of his residency seemed explanation enough, and Dan figured if Lightner wanted to talk about something in particular, he'd talk.

Once, halfway up the most complicated hill in the park, a climb that was arguably not even really a trail, Dan asked Lightner if he was seeing anyone. He snorted, or scoffed, or exhaled loudly up ahead, and asked back, "You still living with what's-her-name? Our All-American Canadian star of track and field?"

Dan said he was.

"How's that?"

"Good," Dan said. "Really good."

Lightner made another noise that might have been acknowledgment or just a wheeze. Mud flew out from his heels and past Dan's head. Then, the hill abruptly leveled out. For a few seconds Lightner pulled ahead, then Dan accelerated easily to catch him after he reached the top himself.

"So do you consciously run differently, on these kinds of trails?" Lightner asked. "Like, try to adjust your footstrike, or stride?"

"I'm just more naturally on my toes out here, I find," Dan said.

"But you can't get into a regular stride, is the thing," Lightner went on. "Ground's choppy."

"I kind of do a curving step," Dan admitted, "where it's really hairy, like this next downhill? Like they say, how your forefoot just naturally brushes against the surface, and pulls back? With your heels kicking up high?" He wasn't thinking about anything remotely like stride; he was thinking about his palm and the meat of his thumb just brushing along Deb's iliac crest, pulling without friction as her hips rose to his hand, as if drawn upward magnetically. It was dangerous at this pace, Dan knew, to think about anything but the trail in front of him.

"Huh," Lightner panted, considering. "I'm just concentrating on posture, on balance, when I go downhill."

"Lots of tiny steps."

"Trash your quads," Lightner countered, "in a race."

"If you lean back, it will." Dan's sentences were getting shorter, punctuated more heavily by breaths. "If it's not too steep, don't lean back. Just keep accelerating forward. It's the trying to slow yourself down," he huffed, "that does your quads." Lean into it, he thought. Plunge forward, don't fight the gravity.

Lightner said something Dan didn't catch. "Right?"

"What?" Dan wasn't even pretending to pay attention; Lightner was still going on about the danger of descending a slope too fast. What really was "too steep" though? If you didn't fall, no downhill was too steep to run down, was it? Until you fell?

## Ten

Birds, Dan wondered now, jogging along the path beneath the powerlines, in the dark—why birds? What was the chain of forking paths and coincidence and opportunity that could lead his Susy to that particular passion?

Well, the first summer she could drive herself there, she had a job at the zoo. She'd expected unexciting work, emptying trash cans or maybe serving slushy cones in plastic novelty cups shaped like monkeys or polar bears. Instead—she still has no idea how—she found herself stationed in the aviary, given a clipboard and a folding chair behind the beaded curtains. When a macaw shit on her arm the second day and she came back on the third, someone must have figured she had the proper prereqs.

She spent four afternoons a week that summer inside a faux-tropical exhibit, the air thick and musty with bird dander. Her ears echoed with shrill squawks and trills the whole drive home, and in her room, exotic feathers fell from her clothes. When she closed her eyes at night she saw afterimages of plumage, brilliant bursts of color.

By June she'd learned to sit so still the parrots would perch on her shoulder, and parakeet pairs would bicker from her knees. She wore long sleeves, and a bandanna over her hair. When Mazie, the African Grey, laid two off-white eggs in the hollow of a fake tree in the back of the exhibit, for a whole day Susan was the only one she'd let near her nest.

By August, her hands were scratched, and her old Asics colorless and unrecognizable. She asked one of the keepers how they'd ended up in that job anyway, and what kind of classes she should be taking.

Of course her parents encouraged her. Why wouldn't they?

# Eleven

Beneath the next tower, Dan waved his hand before his face to dispel his own breath, and stopped, turning his head, then searching above with his beam that picked out nothing except the nearest steel stanchion that rose ten, twenty feet up, then disappeared. He walked over to it, leaning one gloved hand on the cold metal, then his forehead on the back of his hand. He shut off his headlamp and closed his eyes tight. Running at night tires out the eyes, he'd learned, watching nothing but the next steps of trail, focus fixed at the same distance for long stretches of time. Without relief, those muscles got tired like any others, and this led to errors of depth perception, occasionally hallucination.

He was aware of the powerlines overhead by the whisper of air moving past them and by their low almost imagined hum; also it seemed like he could feel an electrical pull, the hair follicles at the back of his neck tightening, lifting up. He turned his head up and looked high, into the empty sky, focusing on nothing. Without the silver diffuse glow of the moon he would have been unable to discern the huge arms of the power pylon above him, or have any indication he was still on the right path, or any path at all. In a moment of disorientation, the sky turned into a smooth surface of deep water, and he was looking down into it, seeing the moon and scudding clouds by reflection. He'd been out here a long time.

For a moment he entertained the thought that he was making everything up, that he'd sustained some head injury and was floating in deep delirium. It was a seductive idea, and he pursued it all the way back: maybe there had been no plane crash. Maybe they'd never left home at all, maybe there were all kinds of unfortunate events that had never occurred, mistakes still unmade in real life—the fantasy glimmered with the relief of waking from a bad dream.

The situation was so perfect—could it be what he'd subconsciously needed all along, some renewed relevance and capability, a chance to be a protector, a savior for Susy and Deb behind him? It seemed exactly what his brain might construct, when he looked at it that way.

As plausibly, he could have been injured in the crash and dreaming it that way, his misfiring mind playing out heroic scenarios while he lay, possibly comatose, on snowy ground, Deb bringing bits of snow to his parted lips. Or it could all be some spiraling shock dream compressed into a split second, and he'd pop awake on impact, into the crash still unfolding around him. Or maybe he'd really set out on this insane mission and his body had given out long ago, and he was coasting now through the last mental unravellings as he died of exposure.

He flexed one leg without thinking, then the other, his muscles already stiffening in the time he'd spent leaning against the powerline stanchion. The tread of one shoe nicked his opposite calf, and he reached down, fingering the hard, deep-lugged sole. They were serious trail shoes, engineered exclusively for off-road use, over hostile terrain. He took a deep breath and exhaled. It was all real. He was here, all right.

It felt sad, a bit, that it took a tactile bit of vulcanized rubber to bring him back, and not some warm memory of Deb or their wedding or her shoulder blades or collarbone or Susy and the way she'd squealed at the sight of him just days ago, no just that morning, and her baby teeth and how for just a few days coming in they'd looked crooked—none of those memories or images had arrived to keep him on task. Just a bit of cold rubber on his shoe. He kept rubbing his thumb up and down the ridge of tread, feeling more than hearing the squeaking sound it made.

Straightening, he slapped himself across both cheeks, medium-hard, and clicked back on his headlight. How much time had he wasted standing here? It alarmed him, to have slipped so far into reverie.

Forcing himself to calm down, pay attention and assess everything, it occurred to him that he hadn't peed in hours, since daylight. Then, he had stopped purposely to urinate on a patch of blank snow. His stream had looked dark, not quite on the yellow spectrum. Leaning close to the steaming hole in the snow, he could see the edges spattered lightly but undeniably pink. Any emergency department would admit him based on that alone, but he hadn't been overly concerned then.

Now he stopped and forced a few trickling drops out over a spot of bare ground. Before it soaked in, in the light of his headlamp it looked the color of weak coffee or burnt motor oil. He imagined a whiff of petroleum.

"Optimal diagnosis," he said out loud. "Foot-strike hemolysis." His own voice jarred him, and he got out his phone again and tapped Voice Memo. This was better, no longer talking to himself. The routine was calming, familiar, like dictating notes after a clinic appointment. That was a process of quantifying and naming, imposing order on the unreliable world of symptoms and feelings. Settling back into a jog, he kept talking. "Repeated physical trauma and impact resulting in tissue breakdown. High levels of hemoglobin, from burst or damaged cells in the feet, filter through the kidneys and appear in the urine. Not an immediately problematic condition in itself, in otherwise healthy individuals." This had happened to him before and was plausible now, considering his effort and the conditions, and the beating his feet were taking, in wet shoes, on rough ground. Visible bruising would be inconclusive though, and there was no point stopping to examine his feet.

"Other possibilities," he narrated, "include Rhabdomyolysis. Muscle breakdown beyond what the kidneys can process. In advanced stages, coincides with irreversible muscle loss. Renal failure, permanent kidney damage. Coma. Death."

He stopped his phone from recording. Rhabdo—he couldn't be that bad. Not yet. If his kidneys were failing, the pain in his low back would be unbearable. The strain on his ribcage from just drawing a breath would probably bring him to tears. He'd be barely able to walk, he'd have to fight for each staggering step at a time. And look: here he was running, still. Here was one stride. There was another. Without backing off his pace too much, he lifted the tube of his camelback to his mouth. He bit the valve and sucked, and got only a dry whistling of air. It had felt light on his back for some time now.

Melting handfuls of snow in his mouth would cost him heat energy, and he was reluctant to risk an unknown stream or bog before he had to. Drinking his urine to conserve fluids would be less dangerous, but then if it made him throw up—the thought made him gag a bit by itself—it would be a net loss. He considered stopping to fill his camelback with snow, and though intellectually he knew this was a good idea, he kept going, too impatient to stop, his better judgment at odds with inertia.

While they were both still in school, Dan's goals and Deb's had aligned. Or at least, they had appeared poised to converge, as Deb trained for distances yet unnamed and Dan maintained focus on the long-term marathon plan. He had allowed himself to become filled with genuine enthusiasm, seeing the marathon as a real possibility, a natural next step for his talents and aspirations. The first one he raced hurt for longer than he'd imagined possible, but there was something in the smooth sustained effort, constantly taxing but never unbearable, and he'd done it in just under three hours, exactly as planned. He cruised Toledo's and Cleveland's marathons at a slightly faster pace the next spring, and nearly ran 2:30 in Columbus in the fall, but never devoted maximum effort or prolonged focus to any one, "training through" instead of tapering off in the weeks before.

It was easy to listen to his own excuses. The timing always was wrong, and school kept him busy and he was teaching an intro survey course too, which would not have been a problem if he had not found that he liked it, and wanted to take the time to make every lecture as engaging as he could, something he felt he owed his department and students anyway. And there was his aversion to the taper itself, how inevitably antsy he'd get with the enforced rest. What he didn't admit was obvious nonetheless: really committing meant risking failure. What if the 2:32 race that had felt like a respectable effort, on tired legs from a hard week preceding, was really the best he could do? What if he was one of those runners just incapable of improvement in that way, who peaked early and then disappointed? What if, when it really got painful, instead of facing it he just crumbled and backed down?

The daunting crucible before him was not the distance itself—he could have kept going beyond the finish each time—it was the pace that intimidated, keeping his foot down on the gas the whole time. Arguably, it was a kind of avoidance that first drove him to longer races, the opportunity to simply go longer instead of faster. Rationalizing this as overdistance training was easy.

When he saw the flyer, just a crummy little Xerox, pinned to the bulletin board in the university field house, it was the typo that caught his eye, the extra zero in "5k." It was in a park he knew, about an hour away; the course was supposedly "95% trail," which sounded fun; registration was only ten bucks; and then there was the bit about a strict eight-hour cutoff. Which…Dan had to admit, seemed excessive for a 5k. Unless he'd missed some detail about crawling the entire distance, which also seemed implausible. Fifty kilometers, he thought: thirty-one miles, on trails.

The morning of the race, he felt illicit climbing over Deb's sleeping body in the predawn dark. He'd told her he was doing a longer run, and would be gone all morning. Still, he found himself gathering his shoes and bag of gear stealthily, creeping out of the apartment, and cringing at the screech of his poor car's tortured starter. He snuck through town beneath the two traffic lights on Main, both gone to blinking yellow at this hour, and glided onto the highway. To the east, the sun was not even paling the horizon. The smell of his instant coffee filled the car, not fresh or invigorating but just burnt, with a whiff of overused motor oil.

He'd had two squares of dry toast, and his stomach felt clenched and too small. He never ate more before racing, though, and even in his marathons he'd never needed more than sports drink and a couple packets of carbohydrate gel. He'd never done thirty-one miles straight, that was true, but a few times he'd put in fifteen or sixteen in the morning and a dozen miles more at night, or lined a couple twenty-mile days back to back. He was familiar with the Wall, and the land where every step took more effort and determination.

The start was in a lit-up park shelter, as casual as any local 5k except for the early hour. As he signed in and handed over his ten bucks for a race number, though, Dan couldn't help staring at some of the other runners. Or, more specifically, their gear. The man lacing his trail shoes beside him wore a backpack with a screw-open valve on its top, and a long blue tube that circled around to bob at his chin. A short woman at the picnic table cut two sections off a roll of duct tape and, with great care, smoothed them firmly over her bare heels. Others under the park shelter wore cut-off knee socks as arm warmers, some kind of folded-down shields over the tops of their shoes, or Legionnaires' hats with long flaps down the back. Those without backpacks carried hand-bottles, though the flyer had promised aid every four miles.

There was no gun for the start, just a short course description from the race director in front of maybe fifty assembled runners, and then a shouted, "Go, go!" If a clock had been started somewhere, Dan didn't see it. And then they were off, to a cacophony of sloshing backpacks and clumping, heavy, jog-paced steps.

Though he kept reminding himself it was an experiment, a training exercise, nearly everyone started so slowly that within a mile Dan was cutting along behind the two leaders, swerving around turns in the path and feeling the cool morning air on his face. The two guys in front were chatting like buddies at a bar after work. Dan was disappointed that no one seemed to be racing at all, but out of politeness, he did not pass and take the lead.

The first ten miles passed agonizingly slowly. One of the leaders peeled off at an aid station and never caught back up, and another periodically ran with them and fell back. "I haven't seen you at one of these," the remaining man commented to Dan. His name was Jensen, and he worked in IT. Married, two kids, Dan figured him for about 40.

A little after twenty miles, although their pace never really changed, Dan unexpectedly had difficulty keeping up. His stomach ached with an emptiness his carb gels weren't denting, and he felt energy-poor all around; it occurred to him that, at this leisurely pace, he'd been out here a good half hour longer than he'd ever run before.

At the next aid table, he tried half a peanut-butter and jelly sandwich. For the next mile, Dan murmured along in agreement as Jensen chattered about bands that hadn't been famous since the 80s. Then, as suddenly as if yanked off the trail by an unseen hand, Dan stopped, grasped a sapling with both hands, and dry-heaved.

"You OK?" Jensen asked. He'd stopped on the trail, clock ticking, just watching Dan.

"I'm fine," Dan croaked.

Jensen lifted his water bottle. "You getting enough to drink? Or, you need a salt pill?"

Dan shook his head. "Thanks," he said. "I'm good, go on. I'll catch up."

Jensen nodded slowly. A wave of nausea hit, and Dan hated the concerned, composed middle-aged guy beside him. "See you soon then," Jensen said. Dan violently retched something red and brownish, along with more water than he thought he'd drunk all morning.

The rest of the race was a blur, jogging down the trail on dead legs. The course was a large eight-mile loop, and Dan and Jensen had been lapping back-of-the-packers for a while, but now he wasn't even overtaking walkers anymore. He got passed once, then again, and every time someone asked if he was OK, he gave a weak thumbs up. A woman twice his age bounced by, the earflaps on her hat trailing behind her. His head felt gripped in a vise, and he staggered by the last aid stop, afraid to put anything else in his stomach. He would have quit, but his car was at the finish.

And when he crossed the lineless line, running, yes, but hardly finishing strong—he hadn't seen another runner to push him, either ahead or behind, for a good twenty minutes—he must have looked confused, because someone from the knot of volunteers under the shelter house called, "That's it, you're done!"

The race director asked if he happened to get his own time. Dan shook his head, and the man shrugged, looked at his watch, and wrote on a clipboard. "Pizza's over there," he was told, "and don't forget your T-shirt."

Jensen sat in a camp chair with his shoes off, munching a slice of pepperoni. "Hey, you made it," he said. "Guess it was the heat, huh?"

Dan felt hollowed out from hunger, but his stomach turned at Jensen's greasy pizza. "I'm usually good in heat," he said. "It's possible I'm coming down with something."

"Hm." Jensen chewed and swallowed. "How'd your fueling go? Were you eating OK, before that?"

"I tried a PB&J," Dan said. "Couple gels. But just water, other than that. So I don't know."

Jensen almost choked. "Seriously? That's all you ate, all day, was one, tiny, quarter-sandwich?" Shaking his head, he said, "Good news is, I don't think you're getting sick. Man. You've got to eat."

And Dan was dumbstruck. It should have been obvious. He'd thought he'd been there before, knew how it felt to run out of ready fuel, but he'd never counted the gels and drinks he took in marathons in their strictly caloric sense. There it was, though, the physiology he surely knew: when stored glycogen ran out, and his stomach had already effectively shut down—that was his stumbling nightmare of the last five miles, his body burning nothing but fat for fuel.

Looking around him then, he saw runners coming through the start/finish with a whole lap to go, chatting, laughing, enjoying themselves and looking for all the world like they couldn't care less about any clock or their time. Most importantly, though, he saw almost all of them stopping, lingering almost lazily at the aid table, taking handfuls of potato chips, pretzels, M&Ms, heading back out to the trail with a cookie or banana.

That summer, it was harder than he expected training his body to accept real food on runs, but the idea was revelatory. If he kept putting in fuel, how far could he go?

Now, under the powerlines' ceaseless buzzing, his food supply was finite and inadequate. Three more nutrition bars, a half dozen gels: the energy equivalent of ten miles, maybe twelve, at most. He knew too well how that dictated everything: his pace, his range, his chance of not dying.

Before he left the 50k that day, he asked another runner about the shirt he was wearing—had he read it right? A one-hundred-mile run? "Tell me about that," Dan said.

There was a website. The race was a month away, and it looked like a three-hour drive to get there. They needed volunteers, especially medical and health-professions types; he'd heard one of the state schools brought their whole podiatry grad program every year, for the one-of-a-kind fieldwork experience. "It'll be wild," he told Deb. He pitched it to her as a curiosity, something to go and observe. "Besides, it's in this huge park and forest. Beautiful scenery, all that."

The race started from a campground, before dawn on a Saturday, and the course stayed open through Sunday morning. Dan had booked what turned out to be a tiny cabin for the weekend; neither of them owned a tent, and Deb had listed advantages including, "Indoor plumbing, electricity, screened windows, a door that will actually close, a bed for Christ sake...."

The pickup truck parked across from their cabin sported a bumper sticker that read, *You Ran a Marathon? That's Cute*, and the gaunt, sunburnt fellow who checked them in to volunteer wore a t-shirt that said "DNR before DNF." Music and beer and laughter were everywhere, though most of the revelers would be racing in the morning.

Deb looked from side to side as they walked, her expression one of suspicion or mild alarm. "You don't want to start doing these," she said, "do you?" She'd asked him this before, a couple times since he came back from the 50k. He kept saying no, and she kept asking.

Literally hundreds of people were there, though, none of whom apparently thought running that far was insane.

"Can you seriously believe this thing happens?" he asked Deb. "How has no one heard of this—a hundred fucking miles?"

"Well I guess I believe it," Deb said. "People...join crazy cults. Or, fast or hunger strike for like weeks. Or, set themselves on fire. People jump out of airplanes, they handle snakes."

"It's like you're reading my whole bucket list," Dan said.

"Ha."

"But you know. Every one of those cult members, or snakehandlers on fire, or whatever, if they saw yours or my weekly training log?" He mocked a shiver of disgust. "'Crazy!' They'd say." He put his arm around her as they walked, his hand atop the narrow shelf of her hip. "'I'd never do that.' They'd say."

She pressed her cheek briefly to his shoulder.

Dan remembered the experience of volunteering more as a series of scenes and impressions, scattered vignettes, even though the reality was prosaic, an afternoon and an overnight of making sandwiches and pouring Gatorade into paper cups at a remote aid station that was little more than a tent, a folding table, and a generator in the forest. Five or six others were volunteering, rotating through and running errands, and when a runner came in, they were to record his or her number and radio it in, but despite the long stretches of boredom and smacking mosquitoes, Dan recalled the sense of energized chaos, of being on the edge of something.

For the runners in the middle of the night, their aid station must have been a welcome sight after miles of dark and lonely trail. Many looked dazed, rounding a corner suddenly onto loud music, their chuffing generator, and such a gross overquantity of light. Most of them lacked the presence of mind to dim their headlamps, and Dan got used to being suddenly blinded. Runners stumbled in shepherded by pacers at their elbow, reminding them to eat something, check their shoes, refill their water bottles. Some flopped onto canvas cots or blankets at the edge of their site, like casualties of battle lined up for triage. Dan could think of nothing more than the scene from *Apocalypse Now*, when the boat puts ashore at a firebase under attack. "Where's your CO?" Sheen demands, as enemy artillery sparkles and hisses overhead like fireworks, and the serviceman answers, "Ain't you?"

Dan recalled the disasters most, the human wreckage, those who came stumbling through in the middle of the night, and often miraculously carried on. One sixty-something guy knelt and breathed gout after gout of orange vomit into the bushes, until another volunteer touched his shoulder, asking if he was keeping any solid food down. Wiping his mouth with his wrist and wiping the wrist on his shorts, the man tilted his head up, jaw stiff against the next wave. "It's twenty five miles," he growled. "I'll do it on body fat if I have to!"

"You know, puking," the volunteer told Dan conversationally, "is like the body's friendly warning mechanism. Before kidney failure. Electrolyte deficit. Hallucinations." He nodded at the man bent over in the bushes. "He'll be OK."

Dan learned that, typically, half the starters wouldn't finish the race, and he thought of their neighbor the night before, camping in his Datsun pickup. A thin guy with honey-blond hair, he sat in a lotus position on his tailgate, orange flip-flops beside him, and said his strategy was just to "never ever stop," to keep moving forward and not quit. "It's a mind thing," he'd said, "and my mind's not going to let me give up." Dan had wished him good luck, but never saw him come through their aid station.

There was the crewcut Marine who called his boot camp the easiest vacation of his life, "compared to this shit." His skin looked shiny, too waxy in the artificial light, and he'd stood before their table for maybe ten minutes, just getting his shit together he said, before shouldering his pack and, with a look of pure misery and disgust, following the arrows down the next stretch of trail. In a silence between songs on the boombox, Dan heard him grunting, "Fuck this, fuck this to hell," repeating it like a cadence as he disappeared.

As the sun began to rise, cutoff times and disqualification loomed, and those passing through their station looked either desperate or resigned. One pacer fumed back and forth over a runner crumpled in a folding lawn chair. "Yeah, every day a lion wakes up in Africa," the pacer, a kid with one side of his head shaved, said, "you know the rest. But, shit." He kicked at the dirt hard. "I'm here to tell you something else, too." Here the kid started to sound like an overzealous high school football coach, giving the locker room pep talk of his life. "We are not the lions in this equation. The lions finished this race hours ago; they're napping right now. Taking a shower. They're probably home getting laid. But we are not the slowest goddamn antelopes!" Sweat flew from his hands as he gestured, his skin weirdly blue-cast in the mixture of electric light and very pale early morning. "Get up." He took hold of a wrist and yanked savagely; the runner didn't respond. "Get your ass up, antelope. You're not dead yet."

Finally, with a sound like a death rattle, the runner lurched forward out of his chair, and just when Dan thought he was going face-first into the grass, his foot came forward. He lunged again, and another foot rose. Two more steps, and he was out of their light and moving toward the path, his pacer laughing and surprised.

"Tough love," Dan joked. Deb shuddered in distaste and turned away.

She was cranky and unresponsive most of the way home, which Dan forgave her; they'd both slept terribly. He was electrified, though, by more than just the joyous exhausted festive atmosphere at the race's finish: until now none of his options for a thesis project were remotely interesting. He'd resigned himself to foraging the same worked-over ground as his fellow grad students—Achilles tendonitis and ACL rehab methods and torn rotator cuffs and all the rest—and all that remained, he'd thought, was to spin the wheel, pick a topic to sleepwalk through with no chance of making any real contribution. "You know," he said quietly in the car, as Deb scowled out the passenger side window. "I bet no one's even researching these ultra races. In any kind of depth, anyway." Even the med staff he'd talked to had been only patching people up, not taking data.

Deb didn't answer, which was OK: Dan was lost in thought the rest of the way home.

Before he pitched the idea to his advisor, Dan conducted an experiment of his own. After all, it would have been naïve, even irresponsible, to make such a proposal without first-hand data. And in retrospect, this experiment confirmed for Dan more than he'd ever expected.

He didn't exactly talk it over with Deb beforehand. Coincidentally, the hundred-miler he found for himself, a state away, was the same weekend as her pre-season retreat with the team. He never confessed all of it to Joe either, who would not have understood. The one person he did tell right away—because he needed his help—was Lightner.

When he got home from the race, it took several long minutes to unpack his stiffened body from the car and climb the steps to his apartment. Finally in sterile-enough surroundings, he opened the blood-draw kit and sat down. His hands trembled from more than just exhaustion, and he had to steady himself carefully before piercing the vein. Only when he'd filled, sealed, and labeled six vials and put them away beside the blood he'd drawn two days earlier, did he shamble back to the bedroom and sleep. When he woke, he ate everything he could put his hands on in the kitchen.

A week later, he staked out an outdoor table at the café across from campus and sat down to wait for his friend. He wandered inside to buy a day-old baguette, and when he got back, Lightner was waiting on the sidewalk. His hair wasn't long but looked tangled, like he hadn't run a brush through it in weeks, and he wore fingerprinted sunglasses. "You look well," he told Dan, "for a dead man."

"Ha, ha," Dan said. "Very funny. If you wash out of med school? You could totally make it as a comedian. I mean it." He tore a bite from the end of his baguette with his teeth, waved the bread at his table and said, "Want to sit? Or, you hungry?"

Lightner sighed, and crumpled into a chair. "I'll get a coffee in a minute," he said. He slid his sunglasses up onto his head and blinked his reddened eyes in the morning light. "Here's your bloodwork," he said, and tossed an envelope onto the table. "Jesus, I see why you didn't want to run it through Campus Health. What the shit have you been doing to yourself?"

Unable to keep playing casual, Dan snatched up the envelope and tore it open. "I told you," he breathed as he scanned the results, his before-and-after. "Hundred mile race. Would you have believed, all these people do them?"

Lightner tilted his head from side to side and gave a little shrug as if to say he was prepared to believe in crazier. "If I didn't know otherwise, based on the first set, I'd ultrasound your kidneys. Possibly biopsy your liver." He leaned back, folded his arms on his chest, and added reprovingly, "And I'd inform you you'd had a minor heart attack."

"Fantastic!" Dan said, waving the end of his baguette.

Lightner coughed to cover a laugh and shook his head. "Seriously. All your stress markers were completely nuts. What was it like?"

"Ahh," Dan said, chewing. "I did get a little light-headed, actually. After I finished. After damn near twenty hours, I was sleepy, you know? I wasn't trained or equipped for the thing, just wanted to see if I could do it or not, hell I barely held on the last twenty miles. But," he said. "you told me exactly what I expected. The standard tests, just aren't calibrated for, for…"

"For the dangerously masochistic," Lightner finished for him. "No. Hm. Come to think of it? They're probably aimed for the 99.9% of people who don't willingly undergo profound physiological distress."

"Lightner, man!" he exclaimed. "It was crazy shit, you wouldn't believe. All these people with their hydration backpacks and head-mounted flashlights, like it was some kind of expedition across the Sahara. Me carrying this dumbass weak flashlight and a tiny water bottle, for stretches where I didn't see another living soul for literally hours, then boom! There'd be this little aid table in the forest, gas generator and electric lights, and a fucking feast out on the table. Oh, and the human wreckage! People puking, hallucinating, you wouldn't believe it. And later on, it's all the young kids falling apart, and these old goats burning by me in the dark, just putting that hammer down all night." He shook his head. "It's like no race you can imagine. All these road races, marathons and all, where you fall off pace for a mile and the whole thing's shot? And you're like, what if I throw up, or take a wrong turn, or have to stop for the bathroom? Or you get blisters, or injure something?"

"Those…don't happen?" Lightner asked.

"That's the thing," Dan said. "Probably all those things happen. To everyone. So there's no point worrying about them. Right?" He added, "I talked to this guy—you talk to people during these—who said, 'It never always gets worse.' Right? I guess it's like, a saying."

Lightner leaned back and grinned at the sky, shaking his head. "Yeah, you were going to be the next great white hope or something, remember? Train up to the marathon, where all that glory was—get fast, surprise the world. What happened? That's off?"

"On hiatus," Dan said. "I'll get back to it."

"Oh, bail it, hell," Lightner said. "Bullshit the girlfriend if you want. Not me."

"No," Dan said. "No, I'm not bailing anything. Just—if I can pull off this thesis project—after that."

"This thesis idea. Which you've yet to really explain," Lightner said, his voice dripping with exasperation. "Tell it then."

"OK," Dan said. "Just bear with me on this, all right? Remember Longer's ice baths?" Their coach had promised a post-workout surprise one day, and when they rolled back into the stadium parking lot, there he stood, grinning and holding a garden hose, behind a row of metal bins from the farm supply. He pointed to a sweating pile of bagged ice, insisting every man had to dump his own in, that it wasn't a thing anyone else could do for you. For three weeks, whether he plopped himself in fast or eased down slowly into the tub with his arms, the breathtaking shock of it never diminished for Dan; neither did the yips, exaggeratedly high-pitched giggling, and cries of 'snap!' from the group. "No major injuries for anyone, though, through that whole peak session."

Lightner winced in the sunlight and affected a shiver. "Parts of my anatomy are still trying to forget. It's not exactly unconventional, though. Anyone trying to absorb a higher training load—I'd think you're already doing those anyway. For the," he said, waggling air-quotes with one hand, "'marathon regimen.' If not simply to build character."

"My character could use it," Dan said. "And, after trail runs, and mud therapy? A little sit in the cold lake is nice too."

"If you like leeches. Is that it then?" Lightner asked. "Drawing off tired blood?"

"No seriously. Stretches. Icy-time. And vitamin I," he said, referring to ibuprofen. "That's like all the prevention we ever did. Isn't it? Does anyone do more?"

"Well I did try chanting," Lightner said. "Lighting black candles to Papa Loa. You see the good that did me."

"But as soon as something did go wrong," Dan went on, "it's like, bring on modern medicine." He rattled off treatments they'd both been through, e-stim and ultrasound to induce more blood flow to damaged muscles, iontophoroesus to push anti-inflammatories through targeted points on the skin, blindingly painful active-release therapies to break up deep scar tissue and adhesions. "So why doesn't anyone apply all that more preventatively?" Dan said, "is what I'm asking."

"Because it would be an enormous pain in the ass?" Lightner asked. "And largely unnecessary?"

Dan shrugged. "I figure, I got nothing in the world but time, right? What if, what if I could get, say upward of five hundred miles a month, with no detrimental effect?"

"To what end?" Lightner asked impatiently. "People are already doing that. You want to research how they do it, ask them. Go out to, back to, one of those hundred-milers, pass out a survey. They'd be all about it, runners are geeks for statistics, you know that. And, you might get an actual viable sample set, with an N value greater than, um, one."

"Well, I have thought of that," Dan answered. "And I'll collect survey data. But none of those people would come spend a month in my lab, you know?" he said. Not to mention that most of his potential respondents were scientifically useless anomalies, flukes of unquantifiable luck and stubbornness. "What I want," Dan continued, "is a complete, day by day picture, from the chemical level on up, of what happens, manageable load through overtrained."

Lightner turned on him his most jaded, intellectually contemptuous look. His elbow rested on the table as he leaned forward, head tilted slightly down, which gave his eyes a hooded look. The very intensity of this reaction pleased Dan immensely. "Thousands of people every day," Lightner said, "die of eradicable diseases. Little kids, stricken with horrible cancers. Somebody in the world just starved to death, right now while we sat here, for the calories of your morning run. And you want to deploy the whole world of medical advancement, to help you beat up your own body, and go for just one more jog than anyone could possibly need to." Lightner sat back, and folded his arms over his chest. "For what? Suppose, even if it works, which it won't, you get the data you want. What possible purpose will this serve?"

"Well," Dan said modestly. "You just saw, how serious tests, don't work for everybody. Under, possibly, important conditions. Witness my phantom heart attack."

"Oh, for…." Lightner shook his head. "It'll never work. You'll injure something stupid. You'll destroy your own body, and no data like that would be useable for anything anyway."

"Possibly."

"You'll be doing nothing but running, eating, sleeping, and treating self-induced injuries. And, I suppose, obsessing over your own biometrics."

Dan beamed. "Livin' the dream, my friend."

"Dream, my ass," Lightner muttered.

Dan grinned then at the unmistakable note of jealousy in Lightner's voice. As Lightner slid his chair back in toward the table, Dan saw how the little finger of his left hand curled in a kind of palsy, and how his expression tightened around the eyes as that trivial load passed through his forearm. "I mean it," Dan said, "thanks again."

He told Deb his plan that night. "It's an opportunity," he said. They'd come from a house party on the other side of town, and were sitting in his car, parked in the lot behind his apartment and a Mexican restaurant. "Not a detour. Look, I don't think many people are equipped to try this, the way I want to do. It's because I've been training that I can handle it, and I'm not going to, to just throw anything away."

She kept reconfiguring her expression, cycling through a dozen kinds of disapproval. "I talked to Joan," she said. "This afternoon, after practice." This was fairly new, calling her track coach by her first name.

"How is Joan?" he asked.

"Persistent, is how she is," Deb sighed. "You know her." She shook her head once, as if bothered by a fly or sudden nervous tic. The restaurant's neon sign, reflected off of low clouds, cast a pale glow on her hair. "She keeps saying, I need to decide on my training, the time to commit is now. That I should be in touch with the groups out west. Or today, she mentioned, the new project in Michigan."

"You should tell her you're moving to Africa. To train at altitude. Run down gazelles on the high savannah."

The curve of her cheek twitched. "Seriously. I have to tell her something. I thought, I'd talk to you about the sponsored training thing, and maybe when we both graduate we'd check them out, the elite camps, together, and—" She turned away. "And here, you're talking all this crazy new shit, all the sudden."

"Crazy temporary shit," he said. "I keep saying the brief, temporary part." It was like no one heard him at all, when he insisted it was about the research. If this idea for a thesis even proved viable, and he carried it out, it would derail him for, at most, a year. After that he would come back stronger, with unique experience, hardened resolve, and an elite-level base. Building from there, he'd get fast for real. He'd knuckle down, he'd quit screwing around. "I'll come back from this ready to burn a marathon down," he said. "You and me both, could—you know. Make a go of it."

She hesitated, still not looking at him.

"You're thinking, what?" he asked. "10k, 5?"

"They're both gambles," she said. "I mean, such long shots. I'm not hoping."

"Joan thinks you could hope."

"You think it's reasonable then," she asked. "For both of us. So that's a plan. Really?"

"Why not?" he said. "Why not."

"Do you believe," she started, leaning across the seat toward him. "You really think we could, both—?" They'd been drinking at the party, and now as she leaned close, an inch from his face, he smelled red wine on her breath.

He slid his arm up her back. She had always secretly struck him as a being of limitless potential, in so much more than the shocking power and grace of her long legs, either in stride or beside him at rest. Some days, riding the thrummed-out high of combined exhaustion and invincibility after a good run, he felt like her rightful equivalent, as if they were larger than life together, a pair of lions presiding over lesser animals. "I promise we can try," he said. "I mean, coming off a base like I'm talking—that's got to be the best chance I'll have."

She studied him a moment.

"And everyone's sure *you'll* make it, you can do whatever you want, it's like—"

She slid her knee over his and flexed, pulling herself closer, and he shut up. Over the cooling scent of tortillas from the restaurant, over her hair conditioner and the lightly flowery soap she used, something heady and sweet wafted in his open window—timothy, maybe, or cornsilk, from the fields.

He dropped into the new plan right away, building base and piling miles on top of miles through the rest of August and September and into October. His capacity for biochemically hellish conditions already strained explanation, and he was excited to test where his real limits lay. Deb's potential exceeded what he could find words for to tell her, too. When he let the fantasy run away with him, he could almost believe they'd both lucked into possession of indestructible biological machines.

On a whim, he suggested they sign up for Boston, to run the oldest and most famous marathon in the world together just because they could. The whole world seemed that easy, some days; Deb had never run that far before, but after he convinced her, they picked a fall marathon and coasted easily and conversationally through a time fast enough for her to qualify. "It wasn't so bad," she said afterward, and, "It didn't feel as long as I'd thought." All through the race, Dan had sensed her frustration with the slower distance pace.

Everything that fall seemed easy in their lives, almost charmed. One day, out for a run around the farm loop, the phrase *Lucky to be alive* struck him so bluntly it almost felt portentous. The farm loop, straight country roads free of any traffic to speak of, was always uneventful, and on this day, the corn was taller than head-high, and meadowlarks chirped raspily from the phone lines overhead. He could almost taste the dry earth that had baked in the sun all day. With a bit of headwind in his ears, he didn't hear the first car until it was almost upon him, and he startled in a way that always felt foolish, like he'd jumped a foot in the air. He swung quickly to the thin gravel shoulder to let the car pass and was just pulling back onto the pavement when his peripheral vision caught the next car, and the one after that, and then the whole line. Though he passed two cemeteries on this route, he'd always thought they were historical, *no longer planting 'em there*, and for a moment he didn't register the fluttering magnetized purple flags on every fender in the funeral procession.

Suddenly he was self-conscious. It was a public road, and he had as much right to it as anyone, but was there some etiquette he didn't know about for this kind of situation? Were pedestrians supposed to stop, put their hats over their hearts, something like that? He wasn't wearing a hat, or even a shirt. Would stopping make him look like a gawker?

So he kept running, looking straight ahead or down at

his feet, listening for the Doppler-shifting whish of passing slow cars to end. There he was, his breath and blood moving powerfully through his body, sweating with the temp in the low 70s and loving the work, moving easily over the land and feeling as alive as he ever had. He felt disrespectful, flagrantly vital, as the motorcade of mortality rolled by, and it was hard not to feel karmically admonished.

The procession passed, and he kept his head down when he went by the cemetery. Then it was back to solitude for a few good miles, the wind and the noise of his own footsteps and breathing punctuated only by the calls of larks and redwing blackbirds. Dry grass in a fallow field shone preternaturally golden, and an early moon hung in the bell jar of a cloudless sky.

He felt, at the same time, an abundant appreciation and a fatalistic superstition of thinking about it too much, that a too-happy life invited its own downfall.

Of course, neither disaster nor eternal bliss ensued, but in retrospect, it had been a sort of charmed time, a calm between complications. It had been contentious, for a while, getting his thesis approved, and then with that resolved, quickly what should have been enjoyable about his experiment got subsumed by details, analysis, and stupefying physical exhaustion. He was getting mileages he hadn't dreamed of, but even as he remained uninjured and his hypothesis bore itself out, all of the time he wasn't actually logging the miles was taken up by mind-numbing work he was too tired to get through.

And even though Deb had a year to finish in her own degree, as she kept talking to the programs out west, Dan began to worry that he was what kept her here, stifling her in the tiny college town like the little lead weight on one of those old-school stovetop pressure cookers. In his more insecure moments, it was only a matter of time before she boiled irrepressibly over and left him behind. The miles were taxing him emotionally too, and as the days shortened into December, his periods of gloom started weighing more heavily, and lasting longer.

Though he'd been holding off a flood of little inflammations, weaknesses and asymmetries, his thumb to the crack in the dike against them, in the end it was his exhausted immune system that shut him down. A sinus infection he would normally have run through left him floored, barely able to crawl out of bed for two days. The data he'd already collected was more than sufficient, and he'd already gotten far beyond any load he'd hoped to sustain. On the third day, when he finally felt almost human again, he decided it was best to quit pushing his odds, leave the table and cash out his winnings.

By January they were both stir crazy, Deb after three years on the isolated campus, and Dan pushing his seventh year there as he finished his three-year PhD in PT. It was a practical degree, a secure choice, but when he talked to Deb about stability, how he'd be able to teach or practice anywhere with it, he could see how such mundane talk depressed her. He kept assuring her he'd resume his own targeted training soon, that he was only backburnering it to focus on a final academic push, but she was less mollified each time he said it.

Meanwhile, his advisor Joe's attitude shifted, from passive encouragement to a sudden piqued surprise as Dan's research began to gel. It was Joe who had suggested he attend the conference in Chicago that March, and even financed his travel out of the departmental budget.

Dan looked forward to getting some scenic runs in along Lake Michigan, but a sluggish storm front refused to even get cold enough to freeze all weekend, and the paths were alternately slushy and frozen, the skyline oppressed by fog. His schedule was filled with panels and breakout sessions anyway, and his dominant memories of the trip were of sitting in conference rooms in the Loop Hilton while sleet picked at the high windows, and enormous overhead heating ducts spilled dry, dust-scented air.

He was surprised how relevant his own work was to many of the session topics, though, and saw why Joe had encouraged him to come. His research was unique, his initial analysis conclusive. Initial queries for publication had so far come back politely rejected, but this hadn't seemed to surprise Joe, so Dan wasn't worried.

The fluorescent lights buzzed in the hot conference room, packed with stale recirculated air. As he listened to one distinguished speaker on a panel of equally revered researchers and physicians, Dan's mouth felt as dry as the synthetic patterned carpet beneath his only pair of dress shoes. "In practice," the red-nosed, white-bearded scientist continued, "muscle group dysfunction or damage due exclusively to fatigue would be a non-existent diagnosis." He smiled. "At least, in human subjects." Dan noted with distress that the man was overweight. The collar of his shirt bit so deeply into his neck that a roll of flesh protruded above it. "Biomechanical malfunction or acute injury would inhibit activity first, and barring that, fatigue of the central nervous system would take over before any muscle group became sufficiently stressed or deprived to involuntarily fail."

Dan was first to his feet when the time came for questions. "But you're not saying it's impossible?" he asked. "That it can never occur? Catastrophic, um. Muscle failure. That is."

The man exchanged a look with the woman next to him on the dais, a smirk almost, and replied, "Well, I'm not denying unicorns exist," he said. "But no one's produced that evidence either." A mild titter passed across the room. In a more earnest tone, though, the speaker leaned forward into his microphone and added, "In anecdotal cases, say, survival scenarios, involving very motivated subjects, for all we know, yes, biological function could continue through the onset of central nervous collapse. Obviously we have no lab data on that. Even animal experimentation, would be ethically dubious, and—" He cocked a wry smile. "And no human would do that to themselves on purpose. Thank you for your question."

"Actually," Dan started, the sentence already formulated in his head. He'd always backed off before running his body into irreparable damage, and while he had no documented unicorns, a couple nuggets of his data would no doubt surprise this panel.

Before voicing any of this, though, he stopped. The opaqueness of his rejection letters had just been explained in a new way—none had been conditional, or suggested revisions. They simply had not believed his results. Or, at the least, they had doubted his credibility. He saw it, of course, now: all those solitary miles, verifiable only by GPS data from his own personal watch, most not even corroborated by running buddies, much less professional peers. With no external validation, everything was suspect—his data, his methods, all the way back to Lightner's false positives.

Dan's mouth clicked when he swallowed, so loud he was sure it echoed through the room. Then he sat down.

That night, the last night of the conference, he sat in the shadows of the host hotel's bar, holding an overpriced microbrew until the bottle grew warm in his hand. Before him, young professionals tired of being professional all day paired off, predictable as molecular transactions. He watched the attendees circling, eyeing each other as unsubtly as boys and girls at a junior high dance. Here, an attractive blonde parted the crowd, pulling along a bookish male friend as a temporary foil; by the bar, an awkward young woman in a party dress made him sad, the way she was trying so hard, but then he thought maybe she'd figured the game out, and knew she had nothing to do but wait, with her mute cow eyes and pudgy fingers wrapped around a sweating highball glass. Over by the pool table, a late-thirties guy in a loosened tie checked his breath, subconsciously touched his empty ring finger, and went in for a run. Dan went up to bed early, before the maneuvering in the hotel bar got desperate and even more unsettling.

"Look, I know you're doing good work," Joe told him when he got back. "I'd recommend you to practice anywhere, you know that." Here he looked up apologetically. He swirled his coffee once, then put the cup on his desk and pushed himself away from it in his chair. "But if you'd been in my position, two years ago. Advising, and one of your students brings you this crazy-sounding thesis. Would you have approved it?"

Dan said nothing.

"You wanted to induce acute and possibly long-term overuse injuries. On purpose. On yourself."

"No," Dan said emphatically, "I wanted to prevent exactly that, and it was working. And I haven't figured all the data out yet, but already, I can see, there are ways to refine—the stress markers, tests for—"

Joe raised one hand in surrender. "I knew you'd find something. I was never worried about that part."

Dan was silent for a moment. "You knew my results would be unusable," he said. "That no one would listen. So—why did you even let me…?"

Joe looked away. Out the window was the new physical plant they were building, and beyond that, an otherwise unobstructed pastoral view from the edge of campus: a stubbled field, a silo, an unlined stretch of road. "I worried what would happen to you, is part of it," Joe said, his face softening. "If you'd dropped out of the program. Fallen out of touch." He went on, still looking out the window. "We'll have a teaching opening in the fall. It's just a one-year appointment right now, but it's full-time. I think you should apply."

"You could coach or something," he pointed out to Deb. "I mean, you know Joan would find you a spot. Or, if not at Marsh—I mean, anywhere in a fifty-mile radius. This part of Ohio, you can't throw a rock without landing it on a college campus."

He sat in his apartment's tight kitchen, picking at a mug ring on the uneven wood of his table. The slant of the roof made the kitchen his smallest room. Deb faced away from him, leaning on her elbows over his sink. The narrow balls of her shoulder joints realigned under the fabric of her sweatshirt as she shifted balance, and Dan thought of the pillars of a suspension bridge, bearing and distributing load. He couldn't tell if she was looking down, or out the tiny dormer window that, on a good day, threw sunlight on his hands doing dishes. Outside, now, she'd see overcast, Midwest in winter, a mass of gray clouds that might as well have been the same ones cloaking him in Chicago. Below, in the sink, would be their undone breakfast dishes, his and hers.

"It's not guaranteed anyway," he said. "I told Joe, he could float my name, so far, is all. So it's not even like an actual offer, I might not get it, you know. And, it wouldn't have to keep us here forever."

"You say that," she said, her back still to him. "And you're right. A year won't kill us. But when does it turn into, one more year after that? When does—"

"I know," he said. "I know I know. It's just, the opportunities I thought I'd have—I wasn't planning this way. I don't, I wasn't, I didn't expect that—" He leaned forward, flattening his chest and shoulders on the tabletop, pressing the center of his forehead down hard into the flimsy pressboard. He reached with his arms, then laced his fingers behind his head. The stretch through his upper back and triceps felt good.

"I know," she said. He heard her turn at the sink. "I understand. I do." She took two steps to stand behind him, and laid one hand on the center of his back. "It's just," she said. Her fingertips played absently over the raised nubs of his vertebrae. "I really wish I knew that we want the same things. Do you know what I mean?"

He nodded, and the table shifted with his movement, but after a second it occurred to him she may not have seen. As he sat up, he felt her hand rise with his back and then lift away. "Well," he said, "this whole training detour? I'm done with that now." Facing forward, he nodded twice, deeply, and said, "Like one more recovery week—then I'm back on it. The serious plan, you know? Our plan. In a year, we'll be ready, to move somewhere and—really try." *You'll see*, he felt like adding, earnestly, ridiculously.

She was still there, standing behind him—he heard her weight shift on the floorboards. When she walked out of the kitchen, he tracked the sounds of her movement through the apartment, to the front window where she paused, then to the couch, where she straightened a cushion and sat. After a moment, the TV came on.

The next night, when he came home, Joan was waiting for him. The light had already gone, and he did not see her outside his apartment. As he walked up the stairs, he swung his keys out from his pocket, flashing a metal circle in the air. Canned mariachi music and the scent of tortilla chips wafted from the Mexican restaurant.

When she stepped forward and said his name, it took him a minute to recognize her, in jeans and a sweatshirt instead of her track suit. "Oh, hey," he said.

"Can we talk? I was hoping to catch you."

"Deb's not here," he said, glancing in the darkened windows of his apartment. "If there's something you want to leave her, I can—"

"No, I want to talk about Deb," Joan said. She took two steps toward him down the stairs, right foot left foot, her rubber soles soundless on the wood, then stopped, forefeet together, heels a little apart. In the light now, she smiled like someone at a negotiation table. "You've been seeing each other a while."

Dan shifted his weight.

"She's going to have real opportunities," Joan continued. "And, possibly, difficult decisions. I imagine you're staying together, after you both graduate."

Dan smiled up at the winter-dark sky. "That's the plan, yes." He wondered who Joan had been talking to, or if gossip about his mismanaged thesis had really traveled so far. Possibly Deb had confessed to feeling trapped. "You know," Dan said, "I think I left something at the lab. I'll tell Deb you stopped by." He turned and walked back down the stairs.

Joan strode down behind him and loped across the lot to get to his car before he did. Leaning over his passenger door, both arms on his roof, she turned up the cordiality, and Dan could imagine her in recruiting mode. "This is just between you and me," Joan said, "but you know that girl has a future." Before Dan could say anything, she raised one hand and went on. "I don't know," she said. "Maybe you're good for her. If you want to be a part of it, what she can be, then great." She looked away. "If not—look, I don't want to rule every aspect of her life, or tell her who to see, any of that." Here she turned back and focused on him hard. "But know this. If you get in her way?" Here Dan almost thought she was going to threaten him somehow, but she said instead, "Every thing she doesn't go on to do—that will be on your head."

Joan leaned back then, as if embarrassed to find herself here in this chilly parking lot, leaning over Dan's rusting car. She opened her mouth to say something else, then closed it, and turned and walked away.

By the time April rolled around, the Boston Marathon had come to symbolize much more than a vacation for them, or a reward. The Olympic Trials were the day prior, and going to watch those took on a whole new aspect if Dan was gunning to run in them himself in four years.

As soon as he found out they were going, Dan's father invited himself along. "You'll want someone to hold your things," he said. "Warmups, all that. And to meet you at the finish." When they lost him in the crowds at the Trials, Deb asked if he'd be OK. "Well he is a grown-up," Dan reminded her, but understood her concern: the man had been like a blinking giddy child since they'd arrived. "He has a cell phone," Dan added, "and he might even remember to use it."

They found a vantage point on Massachusetts Avenue, where the course passed four times. First the women, then the men flashed by like thoroughbreds. The last time, he caught Deb looking after the thinned pack of women at the lead.

"You want to be in there," he said.

"No," she demurred, but only after hesitating. "No."

The next day, they soaked in the pageantry together along the famed course from Hopkinton. As they climbed the Newton hills, he thought about how enjoyable these could be without the stress of competition. Though they were moving quite a bit faster than they had in Deb's qualifier, she insisted she was comfortable, and not pushing pace at all. When she sped up noticeably after mile 22, he quit asking how she was doing.

That night at dinner, at some famous Boston restaurant or other, Dan felt itchy, out of place. The place was packed with garrulous, animated, beaming runners. He couldn't pay attention to the menu, and kept scanning the other tables instead. He leaned forward and asked Deb, "How many finisher medals can you count, just from here? I'll bid two dozen."

She'd smiled at him as if it were an odd thing to say, and then his father returned from the bar, rattling the ice cubes in his rocks glass. "You know, they'll bring you drinks here, Dad," Dan said. "You don't have to watch them make it."

"Oh I know," he replied with a vague smile, "I know," and sat down.

The traffic passing their table momentarily halted, and a man in a brand new blue and gold jacket addressed their table and asked, "Did you run today?" He focused his grin over each of them in turn, settling on Deb. "How was your time?"

Deb blushed, but told him the truth. The man's eyebrows shot up and he very nearly spilled his Sam Adams congratulating her. "How about you, buddy, you as fast as her?" he asked Dan.

"I was happy with my time," he replied.

The man nodded blankly and turned back to Deb. "Isn't that, what, just a couple minutes off the B standard?" he asked. "To qualify for the Trials?" He shook his head reverentially and raised his beer. "That was a show yesterday." Jostled from behind, he did a double take, saw that the way was now clear, and moved on, but not before congratulating Deb again, and nodding quickly at Dan and his father.

Dan shifted in his chair and gestured around the restaurant. "Do you think," he asked, "half the people here are still wearing their race clothes?"

"They're celebrating," Deb said. "They're happy."

"Well so are we. But we showered. The race has been over for hours."

"Four years, Danny," his father said. "You have the time to train now."

"Yeah," Dan said, without enthusiasm. Suddenly, the load, and the caring about it, and the idea of four years of desperate concentrated exhausting training seemed utterly miserable, and so heavy. It wasn't the endurance or the daily time investment or even the pain he minded, so much as the focused speed it would require for him to break into the highest level of the sport. He'd be devoting himself to the training he liked least, for what would be a long shot under the best of scenarios. "I've been thinking," he began. He'd known it at mile 20: there were races he was better suited for. He liked it, cruising at a not-hellish pace; he could have kept that up for twenty, thirty, forty miles more.

As Dan constructed sentences in his head, weighing how much he felt compelled to admit, his father nodded at Deb. "And certainly you could do it," he said to her. "You're practically there already. Don't say you've never thought about it."

And Deb grinned, bashful, admitting, "I have. I have." She looked up then, eyes bright. "I think I want to try it. Really take my best shot."

"There you go!" his father said, and thrust his glass heartily out over the table. Deb found her wine glass and lifted it too, leaving Dan nothing but to join them with the first glass he found, his half-full ice water, which clunked awkwardly against the more delicate glassware.

Back in Ohio, because he could think of nothing else to do about it, Dan threw himself into the speedwork with all he had. Maybe, if he just did the training, the rest of it—the liking it—would come. He started throwing in a set of Yasso diagnostics every week, and the morning after their graduation ceremonies found him jogging yet again, before sunrise, to the track. It was dark between streetlamps, but a pale moon cast its own light. The stadium track was easy to see, and he had it all to himself this early.

The Yasso interval workout called for ten 800 meter sprints, with a modest recovery between each. It was a popular, *Runner's World*-type gauge of fitness: the average time of all ten sprints, in minutes and seconds, supposedly predicted marathon capability in hours and minutes. For example, ten 800s run at two-and-a-half minutes apiece indicated potential for a 2:30 marathon.

Dan was impatient by the end of his third repeat. Every time he coasted to a stop, his tech felt clammy against his skin, the air around him stifling and too humid. As he started the next rep, he knew he wasn't stopping at the 800. With an eye to his watch, he turned a third and fourth lap for a full mile at his old 5k pace. It felt good, his ribs heaving.

On his recovery lap, something creaked in the metal joints of the stands, and a rabbit in the infield twitched an ear, watching him. Above him, almost imperceptibly, the sky was lightening.

He saw that he was going to do it, start over and repeat the whole workout doubled, with 1600 repeats instead of 800s. Same quarter-mile recoveries. More than three 5ks at 5k pace made the proposition interesting.

The first four full miles hurt, in the good ordinary way. After the sixth, he looked around the stadium self-consciously. If anyone were watching, it would look like he was just destroying himself.

But he wasn't, he thought. He wasn't, that was the thing. He was making himself stronger still. Picking a pace and holding it through exhaustion. He was sorting a thing out, determining who was boss here, between his body and his mind.

On his eighth mile rep, the wet air was searing his throat, and he noted the edges of his vision losing definition, a narrowing at the peripheries. Halfway through the ninth, he turned to blow his nose toward the infield, and in the growing light it satisfied him to see a speck of red in the resulting flash over the grass.

He finished the set of ten, and jogging a cooldown lap, wondered how he'd feel after another, if he did twenty one-mile reps instead of ten at 5k pace. Deb would be awake, getting her breakfast, wondering why he wasn't back yet. Passing the start mark, it hardly surprised him at all when his legs spun again into motion.

His times kept equaling up the same, because he made them. When the pace on his watch read too fast at the start of each new interval, he reined himself back, and when it threatened to sag in the despairing belly of every third lap, he lunged forward, keeping his posture aggressive. A couple times, his legs went numb for a whole mile and part of the next, and instead of thinking about the pain's inevitable return, he tried to enjoy its absence, to push hard with the fleeting freedom allowed him. Once he had started each new mile, he knew he would finish it, and that encouraged him.

After his twentieth lap, he wobbled around for a bit, catching his breath and letting his heart rate slow. Certainly, this had been a tiring exercise, but it hadn't been pointless. If he was going to do this, make the transition back to targeted race training, he might as well test what he could really withstand. And twenty miles at pace hadn't broken him yet.

He shambled back to the start line, his legs tired but not exhausted, and cued up his watch for another ten. Every mile got worse gradually and predictably, and he reflected that while it would have been too much to dive directly into the pain of, say, the 27th, it was manageable when he did it this way, with structure and in series. And still, his body kept finding and holding the pace that he'd set, his legs and heart and lungs all aware of it each time the weaker parts of him tried to cheat the workout. It amazed him, and more than once he thought he'd instigated something dangerous. Though his recovery laps slowed to feeble shuffle-stepping jogs, at the end of each, he pulled the first lungful of breath and launched into it again.

Coming into the first curve of his last mile, his thirtieth, his throat filled with hot acid. One heaving breath later, it rolled back and he could swallow, but he still spat and tasted bile, felt something hard pass between his lips. His legs vibrated with pain, his calves and hamstrings all threatening to lock and throw him to the ground, but he pulled them through the same motion one more time, one more time, one more time, rounding the track with six hundred, then five hundred yards to go, still on the bubble of his pace. Cramps wracked his side, like knives sliding up beneath his ribs and feeling around.

Closing in on the finish, that line he'd crossed now a hundred-plus times, he should know how many but his math was leaving him, he wondered if it could really be a matter of oxygen to the brain, but now every step was the last one over that particular piece of goddamned all-weather track, and his vision purpled and his head felt filled with carbonation.

Ten yards beyond the finish, legs pinwheeling just to curb his momentum, he keeled to the right and fell. The pain felt intimate, as he was aware of every joint bouncing over the track's surface, but it felt distant too, like it was happening to someone else, telegraphed in from another continent, irrelevant to him in the moment.

He lay panting, and would have laughed if he'd had the air for it. He'd proven a thing, he was proving nothing, lying here. A ragged whistling sound, like a small baby's crying from far away, reached his ears. For a minute or more it neither diminished nor got louder, unnervingly regular and unvarying in pitch, and he wondered who had brought their child out to the track. Then, finally, he identified the sound as his own breath, keening softly from his open mouth.

The sun was fully up now, and he was alone. Anyone watching, any ordinary citizens out walking laps, would probably be dialing an ambulance. May sun angled gently into his eyes.

He learned multiple things that day. One was that his body was stupid, or maybe just all his switches had been finally overridden: he'd pushed his bag of bones and meat past the point of no return so many times, it no longer cared, no longer bothered throwing up the flags and false warnings of catastrophic system failure. The machine would just do what he told it until it really did break.

Another thing he came to understand was that, while he had more distance in him, faster just wasn't going to happen. He'd strung thirty sub-five-minute miles in a row, and to win anything memorable, to make a real name for himself as a marathoner, he'd have to do twenty-six miles like them, without recovery. Targeted training and a proper taper could do a lot, of course, in theory, but he also knew what his subservient body, too dumb to lie, was reporting in no uncertain terms: muscle fibers have memory, and he'd programmed some of his indelibly by now.

Hell, he'd known this. At least on some level, he'd understood what he was doing to himself all along. And now, trying to undo it, he'd be coming from behind, his body already tuned away from the requisite speed; soon, meanwhile, he would already be getting old for "faster," at a disadvantage against who knew how many starry-eyed kids. Intentionally or not, he'd built his body into what it was now.

The last thing he consciously realized was, simply, he was less than Deb needed him to be. He'd made promises he couldn't deliver, and let wishful thinking start him down paths he could never complete.

Instead of thinking through any of the sensible options, he panicked: later that week, in a frantic, grabbing gesture, he proposed. He had no ring, and no speech rehearsed. He could tell she was taken aback, withdrawing for a moment, composing herself. Maybe he'd wanted her to turn him down, for her to be the one to end the excruciating drawn-out slipping away that their relationship had become.

When she said yes, he'd honestly been surprised.

Since then, three years that felt more like thirty had passed. Dan's father had died. His daughter had been born. Through it all, the world had kept spinning, everything from planets to atoms hurtling down their same blind trajectories.

Back on the taiga, he jogged along, following the stanchions of the powerlines, and in the light of his flickering lamp the towers and twisted foliage became streaks of paint on an impressionistic theater backdrop. In his tired mind, a scene boiled up, unfolding in dreamlike psychodrama, a memory of another thing that had crystallized for him. It had been just after Susy was born, when they were both strung out on sleep deprivation, and a grinding monotone bare-subsistence mental vibe pervaded everything.

The moment replayed for him in silence, like a movie with the soundtrack muted. Deb sat in the glider not gliding, under the lamp on its lowest setting, feeding Susy. He had wondered if maybe she could not see him in the dark, beyond the cone of lamplight, but then something in her eyes told him she did, and in just a subtle shifting body movement, she tightened her arm around the baby, and he was reminded of a running back protectively cradling the ball. He recognized a closed circle, a symbiosis now of not needing him.

It was possible he had only dreamed that scene, but somehow that only intensified its meaning. Nothing had changed between them, because he'd been mistaken about what had been there to begin with. He'd misunderstood, and she'd let him; she'd never lied. She'd only let him think. There was so much of this going around: this passive lying. This letting each other think.

## Twelve

The body gets by, day-to-day and minute-by-minute, through innumerable chemical transactions. For example, while running, compounds are constantly recombined, reconverted into each other, as they move between muscles and bloodstream and liver. A "futile cycle," it would be called chemically, if all these conversions were to occur within a single cell, one thing transformed into another thing only to be synthesized back into the first thing, at a net energy expense. However, glucose converts into pyruvate into lactate back into glucose effectively over space, between muscles and liver across the distance of the blood; this is how energy derives from the cycle. This involves expense: inefficient, diminishing exchange is the way of all things. Every transaction reduces, exhausts, comes at a cost.

It's hard not to apply this metaphor beyond the chemical. Say something, make an attempt at communication. Nothing is understood perfectly; it is sent, or said, and in transmission, meaning degrades. Every thought waits to be misunderstood, to dissolve to neural static, vanishing like a light down a dark hall of mirrors. Entropy is patient, waiting, the only constant.

There will always be things we can communicate, but not make understood. Some of these are best kept whole and private—unsaid, and unexposed to misinterpretation.

# Thirteen

"Wanting it more,'" his father had scoffed once, a short glass of something clear wavering unsteadily under his nose. It was Dan's last year in high school, and he had come home very late. The Winter Olympics were on TV, with a hearty-looking guy in a stocking cap backdropped by mountains. "In the last fifty meters," the man said, "I guess I just wanted it more, is all."

"Such bullshit," Dan's father whispered back to the TV. "The body just does what it will do," he said, and Dan thought that maybe his father didn't know he was there. He was just about to tiptoe from the room when his father said, "Danny, promise me you'll never say something that stupid."

"Are you—?" Dan started to ask. Dan had had a few cups of diluted SoCo at a party, and put a hand to the reassuringly vertical doorjamb. "You're not waiting up for me, are you?" he asked, brave, with no attempt to hide the alcohol on his voice.

The rest of the empty house echoed a stony, listening silence. "Promise me you'll never, if you ever win anything like that, blame it on will, or on God, or on wanting it more. When it's, it's, it's," his father said, gesturing with his glass, "biology." He pronounced this last word, the subject he taught, with contempt, almost revulsion.

After freshman and sophomore Bio, Dan had his father for Physics, too—it was a small school. He tried hard in class, but only because he was a hard worker in all of his classes, and anyway, he respected the subjects, which dealt in absolutes, knowable answers. When he got a problem wrong, even if it were extra credit or some homework exercise that would not affect his grade, he seized upon it and attacked it relentlessly from all angles, like a dog fixated on a bone, until he had it figured out.

Once, in the car on the way home from school, after thoroughly re-examining the single blemish on his latest physics quiz, he said, "Dad. You marked me wrong on this. There's nothing wrong with it."

"Yeah?" his father said, driving. "Which one?"

"It's right," Dan said. "I got a perfect score. You marked it a 97."

"Which question?" his father asked, humoring him.

"Seventeen," Dan said. "The baseball one. 'If a spectator is sitting three hundred feet from home plate, in a stadium at sea level, and—'"

"I know, I wrote it. And what was your answer? Something to ten decimal places?" They were driving past fields, soy and new corn. A hill and a swerve in the road made Dan and his father lean left and then right in unison, twin pendulums maintaining a parallel distance between— as one swung toward the other, the other swung an equal amount away. "It wasn't that hard a question." His father squinted out the windshield. "The girl who counts on her fingers got it."

Dan waited to be sure his father was done, his grin tight and triumphant. "I factored in the speed of light."

"You did what now?"

"Sure, the sound of the ball hitting the bat takes that half second to reach the spectator's ear, but the light, see, the light also takes this tiny fraction of a second to travel that far." He'd known, working out this math during the test, that no one else would think of it.

"That wasn't the question, Danny," his father said patiently. "There was nothing about when she sees, it was just how long after the hit, does she hear it." He pronounced, "97," and glanced over. "Kiddo, you overthought it. You always overthink. Gotta work on that."

"But it was right," Dan said, incredulous. His father mumbled something under his breath he couldn't hear, and he demanded, "What?"

His father smiled placidly and said, "There's being right, and there's the right answer. You've got to learn that." After a beat, "We all ought to learn that."

In a moment of cognitive vertigo, Dan was unable to remember whether he had reached out across the air to Ann that afternoon in his office, so long in the past and less than a week ago, or whether he had done nothing. The peppermint-tea smell of her smooth hair against his cheek, the wordless puff of air she'd expelled when he laid the flat of his hand against her back between her shoulder blades and pulled her to him, maybe he was making all that up. Fact and imagination refused momentarily to line up in his mind.

Then another moment later, when reality clicked back into place, the matter remained unsettled for him, unresolved. There was still the problem that he wished he'd done more, something so simple, put his hand around the inside of her elbow, that would have led to everything else.

Wasn't that another of life's sucker games, though. Can't win. Doomed to play. Clinging so desperately to the idea that our actions make a difference, when still in the end, we all die alone anyway, alone with our experiences and memories of what we did and didn't do. If he had just put out his hand, to her hip or the back of her knee in a way that could not possibly be misread, he would have that experience, that memory now, and it would have been just a narrow single opportunity in life that he had taken, had allowed himself. Or, conversely, not having done it, this was another thing, one less ounce of guilt to the load that made up his life. That was how you built a legacy of honorable choices.

But, he thought: choices. We aren't given real choices. All that's guaranteed is that byproduct of longing, regret. We're never alone, when we have our regrets, the whole unavoidable troupe of them, lifting and scattering and resettling like blackbirds in a field. Every deed, everything you did or didn't do contributed one more bird to the wheeling flock that, in any long-enough life, will eventually blot out the sky. It was a sky he only glimpsed in pieces anymore, and could not remember unbroken.

He knew he still overthought everything. It was who he was. At the same time, he never questioned the right things. He'd spent most of his life dumbly following trail markings, stumbling into aid stations and taking without question what was thrust into his hands. Overhead now, the powerlines were a path, of sorts, but they were no promise. Following them guaranteed nothing.

And the powerlines had turned, a few times. Without the sun he had no clear idea of direction, but confirming it on his GPS seemed a pointless exercise. The way did seem perceptibly flattened in places, and from time to time he could discern a graveled patch, and parallel ruts the right distance apart for tire treads. This made sense: surely the powerlines required maintenance. He tried to believe in getting somewhere, making progress toward something.

The cold humid air clung to his body; he felt the thick moisture dragging at the fine hair of his forearms as he swung them with his stride. To break the silence, to put a sound in his ears, he spoke out loud. He had learned, he narrated to no one, that no matter how terrifyingly hard something seems, how long, how insufferable, he possessed the capacity to do it. "I'll decide to in my mind," he said. "And then I tell my body to do it. And, it happens."

He imagined a combative audience: *But you already knew that. Didn't you? All along?*

"Oh yeah, sure, fine," he admitted, loud, grinning, exasperated. "I knew it. I'd known it. You're right, hundred mile races, hundred mile weeks, never taught me shit I didn't already know." He went on, "No. Yeah. I learned it, from track days. Mile reps. I learned it, when my father. I keep on learning it, fucking brand new every day when I come home, don't I? This, this woman I'm married to, and this kid who's my kid, half the time they both might as well not even recognize me—yeah."

*So, wait. The lesson's where?*

But that wasn't even true—it wasn't that way, or as bad as that. Was it? Here he was overthinking again, fixating, overlooking everything that resisted his narrative, the look to her eyes some other days when she looked up and did see him there, a rounding, a pleased recognition. He didn't know what he wanted, or could never isolate what was missing. Maybe he was conditioned to dissatisfaction, inventing flaws anytime he couldn't find a real one.

He barked a sharp, hoarse laugh. To anything near enough to hear, he imagined he sounded like a kicked coyote, and this made him laugh again. All the world around him was black except for the colorless beam of his headlamp. What was out there, listening? Wolves, were there wolves in this part of the world? If he worried about wolves, would they appear?

"It never always gets worse," he muttered. "There it is, right? Never always." He shook his head at the stupidity of the saying. Sure, it never always gets worse—until the end. When you die. Then it just gets as bad as it can get, and stays there.

Pockets of cooling air swam around his shins, and he felt the outer millimeters of his skin growing cold, capillaries shrinking and pulling back. When the wind blew up or he topped a small rise, the cold flowed past his face. Not that it was that cold. It was well above freezing. But people had died of exposure in milder than this.

As long as he kept moving, he would be all right; as long as he kept moving, he would be perfect. If he stopped, though—he could just imagine his body heat evaporating, leaving him completely in a matter of moments. His right hamstring was beginning to creak like old rope, but rest was out of the question.

Suddenly, a divide appeared before him. It first looked like an abrupt change in the color of the ground itself, a black featureless flatness pulling up. He stopped, glanced up at the invisible space where his powerlines hung, then looked back down to the dropoff at his feet. It felt like a betrayal, an attempt at a trap, the way the power pylons marched on, bridging the ravine without break in their stride.

He peered down into it, reaching with the beam of his lamp. The moon had sunk far enough now that only the tops of the pines were lit, coated with a ghostly blue light the shade of skim milk. A splashing of water reached his ears—running water, snowmelt. Fortuitous for his thirst, but a geographical threat to his progress. Judging from its sound, what he heard was more than a trickling stream.

He shrugged out of his camelback and let it swing from his hand as he paced first one way along the ravine, then the other. One option, he considered, would be to abandon the powerlines and follow the stream, instead of fording it. The bank would be tougher going, but this tributary would inevitably grow, joining a river, possibly leading to a road, a bridge, a village.

He could also turn back. The GPS in his watch probably held enough battery to retrace his route, navigating backwards, if he turned it off for the powerline portion. This was taking longer than he'd imagined, and his doubts weighed fiercely. Going back would be a failure, but he'd be with Susy and Deb. They could rest, reconnoiter, and wait. Pressing on, on the other hand, cast his bet gravely: much farther, and he'd be unable to make it back. Even if he could physically do it, finding his way by visual landmark through that early stretch of forest and bog would be uncertain. And, turning back later, after crossing this stream, would mean getting wet twice.

Still, the miles he'd put in were an investment, a wager on the promise of the only manmade thing he'd seen out here. He decided to investigate, to get down to this stream and see at least what he was dealing with.

He clapped his hands against his legs. Already his muscles were stiffening. Anything but momentum was unacceptable. He tried to make his first step over the precipice gingerly, committing only a portion of his weight, but the crumbly dirt deteriorated almost at his touch, and then he was sliding down, half-sitting, dirt and rocks flying, his heels and hips and elbows bouncing against the embankment.

In a recurring dream, he was delivering the eulogy again. His tie was too tight, constricting his throat. The buzzing of the overhead fluorescent lights reverberated in his brain, and the heat radiating down from them made him feel sick and feverish. An oily layer of sweat had popped up all over his body, making the layers of his suit feel heavier, thicker. To his left, the dusty leaves of a plastic fern cast striped, crazy shadows.

It made no sense for him to be nervous; it was exactly like lecturing, which he did all the time. Here, even, he had the most sympathetic of audiences. Nothing he could say would be wrong. "You know he told me one time," he started, dispensing with the few sentences he'd agonized over as an opening. His own voice startled him with its unevenness. "I remember him telling me once that, in any race, that moment can come, when you consciously decide to accept it all. The discomfort, the strain, the real work of it. And, you decide, to actively engage. Really work your hardest, from that moment on."

He looked up, just to the side of the light, held focus and felt his pupils shrink to pinpricks. He was blind to his audience, had no idea who had come in or left, or if anyone was even listening. When he looked down to his notecards, all he saw was a floating purple smudge.

"The alternative," he went on, "the other side to that coin, and what some might call the sad part, is that, when that moment comes—when that decision's in front of you—it's possible to reject it. To just, withdraw, back down. To allow any of the hundred voices in your head, to convince you, 'not today.' Or, 'it's too hard.'" He looked up from his cards and imagined he heard rustling, whispers from his audience. No one would silence him. He had this floor as long as he wanted it. "I don't know," he said, "what it is, what series of thoughts or circumstances, lead to this decision to commit. Just like, no one can truly know why, after dedicating thousands of miles of training, or years and years of work, a whole life to something—anyone can choose to just give it all up. To quit."

The noise from his audience grew louder. He stared toward the light for a long time. Finally he murmured, "Thank you. Thanks for being here," and stepped away.

At the bottom of the embankment, Dan flexed his knees, rotated his ankles, and patted his joints the way he might check his pockets, making sure everything was still there. Beside him, water hissed and roiled, shaping around rocks and a submerged tree branch. He thought he heard stones clicking against each other. Within his beam, though, the water's surface rose and swirled consistently, and did not smooth to an undisturbed current further out; this suggested a wide flat stream, with no major drop off.

He ought to be able to ford it. He would not hesitate in daylight, but that was hours away. And, sure, there it was, his old impatience again, but for once it was simply, starkly validated. He didn't have hours to wait, until it would even begin to be light, until—his watch, of all its more esoteric features, calculated geographic sunrise and sunset. Absurdly, as if it mattered, he raised his wrist and thumbed the menu button before jolting back to practicality: his watch. It couldn't get wet. While it was adequately rainproof, he was pretty sure immersion would be bad.

He unzipped his pack and fished out his phone in its Ziploc, which he opened and resealed with the watch inside. Then, touching the ground beneath him and lowering himself carefully, he sat. If more marsh or wet ground stood in his way, he'd cross it, but the going had been largely dry beneath the powerlines so far, and he expected more of the same on the other side. He untied his shoes and peeled off his socks. He tied their laces together, balled the socks and stuffed them inside, then slung the pair of shoes around his neck, so they bumped against his chest. The sour smell of his own feet rose to his nose. Barefoot, he'd lose traction and protection from sharp edges, but gain sensitivity and balance, and he'd have dry shoes on the other side.

He grasped the baggie with his phone and watch in his fist, then changed his mind—he'd be more comfortable with his hands free—and jammed it instead deep into his left shoe. Shouldering his pack again, he was ready. Its loose chest clasp swung and dangled, an annoyance, but he'd just be taking the damn thing off again in a moment anyway, on the other side.

Like the old post-workout ice baths, he tried to steel himself against the visceral snap of it, and like always, the shock made a mockery of his preparations. His first barefoot step into the stream made his bones ring with cold, and he drew a sharp involuntary breath. His feet felt smooth solid rock underneath, but as if from a distance; it was like trying to feel someone's face with oven mitts on your hands.

He stepped forward, pointing his light down to gauge his next step, then up to scan for obstacles or the approaching bank, then down again. He held his arms out wide for balance, and felt carefully before committing to each step. The current enveloped his calves, but did not pull more than he could counter. He had made the right choice: there was the bank, and he would soon be across.

Then a stone, when he put his foot down for it, was simply not there, where he had felt it firmly just a moment ago with his numb toe. He jerked back nimbly, feeling all the muscles fire from his hip stabilizers up through his core, but the swinging maneuver that would have recovered him on a trail run failed without that forward momentum. Suddenly horizontal, he thought, that is exactly how it is: if you make a mistake, you can credit one footstep ahead, but beyond that is asking to distribute weight over empty air.

Then he was submerged in black and cold. And, for a split second, silence, then the sound of rushing water again filled his ears, and he was not drowning, but splashing, rolling, his whole body soaked. When his head ducked under, his lamplight instantly was gone, not even shining under the water for a second. Slapping his free hand to his chest, his heart leaped into his throat: his shoes. In the darkness, he lunged out one arm in a desperate swimming reach of a stroke and felt his finger seize rough fiber, and he was terrified for a second he'd gotten only a branch, but then he pulled it in and recaptured the weight of his shoes, heavier now, spilling water.

Panicked, he scrabbled toward where he'd last glimpsed the bank, banging his elbows and knees against underwater rocks with shocks that barely registered, until he'd pulled himself out, shuddering uncontrollably in spite of the adrenaline rush.

He'd lost his pack, which he'd hoped to refill on this far side. Everything that had been in it was gone. Salt tabs, extra gels, moleskin and duct tape for blisters, extra dry socks that were dry no more, wherever they were. His headlamp, ironically, was still fast on its strap, dead weight that might never dry out again.

He touched his pockets: he had left two more gels, and three or four electrolyte capsules that were probably wet now in their unsealed bag. He pulled off his shirt, tighter now and sticking to his skin, and even though the light wind made him that much colder without it, he wrung the shirt out carefully, hearing more than seeing the water trickle out, and put it back on. The wet fabric still clung, but felt lighter; it would rewarm on his body.

He repeated the wringing process with his socks, neither of which thankfully had fallen out of his shoes. His knit hat and gloves had not soaked up too much, but he squeezed a few drops from them as well. His electronics in their baggie were intact as well; he slipped the watch back on his wrist, and guessed he'd just hold the phone. The shoes themselves he banged against his hand and then the ground, to knock out what water he could.

Then he turned back to the stream. Already his eyes were getting more used to the dark, and in the diffuse glow cast by the moonlit cloudy sky, he could make out the restless churning surface of the water in the middle, the smoother eddy at its near edge. He knelt, then plunged both hands into its cold flow.

"Dying," he mumbled aloud, "is untreatable. Everything else, we'll deal with later." He drank, filling his hands and raising them again and again. Schistosomiasis, giardia, dysentery: there were aspects of ignorance he envied. At least exposing himself to a single source was better than drinking from every stream he came across. He slurped noisily, at first trying to filter out sediment with his lips and teeth, then just raising his hands and lowering his face and gulping. Then, hands on the gritty bank, he put his head down and extended his lips to the surface of the water like an awkward kiss. Then his chin was in, and the whole lower half of his face, as he pressed his cheek shamelessly to the pebbly streambed and drank and drank, letting the water flow into his mouth and swallowing, carrying into his body whatever it would. He no longer cared, thinking only of his now and future thirst.

Finally, half his face chilled numb, he stood, turned, and faced the climb on this side of the stream. It was less steep than the one he'd slid down. Eyes open wide to catch every bit of moonlight, he found one handhold, then another, and then very quickly he was more walking than climbing, hunched forward, his fingertips gliding over the ground only for balance. Above him stood yet another power pylon, silhouetted now against the sky, absolute and removed, majestic in its way.

At the top, he kept going, and very quickly, the sky seemed to brighten once he'd climbed out of the ravine. He thought it was his eyes acclimating, until he glanced up. In the slow-moving sky, the moon had just shaken free a scrim of cloud. Under its full light now, he could move almost as well as with his headlamp, but above, a checkerboard of cloud and clear scrolled by, soon to mask the moon again. The old expression about hay and sun echoing in his mind, Dan made time while the moon shone. At least he was committed now. And that was something.

His mind drifted to those inspiring crazy shows he sometimes saw in the gym, on winter days when he chose the university's treadmill over outside, about people who had survived ridiculous, impossible odds, adrift for days in shark-infested waters, lost in the rainforest, or trapped on a mountainside. Or the guy who, pinned under a boulder, had sawn off his forearm with a pocketknife and hiked out thirty miles. These shows reenacted everything with more photogenic protagonists, actors acting brave and terrified in measurable increments. The actual survivors, interviewed quickly near the end of the show, were always off-putting, with their black, frostbitten patches of skin, and sad artificial limbs.

He might just about qualify for an episode himself, Dan thought. Escalating disastrous conditions, prerequisite to make viewers shudder out of schadenfreude? Check. He imagined his story in sober, ominous voice-over, *Heroically, battling on, despite yet another disappointment, against seemingly insurmountable odds.* They'd get some hungry kid to play him, some young actor dying for a chance, far too earnest. Dan imagined himself on set, watching his more visually likeable doppelganger stumble through the snow in some farm field a mile from a freeway, his lip trembling, whispering inanely, "Got to make it…for…." The actor straightened, called out, "What's my daughter's name again?" Dan would let the director tell him.

When it came time for his own interview, he would stare into the camera and say, "Motivation? No, I had plenty of motivation." He would glance away, then back, and maybe shrug modestly to simultaneously deflect and treble the melodrama of it: "Death was kind of my pacer." It would be a flip-side to *Jesus is my copilot*.

Maybe others would want to try what he'd done. They'd helicopter thrill-seeking runners out into the wilderness and leave them. T-shirts would read *Death is my pacer*.

Still, first, he had to survive. They only did shows on people who lived—"I Shouldn't Be Alive." Maybe he'd spark a special series, "Shit, No Wonder I'm Dead!" How much great TV do we never see, just because some inadequate SOB failed to live through it? How many deaths did it take to make an exception, the reason why the star "shouldn't be alive"? If he were setting up someone else's survival special now, would he even make a sidebar, a still photo, a quick VO line—one more who perished?

At least, he thought, he came by it honest: a history of second places, never winning when it counted. Hell, he had a long lineage of also-rans. His father. Longer. He would be in familiar company.

Failure came to everyone, though, really. All of us were locked in this eternal communion of breaking down. An entropy shared by every living thing. A process generally offset by anabolic repair, infinitesimally skewed toward the victory of time. Except, not so gradually for him now: maintenance and rebuilding required input of raw materials, and without those, he was progressing into unchecked decline.

A term worth knowing: catabolism. The process by which the body takes molecules apart. Although all biological cycles use it, it especially aptly describes how the starving body cannibalizes itself for fuel. The word's literal derivation meant "throwing downward," but to Dan it always suggested "metabolic catastrophe."

He hated the connotation he was letting creep in, the lapse it signaled toward unprofessional sloppiness. Biology knew no subjectivity, and no action or reaction or process was good or bad. Really, this was his field's worst and most pervasive intellectual failure, assigning will and intent to nature, and he railed against it in every intro lecture course.

He had eaten one of his carb gels earlier, and though it had done nothing to blunt his hunger, he'd saved the last one. He felt it bouncing now in his pocket with every step. One sad single fucking tiny little gel packet. 150 calories, if he tore it open and sucked every gooey last bit from the wrapper. A single mile of fuel, at best.

Then, it would be nothing but body fat, and his own muscle proteins. Leading to, literally, a death march, until he emptied the tank, burned every calorie he had.

His stomach twisted and growled and felt like it was curling in on itself. He left the gel in his pocket, thinking not yet, and not yet, and not yet. It was not that its presence and feather-light weight bouncing against his leg was so comforting in itself; he just dreaded more the thought of it gone, the feeling of being turned-out, empty-pocketed, with finally nothing left.

As the night progressed, slowed by the loss of his light, his stomach empty and his clothes still damp from the stream, he felt his body temperature dropping. Cold rose in waves from the snow still on the ground, stealing up his calves.

He wished he'd worn more. *And what's happened to your mittens*, a voice that could be his mother's echoed. He'd been so young, he wasn't sure of her voice. A shiver racked his ribcage. Susy, he realized, was younger than he had been when his mother died. He drew a couple short fast breaths and clenched his shoulders and back, wasting energy for a barely perceptible, quick-to-fade shadow of warmth.

Though it felt like a kind of surrender, a dangerous lapse of faith, he pulled out his phone. He opened the seam of its Ziploc, thumbed the button and brought up the camera. He'd decided he wouldn't do this, or at least wouldn't think about it, not yet, but suddenly the greater risk seemed waiting too long.

It was too dark for the camera to get his face, but the audio would record, and that was the important thing. "Susy," he started to say, and coughed, his voiced strangled off. He cleared his throat and started again. "If you're listening to this," he said, "there are things I want you to know." His voice shook and his breath was short. If he stopped or slowed, though, the cold would set in worse, so he kept on, jogging and huffing for breath and keeping his voice as even as he could and trying not to ramble. "Don't hurt anyone if you can help it," he came up with. "Work hard. Be good to yourself, too."

He stopped the recording. Was that really all he had? After *I love you, I'm sorry, I never meant to leave you this way*, he couldn't come up with a whole lot else.

There was time, though. He had a lot of time. He would think about it, and try again. It was important.

As the sky began to lighten, for a twilit half hour it combined with the mercurial moonlight to outline twisted shapes of thin trees and wind-wracked brush. Too many times, his heart quickened at impossible shapes, suggesting civilization and manmade structures that could not be there, only to resolve again into the natural.

He almost passed the crashed truck before he recognized it. It seemed almost regressed to nature itself, its once-angular lines softened and severely rust-degraded, all but the last flakes of its paint weathered away. Now the broken truck hunched nose-down in a ditch like a skulking animal, doing something private just out of view.

Dan stood above it, his breath pluming and dispersing in the ethereal light. While the truck was evidence of civilization, some mark of maintenance under these interminable power lines Dan was beginning to believe had sprung up of their own accord, nothing indicated recent human presence. Clearly it had been abandoned here. He considered sacking the cab for supplies—if not edible food or good water, possibly still a coat or a blanket—but worried what else he might find. A bag of bones in a company uniform, unmissed and unreported? The last resting place of the last human to pass this way, who'd gotten no farther?

The longer he stood deliberating, the more the cold wrapped its fingers around his bones. The sun, visible wholly now above the horizon, was a pale and distant orb.

Dan knew some facts about his mother's death. It had been night, a week before Christmas; there was a slow-moving train, and black ice before the crossing. Dan imagined the headlights of his mother's car, a little Honda painted gray or possibly brown, illuminating the side of a passing boxcar, the lights' double circles converging on one impossibly huge, turning, clanking wheel; then the squeal and crunch of metal.

"She was leaving us," his father admitted one summer evening. With school out, he'd been drinking since noon. Dan was old enough by then to understand the difference between leaving, and running an errand. "It wouldn't have been for good," his dad said. "But still." Surely, Dan always thought, she'd meant to come back for him; arrangements must have been made. But that didn't explain why he hadn't been in the booster seat, with her.

Years passed before Dan thought to wonder whether his father had always drank that way, or had fallen to it in his mother's absence. Always, in photos, his dad held a glass of something, or a can of beer, or, in one case, a bottle of Seagram's Seven aloft like a prize—but everyone, in those pictures, was drinking too. The alcohol and his mother leaving: Dan had no basis to determine cause from effect.

Worse were the memories of things he could not have known. Clear products of his imagination poisoned the data set. The accident itself he could not have seen, the mangled metal of the Honda he couldn't remember as gray or brown; no one would have allowed an eight-year-old to view that. It left him no choice but to suspend judgment, suspect all memory as equally unverifiable.

Dan put the crashed truck behind him, unexplored. As full daylight rose, his feet hurt and kept hurting. Usually, he didn't like to look inside his shoes while on a run, preferring instead to let his tape and petroleum jelly and moisture-wicking shoes and socks do their work. This was getting to be much longer than he'd ever run before, though, and as hot spots began to chafe on their way to becoming blisters, he wondered how much farther he had yet to go. Without his pack, without his duct tape or moleskin or lubricants, he told himself, and with no pair of drier socks to change into, there was little point in even untying his laces. There was precious little doctoring he could even do, and anything he did to interfere could introduce new problems.

He knew blisters, he thought, and took pride in ignoring their fire. He refused to let their trivial pain change his stride now. He could stand it. The tender places that had used to hobble him in his youth had long callused over, and now his feet just inflated the odd blister or two as padding, almost like he could consciously will it. The sore spots burned until they puffed up with water and then they stopped, or if that didn't help and it was the blister itself that hurt, soon enough it would burst on its own. Either way, the pain was not debilitating, and the problems would solve themselves.

As the day dragged on, though, one pain began to stand out over the others, a dull knife stabbing his toe on every step. It was an unfamiliar, sharper pain. Soon he was involuntarily altering his footstrike and, cursing, he slowed to a walk. He didn't want to sit down, as his legs would stiffen quickly, but after trying a few more running steps, there was nothing else to be done.

He eased himself down in the middle of the trail, flexed his fingers, and tugged at his dirt-stiffened laces. Peeling off his sock, he found what he'd suspected. The nail of his big toe floated and wobbled on top of an enormous purple blister. Friction from his sock and hydraulic pressure of the blister had entirely lifted the nail from his toe, but this was not what hurt; it was the sharp edge of his toenail twisting when his shoe came down and stabbing the tender nailbed underneath. Why, he thought, why for God's sake hadn't he just had all his toenails removed years ago?

Now, he wished he had the tiny folding knife he kept in his pack. He wished he had duct tape, or a clean bandage.

The nail was already severed at the root, so that was not a problem. It had to come off, though. He prodded the blister, sickly firm like overripe fruit. He wished he had pliers.

His parents' front door had been heavy and old and made of thick wood, with an enormous brass knob. Dan thought he remembered his mother teaching him how to open it. Though he must have been old enough to come and go freely, he hadn't had the grip strength to work the knob.

"Turn it as hard as you can," she explained, "then, just a little harder."

He'd been amazed when it worked. Before, he'd simply exerted all the force he could, straining until the tendons in his thin wrist stood out and shook, to no effect. Approaching it with a strategy, though, a method, did the trick: he gave it all his strength, backed off a moment, then turned just a little harder. And the mechanism unclenched. The door opened.

The same door failed to latch behind him, the day he found his father dead. He let it swing behind him, to stand open to the cold. He'd knocked out one of its panes with his denim jacket wrapped twice over his fist. His key worked well enough, but when the chain lock stopped the door, the old painted-over chain lock that had never been used against him in his life, Dan knew there was no point trying the back kitchen door, or climbing up to mess with second-floor windows. He'd shaken the sparkling glass from his coat and reached in gingerly, careful to keep his wrist from the serrated edges he'd left, and disengaged the chain.

He'd had an idea what he'd find. He'd called on Saturday and again on Sunday, to tell his father about Deb's first ultrasounds and the tiny globe of the head, the frills that might be fingers or toes, or ribs. He got no answer and his messages went unreturned, and every time he went outside the dry gritty bluish snow under the unbroken lid of clouds looked like weather for dying, going to ground like a rabbit against a hard freeze and just not waking up. He cancelled his Monday afternoon class to drive over, without telling Deb.

The old house made its noises, settling around him and creaking through one more winter even as, deep in the dirt-floored part of the basement, Dan heard the boiler furnace cycle on with a groan. He hurried to the kitchen, where his father's hand lay on the table, fingertips resting against the flaking glaze of his coffee mug just as if he were about to lift it and drink. Beside it were two unlabeled prescription bottles, and a small china bowl Dan remembered eating cereal from. The bowl held two neat domes of powder, one white and one aqua blue, and a few empty halved gel capsules and two more full ones—extra, unneeded.

Impulsively, Dan took two steps across the room, laying the soles of his shoes so softly against the linoleum as to be soundless, and stuck the index finger of his left hand into the coffee cup, half full and two knuckles deep. Though no steam rose from the cup, he had been hoping to be scalded, for the liquid to be anything but so cold.

He retracted his hand and stood a moment, stricken, about to drip. There was no dish towel out, no roll of paper towels. A cold droplet of coffee hit the floor with a tap.

He looked closer. The thin brown liquid clung to him like a wash, lightly yellowish on the smooth skin, collecting darkly in the wrinkles of his knuckle, the recess of his cuticle, the tiny lines where his skin had cracked in the cold. He thought of the few times he had changed his own motor oil, how even after he washed up the stain had lingered on his hands, along with the faint whiff of fossil fuel.

A second drop fell from the whorl of his fingertip. He looked again for some kind of towel, there should be one in here somewhere, and briefly considered popping the wet finger in his mouth, or shaking his hand once vigorously and letting droplets fall where they may.

A detached portion of him looked at the body, the most surely dead body of his father, and felt a small secret relief: it was over, the emergency was past, beyond what he could affect in any way. It would be pointless to check for a pulse, dial 911, or do anything but stand there in a new and completely empty silence. His helplessness was so complete that it was freeing. Alone now, all the expectations for what he should feel, how he'd have to act, were in a blessed stasis. For a moment he believed he might stand there until the still air told him what to feel, taught him what he needed to know.

He waited. Nothing came for a long time. And then, still nothing—nothing but the realization of nothing itself, that no greater understanding or comprehension would be given to him after all. No meaning was going to arrive just because he needed it to.

## Fourteen

Fire, Deb feared, could spread quickly. That was the thing. While the land around them was soggy, mud in the high spots and quagmire under the snow, the spindly trees above them were sticks, kindling, pine branches brushed with dry needles. She'd listened to them sighing and rattling all night, when Susy for a couple of hours had settled into an approximation of sleep.

All morning she'd struggled with Susy over why she must stay in the tent, but her library of distractions was limited. Her daughter frowned, disappointed and skeptical, when her stories started to repeat themselves, and all the games she could make up were dumb, naming the branches that tapped against the side of the tent, telling knock-knock jokes that weren't funny. Susy wanted to get out, stretch her legs and walk around, look and see—she said—where the animals lived, but Deb couldn't override her need to keep the girl close, within fingertip range.

So finally they'd gone outside together. And it was nice in the sun. But shuffling in a circle, testing her leg a little, only woke up the pain all over again, confirming all her fears. She could walk if she had to, but was incapable of outrunning anything—certainly not a fire if it caught in the trees, and the trees from here might as well be unending.

"C'mon sweetie," she said, "I'll find us something more to eat," and Susy's glum expression brightened only a little. She offered to let her play with her phone, which probably had a little battery left, and what was she saving it for?

"That's OK, Mama," Susy said, with a world-weary sigh. "I don't need to."

Deb smiled. Where'd she gotten that? Every day, almost, it was a new expression, some affected mannerism that Susy made her own. It was like being barraged with pictures of the person she'd grow up to become.

They could wait a little longer; it wasn't a decision she'd have to make yet. Back in the tent, she put her hand again in the pilot's survival bag, reassuring herself by brushing her fingertip over the hard contours of the flare gun.

## Fifteen

It honestly amazed Dan when the sun began to set again. He'd been swooping in and out of ever-longer reveries, but had that much time really passed? Surely he could not have been following the trail of these powerlines for a day, a whole fucking night and a day, and gotten nowhere, passed no road, no settlement, not even a branching of the wires. Could he have become confused in the night, turned around, doubled back on himself? But that would have taken him back to the ravine again, the crossing. And he'd been heading roughly north all day, the pallid sun warming first his right shoulder, then his left. It was very possible he'd made a fatally wrong choice, picked the wrong direction altogether, but he was invested far too deeply to turn back now. From here, he figured he pretty much had to keep following the lines north, until they terminated or he did.

Until then, though, unbe-fucking-lievably, here he was heading back into the cold again, of a second night. With no energy, his stores depleted and no real food in his body to speak of, his legs felt both heavy and hollow. His condition was degrading radically. Momentum, forward progress, was about all he had, and he was growing superstitiously afraid to let that falter.

Though he'd never seen them, Dan had heard about "black mice," another biological quirk and facet of ultra lore. "That's when you know to pack it in," a veteran had told him. "Your race is over, there's no coming back. Once that shit starts."

Black mice were hallucinatory dots in the peripheral vision, that occurred at night, under phenomenal physical distress. They would skitter in and out of a flashlight beam, disappearing faster than you could look directly at them. The black mice were uniformly a harbinger of disastrous, impending deterioration and collapse.

Physiologically, the dots were tied directly to central nervous system fatigue, the limiter that led to catastrophic muscle group exhaustion and real red-line depletion of the body's reserves. Such fatigue came down to non-negotiable, chemical, biological fact.

The fatty acids exclusively fueling Dan's forward progress were being transported by the same carrier protein as tryptophan, which the brain converts to serotonin. Limited capacity knocks tryptophan off the protein conveyor belt, and it builds up in the brain, producing excessive serotonin, and causing intense fatigue.

Keep pushing, and the brain begins biologically prioritizing systems. Like a powerplant directing blackouts in a damage control scenario, critical operations—the hospital, the nuclear cooling towers at the edge of town, emergency communications—are fully served, while across the residential and light industrial districts, whole grids go dark. Dan imagined a night watchman shuffling through the empty plant of his brain, calmly pulling shutdown switches.

Some biological systems can go dormant for a while. The greedy brain, however, demands a constant supply of free glucose. Once that is interrupted, peripheral systems, like the visual cortex, become erratic.

Dan at first thought it was only something stuck in his eye. When the smudges began darting of their own accord, and he couldn't wipe them away, he tried ignoring them. *Facing forward, eyes ahead*, he repeated like a mantra, but the dots got bigger the more he avoided looking at them. Soon the mice were squirrels, chiding him and chucking their tails and competing for his attention. Then they were gophers, weasels, raccoons doing jumping jacks. Pinwheels, flailing arms, helicopters.

Then he rounded a corner and the scene seemed to flatten before him. His first fear was that an entire horizontal band of his vision had gone static, but then as he slowed to a walk, listening more than anything else to find his bearings, a low white noise reached his ears. As his heartbeat slowed, the flickering black spots receded, and he saw what lay before him.

Down a gentle slope of perhaps a quarter mile, a river, a vast and unfordable one this time, swallowed the path he'd been following. Tentative and horrified, he picked back up to a light jog and approached, waiting for a solution to present itself. He could make out white foamy movement where the current split around boulders, and the powerlines, his promise and his lifeline, did not divert at all.

Just then, the moon burst from behind its scrim of cloud, and hung lemon-yellow in front of him like an oversized Chinese lantern. It illuminated the river cruelly, and the sound of the rushing water amplified in his ears.

The powerlines, in three great strides, bridged the entire river, cement shorings bracing their pylons against the water's rush. Boulder-heads dotted the surface, and slabs of ice clung to little islands and careered up from the water at angles, but formed nothing he could possibly hope to cross. A few weeks earlier, he supposed ruefully, it would have been frozen hard; a few weeks later in the season, unswollen by snowmelt, high spots in the rocks might have been manageable. And that, he realized, was what had become of his path, the thready two-track beneath the powerlines, and why no bridge existed for maintenance access: for much of the year, the river was probably passable here.

Indeed, the smooth, beach-like bank he stood on, extending as far as he could see upstream and down, suggested the river had once been much mightier. Possibly it had been artificially dammed or diverted, something to do with the mad marching powerlines to nowhere, but if so, it was the mark of a human hand now absent. Nothing bore the remotest sign of habitation, not even the most abandoned of structures, no forestry station or settlement or emergency cabin fallen to neglect and ruin with wild grass seed heads nosing up around crumbled brick foundations.

A cold scent filled his nose, more gravelly and metallic than the pine he'd been breathing. The flickering reflection of the moon on the water made a mocking path, casting a line right to his feet at the water's edge. Grimly, he knelt, pushed down his cupped hands, and drank. The water was achingly cold.

Clearly, Dan had two choices now: turn left or turn right, follow the riverbank one way or the other, upstream or down. He took a few idle steps just to keep his legs from cooling, and over the white-noise rush of the river water his shoes kicked clicking rocks, and crunched in the coarse sand with a brushing *whch* sound. The nearest ground to the right was more rock-strewn, while the left sloped in a long silty beach around the next bend.

His watch had begun chirping "Battery Low, press enter" around dawn, and he'd shut it down to conserve it. He held the power button down now for a long three-count until it finally responded, and then he stood stupidly with his wrist raised, bleeding body heat off into space, while the watch acquired a satellite.

When he did finally reach help, he could power it back up to retrieve the GPS coordinates of his starting point. He'd been stupid, so optimistically naïve, not to have written the numbers down when he left, or stared at them until they burned into his retinas or made up some rhyming song to memorize them.

Firing it up now was jeopardizing its battery, and he'd gone this long without the comfort of the accruing hours and minutes and seconds on his arm, and the beep for mile splits, even if they were discouragingly slow. He'd been tempted many times, too, to turn it back on and access its navigation screen and the jagged line that marked his progress, as well as the way back, the trail from where he started.

He rationalized now that he had a choice, was at a real crossroads here, and should at least affirm he wasn't doubling back on himself. Zooming and scrolling, his last reading gapped by a day's progress now, he squinted sentimentally for seconds, for far too long, at the pitiful thread that still represented the most tangible link between him and Susy and Deb.

Snapping back to business then, he toggled over to get a read on his current position, let the compass rose settle, then compared it with the curtailed thread of his previous path. The little picture, backlit with precious battery glow, confirmed that the powerlines had led him in a consistent direction, but offered little guidance now. Neither left nor right, east nor west, seemed a better gamble than the other.

Turning back was, for so many reasons, out of the question by now. "I'll crawl if I have to," Deb had said before he left. How long would she wait?

He could now remember Deb looking at him coldly, calculating, weighing the chances of him seizing this opportunity to be rid of them both, saving himself and sending no help back. You heard about those cases in the news, some unsuspected sociopath, a father, always the father, who engineered an accident and made his young family disappear. After all, if he walked out of this wilderness alive and alone, no one could suspect him.

Or maybe this hopeless exhaustion was what Deb had wanted for him. For there to be suffering, for him to complete a penance. She wanted him to keep going until he hated it, and felt each footstep ache without a ghost of hope left in him.

He shook his head hard, making both temples throb like his brain was a loose ball, bruising and rolling around in there. He had to cut that shit out: the weirdness, the paranoia. Really it was like one of those holographic toys: tilt it one way, and the bunny smiles, another way, the little animal snarls with a mouthful of fangs, bloodshot eyes. Deb turned her head in the unreliable light filtering through the tent, her face a multitude of tiny facets and refractive surfaces, compassionate from one angle, vindictive from another. The illusion, of course, was that the toy bore both images, and only changed according to your point of view; you could get the same effect by holding it still and swinging your head around to look at it from different angles, so it was really what you did that made it different, that controlled what you saw. Deb's lip curled in a sneer that, when he looked closer, was a concerned and genuine smile, distorted by light and perspective.

He had to keep it together, he thought. Pay attention. His mind felt dangerously unmoored, like if he let it drift too far, he might not be able to find his way back. Had he really been constantly moving, awake and running, for— how many hours could it be? Thirty-six hours, forty? He had no clear idea what time it was now, and numbers moved sluggishly in his brain. But, a day and a half, anyway, probably closer to two. With no stops or demarcating walls of sleep and waking, it felt like a single hellishly protracted day.

His hands themselves were filthy, and he knelt at the edge of the river to wash them and drink again. The frigid water chilled his throat as he swallowed it, and froze his hands. As he shook his hands dry, the droplets shone clear and cold in the moonlight, arcing onto flat cracked rocks and mud. He watched the paths they made in the air, light against the dark, sparkling briefly then out.

He was at a crossroads, about to depart the trail he'd bet everything on. If he was never seen again, just flashed out in the darkness out here, he'd have left no trace.

Dan bent down and ran his fingers along the edge of one dinner-plate-sized rock. He pulled, and it lifted easily from the mud. Behind him, farther from the water's edge, was a darker patch of silt. There was no shortage of rocks for him to work with.

Straightening, he lifted his wrist and toggled through the options on his watch. "Back to Start" produced a slow incremental bar as it processed, then a compass arrow and a distance. He held still as the arrow settled, then sighted along it to a spot in the dark, drawing a mental line over the darker ground.

As he lifted and placed rocks, walking back and forth, the work was a nice change, even though he was exhausted. The rough texture against his hands was welcome, along with the good pull of muscles in his arms and back that he hadn't been using. As he laid out first his arrow and then the letters SOS and finally the distance in kilometers, he felt like he was doing something ancient, making something, marking out his posterity on the surface of the earth. He had to rest before lifting the bigger stones, and a couple times closed his eyes, kneeling down, his forehead on one knee, collecting his strength and his breath. He'd blink and the blue-white texture of each stone seemed pillow-soft. Each time he opened his eyes again, it got harder to remember who and where he was, and how long he'd been gone.

## Sixteen

"You say this with me now," Gilda intones, staring around the circle with her usual fierce posture, head forward, shoulders back. Gilda is a solid woman, Haitian or Cuban—something Caribbean, Dan can never remember what—and has done mission work in places the UN fears to tread. Her skin is so utterly saturated black it's colorless, not even a bitter chocolate hue, and when she speaks under the dim light of the church basement, her features seem almost to float, Cheshire-cat like, her eyes and tongue and teeth blinking in and out of existence.

"You say this with me now," she repeats, staring around the circle. "Being alive today, is no my fault. What happen to others, what I could no do anything about, is no my fault."

They all repeat it, some mumbling lower than others. Gilda glares at one boy, a haunted-looking kid in an Army Strong T-shirt and camo fatigue pants that button to a clean closed cuff below his missing left knee. "What happen to my buddies, no my fault. I going stop living in the past, right this minute. Robert," she continues, "I thought I told you, you don't come back in here wearing those Army clothes."

Robert flinches.

Dan has quit his insurance-sponsored therapist after just two sessions, and has never called the referrals colleagues gave him after the funeral services. He's not sure why he keeps coming to the Survivor's Guilt Support Circle in the Mennonite Relief Fund church basement every week. Maybe it is a perverse interest in other members' stories, maybe it is the whole small-town, half-assed laughable quality of it: Gilda is in no sense a professional, credentialed or otherwise, and from the grim set of her jaw every week, she doesn't much relish her task of marshaling these shattered self-pitying white people.

Rumor has it she lost a family, two baby girls in a carriage and a young husband pushing them, when some building collapsed in Trinidad or Port au Prince or somewhere like that, bricks and mortar just raining down and not touching her as if she herself were made of light. According to this rumor, running this group is the latest installment of her penance for being alive.

Maybe another reason Dan keeps coming is the Narcotics Anonymous meeting before theirs, the over-caffeinated, sunken-eyed walking dead shambling up from the basement as he goes down into it. Their jaws rotating chewing on a toothpick or coffee spoon or corner of nothing, eyes fixed on nothing, contemplating not scoring on a minute by minute basis; maybe the idea appeals to him of becoming one of these, just checking out of the whole loser's game, driving an hour to the nearest real ghetto where he can buy enough of something and a needle to shoot it, enough to keep him on a numbed-out cruise for a couple of days straight, a ticket he'll never have to pay back in hangovers or withdrawals if he saves back enough to OD on.

He talks to the junkies sometimes, leans against the wall with, maybe, Katrine while she smokes cigarettes down to the nub of every filter. Katrine is his age and looks double it, a wrung-out dishrag of a woman. All of them are lost causes, and will never be new again.

Robert, the paratrooper amputee, asks bitterly if Dan still runs. Gilda shoots him a stern look and he says, "What? Physical activity is therapeutic."

"Not so much," is all Dan answers.

Which is funny, a bit, he supposes. If he'd kept at it, he might be much better off now, both physically and emotionally. Swelling of both legs threatened deep vein damage, and he of all people knowing exactly how important it is, just hasn't kept at the PT, and now the muscle loss is probably irrevocable. Not to mention the number the whole thing did on his kidneys; the cellular carnage and chowed muscle tissue has left his body's filtering capabilities on par with an 80-year-old diabetic's. In the first hospital, an intern guessed from his chart that he'd been struck by lightning.

Still, he has tried running again. Once. He had to sneak back up on it, accelerating gradually from a walk so his body wouldn't see it coming, but before he got a quarter mile in a shuffling jog, everything clenched, his muscles wouldn't work, and he fell to the side of the path and puked bile in the crabgrass. He felt it coming hot and acid up past his back teeth first, and tasted salty tears sliding down his face.

He tries lots of things again, sort of.

Elena is blonde and, he supposes, pretty enough, if you're into that drained and stricken look and don't mind the way she fixes her gaze behind you in conversation. Maybe a month after she joins the group, Gilda insists they go out together.

"Not dinner," Gilda prods, feeding them lines, one night after group. "Just coffee. You will see what happens."

Dan tugs at his shirt collar and tries to catch Elena's eye with a commiserating look, something that will team them together against Gilda, make a joke of it, but Elena just frowns fiercely at the red plastic coffee stirrer she is bending back and forth in her hands, whitening its plastic at the joint, applying just enough pressure to not quite break it and then bending again, stretching it the other direction.

"You will go do this now," Gilda says. "The shop it's open to ten. Neither of you doing nothing but going back to your empty old houses anyway."

"Look I'll walk with you," he bursts. "It's a nice night. What do you think."

Elena shrugs, opens her mouth to speak, closes it, and shrugs again, still staring down at her hands.

"You will have a nice time," Gilda says, more commanding than assuring.

Outside, Dan tells Elena she doesn't have to do this. "I just thought, so she'd leave us alone. Is all."

"I know. I know," Elena says, nodding, brow pinched. "You don't have to either, I was going to tell you."

A long period follows in which Dan feels he can either walk to his car or past Elena, and since he doesn't really care which, it is easy to choose one arbitrarily. If she stands still and does not walk with him, he will have a coffee on his own, and that will be just fine.

Outside the store, she says, breaking the silence, "What are you getting? I never, I never know what to get at these."

"They have just regular coffee," he points out.

"I know," she says. "I just feel like such a—" She looks up, pulling a brave half-smile, and because he can tell how much work it is for her, he returns it.

"They make a good chai tea," he says, and her smile broadens, grateful.

Elena's husband was killed in a farming accident, a tractor that overturned on a slope near their house. "I'd been after him to mow it down," she said in her first group meeting. "Before the wild mustard spread. And choked out these, these daylilies I was trying to grow. These, these stupid two-dollar little flowers. That don't even look like anything." Someone handed her a tissue, and she took it, quizzically, dry-eyed. "The thing rolled, you see," she went on, squinting into space, "and it pinned him into some mud, under, I guess, the tractor's tire. One of those kind of puffy tires, with a little give. It was just a small tractor, not like for in the fields. And I guess it didn't break anything, immediately, it was just like this slow slow pressure—every little breath, he couldn't inhale quite as much as before." Here she made a series of shallow exhalations, emptying her lungful of air in hitched bursts, in demonstration.

"I don't really remember how to do this," Dan confesses, bringing both chais back to their table. He's never liked the spice in these, and doesn't know why he ordered himself one. "It's been a long time."

"Sit down," she says, patting the chair beside her once. "We talk, is how we do this. Or not." Lowering her face to her Styrofoam cup, she nods, as if confirming an expectation. "Their milk is burned," she whispers. "Isn't it."

He has tracked down Ann, dialed her number in Nashville. He left her a message, then was relieved when she never called back, or picked up when he tried again. Good for her, he thought.

Four burnt chais, four group meetings, four weeks later, Elena asks him to drive her home. "Unless you don't want to," she says, emotionless, looking directly at him. "It's OK if you don't want to. I want to. But it's OK if you don't."

Her farmhouse is down a long lane from the road, and the sun is still up. Dan feels conspicuous, easing his Hyundai over ruts, even though no one is here to notice him.

She gets out and Dan watches her walk to the door, her hipbones rolling under denim shorts. He notes a dull physical stirring.

Inside, a pair of muddy men's boots stand upside down beside a radiator.

Someone asked on her first day of group, "The farm. Is someone taking care of it?"

"Clay has brothers," she replied. "They're…doing something. I don't know. Contracting, to harvest off, then lease out the land." They had no children. "One miscarriage," she said breezily, waving it off.

Dan doesn't ask whose the boots are.

Her mouth and dry lips brush over his collarbone and pectorals light as a moth's wings. He moves to kiss her lips once, and she returns it briefly, then turns away. She pushes her forehead against his sternum and wraps her fingers around his penis instead. Her breath tastes like burnt milk and chai spice.

Afterward, lying still, side by side watching the ceiling fan, she says she needs him to go.

"I understand," he says, trying only not to flee too fast.

He drives aimlessly for some time, executing mile-wide squares and cloverleaves over the farmland as the daylight dies upon it. It's the same ground he's covered so thoroughly on foot, over years, and using the gas engine to do it feels tired, impotent.

At home, as he parks the Hyundai, he still smells Elena's burnt milk breath and the dry scent of her soap on his body, and he laughs out loud, bitterly, once. He has no one to hide anything from, no reason to be ashamed.

The scenes splice so neatly that nothing strikes him as unusual, hanging up his keys, slipping off his shoes, and entering not his own kitchen but his father's. "Dad," he says evenly.

"Danny," his father greets him, as if he's been waiting. The mug-stained old table, round and wood, floats in an island of light, his father an actor on a sparse stage set. His father raises a cup. "Coffee's on," he says. "If you want any."

"I've had too much," Dan says. "Thanks."

His father pulls a tight smile and nods. "You're going to meetings," he says. "That's good."

A draft of winter air blows into the room, and he thinks some window must be open, or the door has not properly closed behind him. And then the telescoping, anguished contradictions pile all up on top each of other, and Dan understands, not exactly what is happening, but at least he has a sudden clear idea of what isn't. He never left the riverbank, and is inside a magnificently detailed caesura, a hallucination. "You're not here," he says, nodding slowly, realizing, "I'm imagining you."

"'Here,'" his father says, gesturing like the words mean nothing, semantics, "'not here.' What's important is, I wanted you to know—" Here he sits his mug down and leans forward.

"I'm imagining you, to talk me in," Dan says. Finally, something: he seizes on the idea. Wasn't that what people talked about, all the unlikely survivors—a feeling of being not alone, a sensation of supernatural support?

"No. Danny. It can be easy, you know," his father says. "I'm here to talk you *out*." He tilts his head back, and pauses to let this sink in. "Don't think it was hard for me, OK? You don't have to fight it—just, let it slip over you. A warmth. Like falling asleep."

"No," Dan says petulantly. "No, I can't. Look." He steps backward to leave the room, but there is only blackness there.

"You've had a good life, Danny," his father goes on. "Think about the good things. Just—relax, and remember the beauty that's been in it. That's been in everything, all along." He sips from his cup, and smiles slightly, as if savoring the bitterness. "Sit with me, Danny."

Numbly, as if not fully in his body, Dan pulls out a chair. The legs scrape on the floor. He sits gradually, relaxing only one part of his body at a time, and a warmth does begin to creep up him, like a buoyant, body-temperature bath.

"If it wants to slide over you, Danny, it's all right. Let it. Think about the warmth."

Dan starts. Had he spoken out loud? About the warmth?

"Think about the good things," his father repeats. "Your little girl. You have a beautiful little girl."

Dan stiffens, and tries hard to move his arms, but it's like being asleep, and the strongest signals his mind can send evoke only twitches at one wrist and the other elbow. He feels his jaw clench, the muscles in his neck trembling. "You haven't met her," he says. His father was dead before Susy was born. "You've never seen Susy."

His father shrugs at this. "Sit with me a while, Danny. She'll be here soon. With her mother. They'll all be home soon."

Dan shook his body awake, and the warmth was pulled out of him hard, joint by joint. As his feeling came back, everything hurt, like he'd been hit by a bag full of billiard balls. He was shaking, trembling, and as he stilled his body, the bumping against his bones stopped. And he opened his eyes, not to his darkened house but to the same riverbank, eternally the riverbank, the white noise of the water ringing in his ears. Had he lain down? Fallen? Was he awake now? His cheek felt the imprint of many tiny rocks.

Guilty, exhausted, and furious, he hauled himself up and looked around. A pale neon wave rippled the sky, and he rubbed his eyes. When the afterimage failed to clear, he blinked dumbstruck a moment before registering the Northern Lights. Dear God, he thought, how far to the northern ends of the earth had he come? And what was he doing about it—sleeping?

His nearly-finished SOS glowed accusingly on the dark bank. Moving jerkily, he threw two more rocks onto his sign, then another, then stood back, breathing hard. Then he wrenched himself back into motion, putting his work on the bank behind him and following the river's flow. Downstream felt like the right decision, the direction of civilizations and culmination, not emptiness and obscurity and origins. For a time, the rocky, part-frozen silt of the riverbank opened out before him as wide as any country road.

He and Deb had honeymooned in Honduras, and the first day, his shoes kept sinking into the wet sand of the beach, weighting him down. Barefoot, though, they sped over the sand. The scouring texture had been invigorating, even as he tensed with every step at the possibility of meeting a sharp shell or piece of broken glass. If he tried running barefoot here—fifty degrees colder, on this beach that was the polar opposite of that Honduran resort—the rocks and ice crystals would mutilate his feet immediately.

While he had been asleep, his watch had exhausted the last of its battery, and now with its screen unlit, its face zipped to blank, Dan felt utterly abandoned. He morosely imagined someone finding the watch years from now, here on the riverbank if animals had not dismembered his body and carried it off. Chipset and serial number would trace it back to him, and if anyone plugged it in to decipher his story, perhaps in combination with the arrow he'd left where the powerlines met the river, he didn't see how any of it would point to anything but two corpses in a tent, and another in the plane. His whole idea had been to use the coordinates in the watch to send back rescue, and now he'd completely failed at that, letting it power down while he slept. Without electricity and a charging cradle, the numbers were irretrievable, and he was the one who had let them go, not even taking the time to memorize them or write them down or carve them with a sharp rock onto his arm.

Fault. Oh, fault. Failure, culpability, was his story ever about anything else? Fault was such an encompassing word, though, along with its meanings other than just blame: an error or imperfection, a tectonic line of stress. A character flaw.

He saw Deb back in the plane, before she had tested her broken leg but still knew what it meant. Her bangs had fallen out of a clip and hung down, on each side of her eyes, shaking. It was as intense as he had ever seen her, lips parted enough he could see edges of teeth top and bottom, purplish smudges flaring under her cheekbones. Every one of her nerve fibers shook with tension, the cord in the near side of her neck standing out, just beside where her pulses fired so rhythmically he could count.

In his imagination, she intoned, "This is your fault," not accusing so much as just desperate for him to understand. True, the scene was shifty in his head, but the details, if uncertain, were so vivid. The sound of air between Deb's teeth. Neither of them had even looked at Susy yet; Deb, he understood, was laying out the ground rules first, establishing responsibility for the unthinkable. She breathed, eyes on him, lips trembling. Eager.

And he thought, it was such a simple thing he could do. A favor, costing him nothing. An acceptance, the word "OK" floated up from his chest, poised like a wafer on the middle of his tongue, waiting only for the breath to make it real.

There seemed little point in fighting it, anyway. It was hard for him not to see the whole sequence of events as predestined, ordained, down to the one specific treetop that had strained upward all its life just to catch the airplane's wingtip, the wood and bark and metal colliding perfectly. The two geese, rising up before the windshield—it was stupid to think such omens could have been avoided. One unique patch of forest, back where the plane had crashed and the tent was pitched, had been designated for the end of his little family's progress, and another singular spot on the surface of the planet awaited his own end.

There was no such thing as probability, he thought; time was a constant transformation of chance into fact. Each footshape of dirt and ground ahead of him, waiting for his step there, and there, and there; every footstrike changed one of those possibilities into the trail of decided steps behind him. The number of footsteps he had left was determined, even if he couldn't know it. And the path ahead of him was exactly like the one behind, excepting only the variable of time.

There were only different kinds of facts, the not-yet-known and the already-proven, both equally true.

The waved aurora above him softened, as if relenting, taking pity on his harsh situation. By looking just to the side of his path, avoiding the blind spot at the center of his vision where the optical nerve itself interrupted the field of his low-light receptors, Dan could see well enough to run, and he tried to keep his breathing easy, his gaze loose. He watched his peripheral vision for flickering, or signs of the black dots moving back in.

He was aware of the minute decisions that went into each individual step as he leaned forward, felt for the ground for a split second before he put his weight down, then rolled through, pushed off, and began reaching forward with his other foot. In this way, combining faith, proprioception, and a fearful sideways scanning of the ground he could not look directly at, he kept moving. When he misstepped the first time, he was too exhausted to recover his balance. A stone shifted beneath his step, rolling his ankle outward, and he threw his whole body limp, just let himself go weightless on the treacherous piece of ground. "Judas rocks," they were called: footing that looked firm, until you committed your weight.

It kept happening. First he skinned an elbow, then refreshed a scabbing knee. He picked himself up and kept going. Twelve-minute miles, he figured he was doing, though the incredible concentration and repeated falls made it far more taxing.

For stretches of time that might have been minutes or hours, he half zoned out and couldn't tell the sounds of his footsteps from his heartbeat in his head. He was powerless to alter either cadence, his pulse staying mostly the same aside from a sick loud thud here and there, and his footfalls only varying a little bit, like the meandering rhythm of a song he couldn't remember. He pondered the miracle of his ankles, the most essential and improbable joint of his body, swiveling and hanging on each stride and then accepting whatever angle they met, locking, pushing, and opening again. He was very nearly shuffling, lifting his feet just millimeters off the ground.

When the next foot caught and he fell again, this time he didn't even react, just toppled like a tree. Both elbows hit hard, and the pain was a sick ache that nauseated him briefly but centered his mind in the present. He couldn't keep risking these falls. A long new scrape radiated bright pain down his right forearm, and as he got up, his left arm was numb.

He was deep into it now—the process of his mind and body becoming diffuse, all his material components beginning to disperse. Flesh of my flesh of my flesh of my flesh, he thought. This was it, his body was eating itself. He imagined devouring himself into nothingness, diminishing until his last atoms were split, their energy dispersed.

He'd never really prayed, and didn't think he knew how to mean it now. Who or what could he appeal to, what was there he believed in? *O Glycogen*, he thought, as much lamenting as mocking, *in which we trust*. Sad as it really made him, contemplating the end of his poor fucked self, still he reached and all he came up with was parody: *Holy trinities, chemistries, triglycerides*. He would not be swayed by temptation, or place his faith on fickle adenosine triphosphates. Lead us not into unsustainable lactate loadings. Gluconeogenesis, an everyday miracle, real transubstantiation; as close to energy from nothing as it got. He believed, he believed. Saint dopamine, saint epinephrine, saints adrenaline and endorphin. He would transmute body fat and protein, his muscle tissue and corporeal being, into energy; he would cannibalize himself and be reborn. Eat, flesh of his own flesh. Be nourished, be devoured, move forward.

He believed. Yes.

The ribbon of neon-lit riverbed kept on, and he kept on it. Eventually, when he had lost all track of time and forgotten to hope that such a thing might ever happen, the sky began to lighten above him, rocks and gray trees and gray brush coming into focus in achingly slow degrees.

As his surroundings became more visible, he noticed that the river, though he was following it downstream, was greatly diminished. In places it was more boulder and dry rockbed than rapids, and the beach he was running on had significantly broadened. What kind of river grew shallower as it ran, he wondered. It fit, in a way, that in this cruel land of absence, where every path he took led to dissolution, even the rivers had gone away.

Thinking rationally, though, he guessed the stream must have been diverted or drawn off, possibly even dammed at some point he'd passed in the night. If he wanted to cross now, if he had reason to believe the other side was better, there were places he could almost walk across.

As he proceeded down the rocky beach, now as wide as a two-lane road, a swath of uniform gravel appeared before him. As he drew near, he saw the gravel continued, off to his left, away from the river: a road. An actual road!

In lieu of falling to his knees, he stood at the brink of the road and stumbled in a circle for a moment. He was elated, validated: now surely, he would get somewhere after all. And in the midst of the joy, he felt a helpless anger, too, at how many similar turnouts or trailheads he might have already passed by in the dark, oblivious.

Still, his next thought was that this chance, however he'd gotten it, was more than he rightfully deserved. So many things made him feel small and selfish anymore, emotionally stunted, as if incapable of feelings that were native to everyone else.

When Susy was born, for example. He'd been expecting new revelations about the fragility of life, whole new dimensions to love he'd never dreamed of. Sure, he would have died for this squalling, puffy-eyed ball of limbs, but he'd assumed that was hardwired in his DNA anyway, before he even held her. There was no welling up or sudden rush of new feeling, as he self-consciously wondered how long until he ought to hand her back.

The surprise, the change that did come, was his new take on stability. Or, to put it more precisely, it was the realization that he'd always fantasized about shattering news that would change everything: the next 9/11 bombing, a pandemic or fire, a fierce cancer within Deb or himself. Part of him had wanted his world ripped apart in a holocaust of grief, something to plunge him into the raw core of transformative experience. The nibbling urge that said *jump* when leaning over a huge drop, the idea of steering a good relationship toward the abyss just to dare the loss: before, tragedy had held some perverse, seductive appeal.

After Susy, he could not desire anything but tranquility. He rightly feared the real and possible horrors of the world. Now he wondered superstitiously what restless yearnings had invoked this ordeal. Two days ago, he'd been on a mild adventure, an excursion, a chaperoned funhouse ride that never broached real danger. A week ago, he'd been engrossed in his end-of-semester routine, safely in the palm of civilization and bulwarked against change. To be ripped so abruptly from such safety now felt like he must have caused it, signed up for this somewhere, wanted it to happen. Had he lived his whole life at the edge of this precipice, constantly oblivious to catastrophes narrowly averted?

Even as his rational mind refuted the idea, the possibility of self-sabotage ground at him. Smug fragments of his own psyche taunted him, reciting lists of traps he'd laid against his own complacency and happiness, and every self-destructive thing he'd ever set in motion that it was now too late to fix.

He was making pathetic time on the smooth-surfaced road. He was barely lifting his feet over the gravel. Air burned and wheezed in his throat, and his arms and legs no longer felt clear warmth or cold. Every time he turned his head, the world spun giddily. He was far from saved. The road meant nothing for him if he couldn't keep moving along it.

After a while he felt someone else, a presence with him on the road. He wondered how long Craig had been jogging alongside him. "Don't let me slow you down," Dan muttered. Speaking aloud made him taste iron in his throat. "I'll make it."

Craig waved him off with barely a gesture and stayed even. Dan marveled at his fluid stride, even at this shambling walk-jog. Craig made every speed look effortless. That hadn't changed since college, and neither had anything else about his old friend: the sunburned skin stretched too shiny over the bones, his eager smile and the startling white of his teeth.

"How's training? You been getting your miles?"

"I guess," Dan said, unsure what Craig already knew or not.

"National championship," he said, as if in answer to Dan's thought. "Sounds fun."

"I was never going to win or anything," Dan said reflexively.

Craig barked a sharp laugh at this. "Bullshit. You've never in your life tried hard for something you couldn't win."

Dan tried a laugh that just came out a weak cough. He squinted down at the road. "No. No. I've," he said, "got some damage going on here."

Craig nodded. "Some other year then."

Dan started to shake his head, but the crashing in his temples made him dizzy.

"Let me tell you something," Craig said, suddenly impatient. "You will never win your championship. You will never ever get that. You just won't. If you did, you'd have the chance to understand that that doesn't mean anything either, there's no winning anything that's enough—but you won't get to learn that. Here: feel the air in your lungs. Blood, pushing through your body. That's what you get, and it's all that you get. As long as you keep putting one foot in front of the other, you get to live." He added bitterly, "That's all anyone gets."

After Craig evaporated, Dan found himself thinking in terms of cycles. Cori Cycle, Krebs Cycle, the Citric Acid cycle, spinning in the little diagrammed wheels that made bigger wheels go: changing glycogen to pyruvate to lactate, then it was off to the liver to turn lactate back into pyruvate back into glucose. And, it costs, every step costs. Energy must keep feeding in, driving the cycle like feet pushing the pedals of a bike, or the diagram breaks down and stops. Nothing comes from nothing.

Carbs to energy to shit to plants to corn or wheat or green leaves or whatever, the whole wheel pushing itself on as long as there's energy, energy being shoved in, fed in, used and broken and transformed, every step of the way. Right foot, left foot. Pushoff, toe-off, left heel in a backwards kick, contact, brush, pull, toe-off again. The Achilles and the arches eat shock and spit it back out again, absorbing energy and rebounding a little less. Even though he was barely lifting his feet, every few more inches forward still involved millions of chemical transactions, cycles burning and turning.

Cycles, circles. He was born, his baby was born, he will die, another day if not today. Life, death, whatever after that. The cycles don't need you to care, they push themselves.

The sun, the sun, it couldn't be over fifty degrees, but it felt like it was cooking him. And when he passed through shade, he shook with cold.

From the hip, from the knee, left foot, right foot. Foot forward, contact, pushoff, body forward, foot up, foot back.

Then Nate was there jogging beside him. Nate looked older, aged in a way Craig hadn't. His head was clean-shaven. "Craig oversimplifies," Nate commented. "As he also makes it more complicated."

"Riddles," Dan said. "Thanks. You always knew what I didn't need at all."

A tiny smile spread and relaxed, and Nate kept his eyes forward. "It's like when Longer used to tell us we chose the pain," he said. "Remember that?"

Dan suddenly remembered, or thought he remembered, itching to speak up that time, during that particular pep talk. He'd felt so strongly that he was never choosing pain as much as was embracing life. Feeling his blood move.

Nate replied as if Dan had spoken this out loud. "You're right, when he called it pain, what he meant was embracing death. Not what you meant. But the thing is, they're the same. You're both right. Choosing pain is choosing death, true. But understanding suffering is being alive."

And after that for a few seconds there was still the sound of his feet, a rhythmic pat and scratch in gravel, until Dan realized it was only his own steps he was hearing. He'd been talking to air again.

Once, he'd gone on a hunting weekend with Deb's father Bernard and her brother Bradley. Their cabin was dark, with tiny windows, and smelled like old wood. The first afternoon, Dan went for a hike alone.

"About time," Bernard said when he got back. He scowled when Dan hesitated at the door with his muddy boots. "It's no mansion," Bernard said. "Don't embarrass it with pretending."

Dan tracked in a few steps, to the nearest chair. Bradley was nowhere to be seen.

Bernard had been oiling a rifle. He lifted it to gaze wistfully down the lightless tube of its barrel, then put it aside. "Who'd you say kept all those hunting cabins? Hemingway?"

"He liked to get away," Dan said, pulling off his boots.

"Got that right," Bernard muttered. He put the gun down and lifted a small glass of something copper-colored. "Sometimes," Bernard said, tilting his little glass, "in life, you may think, you've come to a real bad room." He stretched the side of his mouth in a yawn, drank from his glass, and continued. "But it's only one room. Outside that room—"

A gunshot echoed off across the lake, followed by the honks of frightened geese.

Bernard shook his head and finished his drink.

Now, alongside him, men Dan didn't recognize flickered in and out in between the trees. Their skin was the color of clay, and he heard them snickering, "He's in a bad room." They kept pace effortlessly, without moving their legs. They giggled and elbowed each other.

"It's his body slowing him down," one observed. "Remember how slow we ran? Back when we had bodies?"

"Wait," the other said abruptly. "Do you think he can hear us?"

Alarmed, Dan stared straight ahead, and thought of nothing but moving his legs.

"Hah!" came the other voice, and derisive laughter. "You're saying this dork can see through time?"

"It's not time," the first voice insisted. "It's geometry. All he has to do is look at right angles to the right angles. And there we are."

The other disintegrated into a barrage of snickers. "Bullshit. You're so full of shit."

"No," the first insisted. "You know, there's more ways to be parallel, than two lines."

"OK, OK then, let's try it."

Dan felt his attention drawn to the side, and he was in a clearing. There, the men with clay skin stood with their arms crossed behind a folding table with some half-full paper cups. One held out a cup to Dan, but as he reached out, the man withdrew it, snorted loudly from his throat, and spat into the cup. Smiling meanly then with a mouthful of black and graying teeth, he threw the cup in Dan's face. It felt like nothing, just like a splash of room-temperature seltzer that evaporated before it touched him, leaving his skin dry.

The other man leaned forward to swipe a finger down Dan's arm, leaving a smooth gray streak. He lifted his fingertip to his lips to taste, and said, "OK. So, he can see us a bit."

"He'll become one of us, then?"

"No," the other answered immediately, then reconsidered. "Well. Never one of us, exactly. But the land will still receive him. It will swallow his corpse."

"It receives everyone."

"Hm," the other answered wistfully. "And the lichens filigree our bones, yes."

"He will move better then. With the weight of his body lifted off him."

"He's not going so well now though."

"No."

The thread of his narrative was unraveling, he felt it, and it took concentrated effort to stop his mind from wandering. He knew what drove this mental diffusion, a dearth of glucose to his brain compounded by lack of sleep, and it was almost fascinating to passively sit back and watch his awareness disintegrate. Associations from real life and dreams alike bubbled to the surface and evaporated.

From nowhere, he remembered his last chocolate carbohydrate gel—had he eaten it already, had it fallen from his pocket over any of the last hours? Frantically, he slapped along the back of his hip, his mouth and stomach and brain already craving the thick briny too-sweet chocolate paste, and he felt the preliminary heartbreak already if it should be gone. But there it was, the only weight left in his pockets, tapping against his leg so long he'd become attuned to its presence.

His hands trembled, but he managed to tear off the foil top, which was sharp against his chapped lips. In the cold, the gel had thickened, and he squeezed out just a bit of it, like the last toothpaste from the tube. As it touched his tongue, his mind screamed *Food* and a wave of dizziness almost knocked him over. It stuck in his mouth and he couldn't make spit and then as he tried to swallow, his stomach revolted and he did hit the ground, his knees jolting to the gravel as he dry heaved nothing and then nothing again. Only after he spat bile could he take a deep breath and look up again.

So, he thought. He'd forgotten, and waited too long. Unable to stomach any nutrients at all, for now at least, there was nothing left for him but to wait in the empty movie theater of his unwinding mind, watching as increasingly insensible images flitted through an untended projector.

Standing up again, brushing gravel from his knees, he resumed moving and tried, just experimentally, to commandeer control of his brain for a bit. Reaching, he came up with a few images, all of them a step removed from the authentic. Susy's birthday, the desktop image from his laptop: he could see the picture itself, with yellow and green frosted cake and balloons, yellow frosting on his daughter's cheek; her nose had needed wiping. He couldn't remember a single thing outside the picture's frame, though.

Had his memories, his perceptions, ever been completely present? Was he just so nutritionally and electrolytically deprived now, or had there been something really always absent in him, a broken deficiency within his brain? He recalled last spring, picking Susy up from daycare and not recognizing her among the half-dozen toddlers in the play area, because Deb had dressed her in clothes he wasn't expecting. He'd never admitted that moment of guilty disorientation, and his impulse was to cover and fake it, let no one read it in him. It was like some pattern recognition ability had never properly functioned for him.

Other times, he had jolted unexpectedly at the sight of an unknown woman striding across the lawn outside his window, failing to recognize Deb just because she was not where he had expected her to be. These incidents made a pattern, and now, when he was this stripped of himself, he was unable to ignore the huge emotional blind spots that haunted his everyday life.

There were the things you were supposed to do, losing yourself in the wonder of watching your kids sleep, the innocent breaths rising and falling; he'd only, in those moments, been conscious of escaping the room quietly, not popping the loose floorboard that would wake Susy up. Or staring into your loved one's eyes, though he and Deb had never gone in for that kind of sentimental schlock.

He had to do better. If he made it out of this, he'd pay attention, he thought. There was all this he was missing, and it made him feel not a good person. His every day was this glaring series of sins of omission. Oblivious as a parent. And Deb, their whole marriage a history of things done and undone to each other, or for the wrong reasons.

Maybe what he lacked was like patience, he thought, or bravery, things that with unflagging willpower and concentration, could be achieved synthetically. He wondered if he would remember any of this or it would be forgotten as conveniently as a drowning man's resolutions to God.

But if he could hold onto this understanding of himself as a fundamentally flawed, admittedly deluded person — if he could preserve this conception, sequester it away somewhere in his shattered body or sheared-raw mind, protect it through re-entry into his daily life, then maybe he could address it like anything else: a single step, a single failing, at a time. He could do it. He knew at least that about himself. Send the order, execute, and accept it if it hurt.

He'd missed chances. Waited too long on things, it was true. Like his last gel, the last edible thing he carried, which he was mildly surprised to find still in his hand. Competing waves of hunger and revulsion wracked him instantly. Overpowering a nausea that began behind his back teeth and shot all the way down, he squeezed a little more chocolate goo between his lips and fought to neither taste it nor swallow. That worked, and he took a little more. If he couldn't eat maybe he could at least hold it under his tongue, absorb a bit of sustenance from it that way.

When he'd squeezed the last bit from the packet, he tore the plastic down the middle and placed the two halves on his tongue. He remembered the last gel he'd eaten, hours ago, yesterday—without thinking, he would have folded and put the sticky wrapper back in his other pocket. It was a pretty ingrained habit, from running in so many nature preserves and parks, not that the worry of littering was anything but ridiculous out here. He brushed his pocket and, yes, there it still was.

A tiny pearl of brown goo still clung to the wrapper, gummy and half-coagulated. Carefully, he split this last packet in half, fileting it, and traded it for the one in his mouth. Then he began staggering forward again.

With every breath, the plastic rattled like a husk against his teeth.

*All mammals exhibit similar end-stage metabolism in response to catastrophic disease or injury. The brain interprets hypoxia, muscle breakdown, and starvation and assumes that massive energy expenditure is required for survival, and releases endorphins, enkephalins, and endocannabinoids, all natural painkillers.*

*Endorphins and enkephalins bind to receptors within the central nervous system neurons, to hold more dopamine in the synapses. This alleviates perceived pain. Beta-endorphin in particular binds to µ-opioid receptors, the neurological targets of morphine and other opiates, which all alleviate pain and produce euphoria. Euphoria from any cause, incidentally, enacts over the same chemical pathways in the brain, profoundly influences behavior, and is potentially addictive.*

Fugue states intruded on his waking time. He felt himself returning from absences, detached half-dreaming states when his eyes saw white and he had no memory of physical sensations. He re-entered himself mid-step, just about to put his weight on a flat stone that looked as secure as any other. Instantly he recognized it as the Judas rock, the inevitability, the stone placed here just for him. It shifted under his foot, throwing him sideways, and he was unable to stop his full weight from bearing down through his buckled ankle.

As he both felt and heard a loud pop, he knew this was the moment toward which his whole life had been magnetically pulled. A sparkling revelation of new pain shot up like stop-motion lightning, tickling in his brain before the hyperextended tendon had even snapped back. It was a relief knowing how it would end for him now; all of this he thought before hitting the ground.

He took off his shoe and peeled down his sock to assess the injury. Gently, cradling his bare foot in both hands, he turned it, cataloging the directions it would still bend, and saving for last the one in which he knew it would not, with the foot turning under and the tendon in his ankle flexing obversely. Very gingerly he held it at just the point of tension, causing twinges of pain to shoot up the side of his leg in time with his pulse. The pain did not diminish as he held it this way.

With just his fingertips he pressed where it hurt the worst. No bones felt broken, which meant all was not finished for him, and he still could not honorably lie down and wait to die.

The flesh was already spongy, where there were no structures but tendon and bone. Awed, he watched as the swelling grew and a bruise purpled before his eyes, each push of his pulse seeming to inflate it like a bicycle pump slowly filling a tire.

Although he knew this was the worst thing, letting it swell, it was still a minute or two longer before he could tear his eyes away and move fast. When he did break into action, his hands moved clumsily, and he could not think what he was reaching for. The little roll of duct tape, he thought; but that was in his pack, lost miles ago and washed down some nameless stream. His hands clasped jerkily at his empty shoe, and it felt like operating one of those claw games in a coin-op arcade.

His junior year of high school, midway through the track season, his father had given him a faded shoebox. "I don't know if you'd want to use these or anything," he told Dan. "They're probably all old and stiff. Ready to fall apart. Like me."

Dan had been doing homework, algebra or something with both numbers and letters, at the kitchen table. He hadn't moved to take the box from his father's hands, and waited until he set it on the table. *Tiger Marathons*, the box read. He looked up, questioning and annoyed.

"They did all right for me," his dad said, oblivious or pretending to be.

He'd been champ at something in high school, Dan forgot what, and had been promising for a while in college, until some injury. Or maybe it wasn't an injury, it was getting married, graduating, his first teaching job. Maybe he'd never meant to give it up for good, and kept those old shoes on purpose, for a while, at least until Dan was born.

His father smiled. "Feel how light," he said, taking one shoe out of the box and tossing it in the air. It was a dull, faded red, with white stripes. "Terrible support, back then." Dan had never asked if he'd been planned, but knew it had all happened at once, the same year: his dad finished school, was working some factory job, his parents got married, he was born. It would have been a terrible decision to make on purpose. And he was an only child. His father mused, "I'd get, I remember, road dirt on my socks, the soles were so thin."

"Thanks," Dan said. His father waited. "I'll try them later, OK?" He was still in his school clothes, baggy jeans. And he didn't even have socks on.

"I really think you're just about there, Danny," his father said. "You're getting up on top of it, really rising onto your toes when you finish. The biomechanics are coming together for you." He dropped his hand awkwardly on Dan's shoulder. "You could be strong," he said, and walked out.

The shoes stayed in the back of his closet until Halloween, when he permanent-markered an old T-shirt into an Oregon jersey, penciled on a cheesy mustache, and went to a party dressed as Pre. It was a costume no one got, and the shoes, a half size too small, pinched his feet all night.

On the gravel road, his ankle slowly swelling, Dan held one of those ancient Marathons in his hand. It really did feel feather-light. When he tugged one of the laces, it disintegrated between his fingers, dissolving like the scales from a moth's wings. And then the whole shoe vanished, a puff of dust that coated his hand. For a moment he wondered how his sad heavy trail shoe had gotten there instead, on the ground beside him.

Then he came back to himself. He'd have to walk now, and would keep falling even more, this injury begging new injuries the longer he put weight on it. If he had tape, he could work wonders to brace and wrap his ankle, but he had nothing to work with. Clenching his jaw and aiming, he jammed his foot back into the shoe, where it fit tighter than before. He ground his molars hard as a sensation bright and crunchy as broken glass crackled all the way up through his hip and spine. Closing his eyes, he took a deep breath and held it, wound the loose laces twice in each hand, and then pulled hard, lacing the rigid trail shoe's upper as tight as it would go.

So Nate told me to tell you this thing," Hughes said, and it was like they'd never missed a workout since Dan's last season of cross. "From like the 'Samurai Code' or some shit.

You know how he is. Anyway, it's, if I don't fuck it up: 'Go into battle hoping to live, and you will most surely die. Only if you are determined to die, by chance you may survive.'"

"Ha," Dan coughed. "So what's that supposed to mean?" By which he meant, why am I hearing this now.

Instead of the laughing answer he expected, Hughes turned to him sternly. Dan could see now that his shoulders were bobbing to a faster pace, a runner's pace, and his feet were sometimes not quite brushing the top of the ground, other times dipping gently through it. The effect was ridiculous. "It means commit already, dumbass," he said, "It's not like you're getting out of this whole. You know that by now, right? If you don't quit dicking around and commit, you're not coming out alive at all."

"Thanks for the cheery note," Dan muttered, adding, "Asshole."

"I mean it," Hughes said. "What are you saving it for, right?" When he disappeared, his white-striped running shoes faded last.

Dan thought back to his initial vision of rescue, of shouting and waving down some logging crew or hunting party or even a search detail already on the lookout for him. He'd imagined relaxing finally, exhausted but hale, under blankets in some rescue cabin somewhere as a Mountie brought him hot cocoa; he'd seen himself insisting on the accuracy of his coordinates when no one could believe what he'd done.

That vision, he saw now, had been bolstered with a bravado maybe he'd never really felt, ever. Two days and two nights of stark reality had burned that away; he was raw, egoless, frantic for help in any form. All the ideas he'd had of proving something had boiled off and left just a pathetic hope to survive, salvation he'd accept on any terms, no longer caring how broken, how beaten it revealed him.

## Seventeen

Susan remembers her mother breathing slowly, leaning against a tree to support her injured leg, and watching the wrecked airplane. Nothing moved, and she asked her mother what she was watching for, but it was like she didn't hear. She held the gun far away from her body, and the whole forest held its breath. Pale low sunlight lit its metal barrel.

It seems unlikely, in retrospect, that her mother would have let her be so near at that moment. But the fireball that followed is one of Susan's clearest memories, and also unshakably dreamlike. The gun fired with a little hollow pop, more like a weak firecracker, and a flash of sunlight sailed slowly into the hole torn in the plane. Nothing happened for a moment.

Then, heat. Like hot breath from an open oven, with a wet chemical smell. Her mother's arm around her chest, lifting her like a toy doll or a piece of luggage, and she remembered her mother's hurt leg and thought they'd fall. But then they were flying. They were birds and they were on fire, lighting the treetops beneath them. They were two flying flaming birds, and child-Susan was angry that her mother had always known how to do this and had simply been holding out, but then it was beautiful and her throat was full of cool air and she forgave her. They were flying and never came down, until the next minute when they were in the helicopter.

Sometimes she feels a little like she never woke up from that dream, unsure she completely exists, or where exactly she is on the impossibly thin membrane between what really happened, and what might as well have.

## Eighteen

A clattering shape materialized above him, and Dan flinched from the shadow of a big bird. He flashed on, unbidden, the lone goose that had whistled over his head so many years ago, working so desperately hard he could hear the grunt of breath powering each individual wingbeat. He wondered if that goose had ever caught up, earned anything for all its trying so hard, and where it was now. Surely that goose was long dead. Surely all of its flock and its V were dead by now.

The sky above became interlocking shapes of white and black and dun, all birds, all the birds that had ever been, layered to create a smooth domed ceiling above his head. Their shape reformed as a deafening noise, and the noise exploded into a helicopter, low enough to fill his vision and shatter the sky with its individual spinning rotors so close above he could count them. The thing tore overhead, moving faster than he'd imagined possible. He'd never seen a helicopter tilted so far forward, hadn't known they could even fly that way, nearly more vertical than horizontal, like an extreme ground-strafing military maneuver.

He was too dumbstruck to do anything but stare openmouthed after it. Then a choking rose in his throat and his eyelids began to burn, and he dropped to his knees in the dirt, like that scene from every old war movie. He might as well have been passed over by an angel of the Lord, terrible in its glory, instead of just an earthly machine made of metal and parts.

He felt an existential dyslexia, between the doomed goose all those years ago, and the helicopter, and himself here unseen in the middle of the path. There was a congruence, two ends of time he couldn't imagine ever matching, now mated.

He wondered what miracle had occurred, whether someone had seen Deb's flare or spotted the wreckage, but right away, his relief evaporated again. Because Susy and Deb were not saved either: unless he'd traveled in some huge circle, he'd come too far. No rescue chopper here could possibly be for them.

And the second the whop of its blades died in his ears, Dan suspected he had hallucinated the helicopter. Now the empty sky hung, mocking him. He could picture the call sign on the helicopter's belly, and the electric zigzag letter Q insignia of Hydro-Québec—that was too specific for his mind to have made up. Then he remembered where he'd seen the electric Q emblem: through the rust on the rear panel of the abandoned truck, beneath the powerlines, the wrecked truck he'd superstitiously never looked inside.

He rubbed an itch by his temple and his skin felt sandy; he squinted and rubbed his fingertips together, scattering tiny salt crystals. He looked down: his forearms were traced and marbled with the stuff, and his dark tech shirt showed elaborate maps and coastlines of evaporated sweat. Fractals blossomed the hems of his shorts as if he had been dusted with snowflakes, or started to mold.

Salt. He scratched a fingernail down his arm, then popped it in his mouth. Then he had the back of his hand to his mouth, gnawing against his carpal bones and working up the wrist.

Metabolically, everything good had already happened for him. His second winds had been done with a day ago. This morning, when the sky first began to lighten, he'd felt a little bump of energy, a brief respite between crippling periods of fatigue.

Now he was drained, wrung out. His legs echoed with tiredness and his ankle throbbed sickly with every step. He was able to walk with a slightly uneven limp, but any faster was out of the question. Now and then he glanced to the side of the road in case a crutch-sized branch might magically appear, but it wouldn't have helped much anyway. He had no energy left for anything but this plodding, one-two, lurching forward march.

A fifth wind, he thought, that was all he needed. Or a fifteenth. Only that. The spells of exhaustion were getting longer, and he imagined how it must be to drown. To keep swimming, holding yourself up, until the will falters to drive all that relentless physical churning. To swallow water and stop resisting.

Shivers wracked his shoulders, and he wondered how long it had been since he'd last felt OK, any passing shadow of not-pain. His body was closing in, rationing, getting stingy with endorphins and dopamine and the drugs that would allow him to go on. Hypothermia victims, he had read, actually feel flushed and too warm by the end, and in documented cases have stripped off all their clothing and thrown themselves in the snow, as the hypothalamus and all the body's thermal regulative mechanisms go haywire. And those in the end stages of starvation have described finally a lack of hunger or even desire for food, accompanied by overpowering tranquility and mental clarity.

He wondered what form his relief would take, which bodily system would fail first, giving up and sending out false signals of comfort. There was no documentation, as far as he knew, on what gives out first in a human being running himself to death.

He waited and waited for that next fifth wind, that sip of air over cold waves, expecting nothing yet still hoping with each next step, each next step. It never comes. It never comes. It never comes.

*Metabolically, running a marathon or longer presents immense problems. Skeletal muscles need glucose to drive the body forward, but after sixteen or so miles, glycogen deposits within the liver and muscles are depleted and the liver must begin to juggle biochemical chainsaws to generate fuel and keep running. Under the starvation that takes place after glycogen depletion, adipose tissue starts to release triglycerides into the blood. Liver cells break these down into glycerol, which is converted into glucose by gluconeogenesis, and fatty acids, which are sent to the mitochondria to be broken down as fuel.*

*Since the brain consistently demands glucose, however, and since the muscles still require exorbitant glucose for power output and speed, the liver must find more compounds to convert into fuel. It is chemically unable to convert fat directly into glucose, so liver cells process fatty acids to drive the conversion of mid-level metabolites. These are important intermediates in many other biochemical pathways within the body. To replace these intermediates, liver cells begin reprocessing amino acids from the blood, broken down from actin and myosin filaments in skeletal muscles. So, once the liver has used up its glycogen, it begins to process fat for energy almost exclusively, while breaking down the protein machinery in skeletal muscle cells to produce glucose, ultimately needed to drive those same muscles and maintain forward progress. The body eats its own muscle to live.*

*This is untenable. As cycles progressively fail, cells starve and die in apocalyptic waves, intracellular walls rupture, wastes and toxins accumulate, nerves misfire, and whole systems go offline. Biological entropy increases dramatically. It is a process indistinguishable from death.*

It was like the few times he had struggled to keep himself awake behind the wheel, when the road changed to other pictures somewhere between his eyes and his brain, and he found himself asleep with his eyes open, not comprehending what he saw until the noise of the tires over rumble strips jarred him awake. This pulse-pounding terror, the realization that he had almost crashed, should have boiled off his haze and kept him awake for a few minutes, but then the next thing he knew, he'd wake up and be almost dying again. Now, even with his eyes open, shadows under trees took on obscure personalities and dream-significance.

The idea took shape that he would keep running, or walking, or limping forward, no matter what, just like the car kept moving with him asleep at the wheel. He saw that even death would not mean stopping, in that it was just another threshold he had never crossed before. Even when his biological activity ceased, when his blood quit hauling oxygen and his brain stopped registering it, he would not be released from forward progress.

Death could look acceptable if it meant rest, but he saw now it was just another step in that endless progression by which all things just get harder. Seeing death as only another wall, another room, was to realize it made no difference which side of that wall he was on. It became increasingly plausible that he was already dead, and traversing this empty wholly uninhabited landscape eternally was in fact his hell or purgatory.

Beside him then, he saw Nate was running in some kind of flip-flops or huaraches, and Dan's heart fell for a second. He'd thought Nate was too sensible for that particular craze. When he looked again, though, he couldn't see Nate's feet, just a blur where he faded out below the knees.

"'A warrior,'" Nate quoted, "'should be able to perform one final action with complete certainty, even should his head be separated from his body.' So what do you make of that shit?"

Dan wheezed an affirmation. "It is horseshit," he said.

Nate agreed, waving them past this point. "Of course," he said. "But how many miles do you think you're going to cover, dead?"

"All of 'em," Dan muttered, keeping his head down, focusing a meter in front of his shambling feet.

Nate laughed. "OK, good answer. If it were a koan. Or a riddle. Which it isn't. What it is, is an illustration. Of commitment. And, I guess, muscle memory, you can call it. The idea is, one gesture. I don't think it applies much longer than that, you know? Headless chicken jerks a while. Goes a few more steps." Dan hated how Nate had so much breath for lecturing right now. "But I'm here to tell you your body's not going to keep moving, with no one at the wheel."

"It's been working," Dan huffed, "so far."

Nate said nothing, just emanated a strained, superior silence.

Dan frowned obstinately for a minute. "Maybe," he said finally. "It's when you define 'death.'"

"What do you mean?" Nate sounded uncharacteristically alarmed.

"Maybe it's not when he's beheaded," he said, then took several more deep breaths to recover from the exertion it took to speak. "Maybe it doesn't end," he said, "until his body finishes," gasp, "what it started."

"All right," Nate said airily, as if suddenly bored of the conversation. Picking up pace, he loped off ahead of Dan easily, dumb-ass sandals flapping again at his heels. "That's fine. See you when you get there," he called back over his shoulder.

Alone again, Dan thought how every race or workout he'd ever done had a defined finish. Calmly, he began squinting at the ground, evaluating one patch after the next for the best spot to lie down and die. Each seemed more right than the next, until he had to stop moving, stand still, squeeze his eyes shut and turn his face upward.

A puff of wind blew by his cheek and he felt his knees wobble. The soles of his feet throbbed, and his ankle ached sickly. He stood still for what felt like a long time. Experimentally, he tried to move his leg, to take a step forward, or not even a step, just flexing his left hip and lifting his knee. The message formed in his brain, was sent, and then either did not arrive or was refused: not even a muscle twitched in response. So, he thought. So.

Finally, he thought, he had broken the machine. Impossible, he'd thought at times, but there it was: his body would no longer obey his commands. He'd beaten it. He felt neither joy nor despair nor anything really identifiable. He thought, he'd atomized his self. Obliteration, this was it. This was what had been waiting, the destination drawing him, all along. He'd dismantled all his mechanisms, deconstructed himself beyond any hope of coherent reassembly, pried every single piece apart to determine what drove it. He'd gotten there—and now, what was it he had ever hoped to learn?

"You will want to let the pain go," Longer said, "let it rise from your body like a balloon. You'll want to think of it in that backwards way, forgetting that you are the balloon. Without the pain, with nothing to hold you down, you will float away."

His old coach's voice did not sound like him, and Dan did not trust the imposter.

Then his father was there again, holding out to him, always offering, that pair of antique Tiger Marathons in their beat-up box. "Danny," he said, "those heavy things you've been training in. It's time for a change, a change. You're ready for something light—for racing, you want something light. No heel. No support. No extra weight. It's like being weightless...like the ground pushing you back up and forward, from every step."

Dan remembered sitting on a porch somewhere, at a party he must have gone to in college. A black-haired girl, her shining skin tattooed with birds, said, "If you don't enjoy running, why are you still on the team?" He wondered what had become of that girl, where she was now. The sky above him echoed the lines of her birds, and the clouds appeared lit from within, just like the smooth skin of her neck and shoulder.

# Nineteen

In the helicopter, Deb held Susy stiffly to her; the seats were not made for a small child, and the whole craft leaned forward in what seemed like perpetual acceleration. Even with the sliding door closed, the noise of the engine and whopping rotors overhead was deafening, and rushing air swirled through the space.

Susy was cranky with cold still, after the day and the night and the day in the tent. Hungry, too, but for something warm, and Deb couldn't get her to take more than a bite of the sawdusty nutrition bars, and the last of her fruit snacks had been that morning's breakfast. The royal blue blanket imprinted with a fleur-de-lis and the words Sûreté du Québec was scratchy at her throat, and she pulled it tighter around Susy with her free hand without looking. Her leg throbbed every time she shifted Susy's weight on her lap.

Back at the crash site, shivering in the tent, before Deb had finally gotten the flare gun to work, firing it into the wreck, the round guttering then catching finally and igniting more fuel than she'd thought had spilled, immolating the dead pilot she couldn't have moved anyway, flinging the baggie of her father's remains at the flames weakly and it blowing back at her from the heat, the plastic melting though and the ashes hitting the snow in a sad clump—before then, before she'd started the black smoke roiling in a twisting column into the sky, before the helicopter—Susy had sat staring out the tent flap all that second day, asking, "Is Daddy coming back yet?"

And she'd answered, not yet, not yet.

"Well when will he?"

"I don't know, sweetie," she'd told her. "I don't know."

Susy squirmed in her lap now, and Deb looked down, quickly brushing a loose lock of hair from her daughter's eyes and then snapping her gaze back up, guiltily, staring over the ground below. Hundreds of feet below. Flat marshes and scrubby forest flashed by, brown mud and white snow. She thought she saw a scrap of color—was it Dan's red tech, was that the shirt he had been wearing when he left? "La bas," she said, yelling over Susy's head, over the roar of the rotors.

The pilot looked back, shook his head. Shrugged quickly in apology. There had been no search, no report they were even missing, and the smoke from the burning wreck had first been attributed to lightning, a naturally occurring fire in the wilderness. Only after some kind of marker, an SOS apparently indicating their position, had been spotted from the air by a survey crew for Hydro-Québec, had the rescue helicopter been dispatched. It was getting late, and they had neither time nor fuel to mount a further search today.

"Maudit—!" she yelled. "Merde! Retournez-vous. Faites demi-tour!"

The pilots exchanged a quick glance, then a nod. The world lurched sickeningly to the right and dropped, and she clutched hard at Susy's shoulders, never mind the belt around them both. Below, straight out the window, trees and rocks and dirt swung past, and she strained her eyes to take in as much of the scrolling scene as she could. Nothing stood out, no movement, not a speck of manmade color. Anyone moving or waving on the ground could not be missed from this height, and from time to time the late sun threw red or orange glints on patches of snow that disappeared when her angle changed.

"Encore?" the pilot asked. A dark visor hid the top half of his face, but she could tell he was impatiently humoring her. "Nous n'avons pas de," he began, but Deb stopped him with a shake of her head. The craft steadied, rose, and tilted forward again.

"Mommy, what does that mean," Susy demanded. "La bah. Mo-dee."

She caught herself, forced herself to be calm. Absently, she raised her hand to smooth the same lock of flaxen hair buffeting about the girl's temple, and as soon as she took her fingertips away, the wind plucked it back loose, set it flying and fretting at the girl's head again; Susy waved, as if shooing a gnat or mosquito. "Nothing, sweetie," Deb said then. "It doesn't mean anything, don't worry."

"Demain," the pilot assured her again. Tomorrow, a search would begin from the SOS marker, expanding outward in circles; they knew how to do such things, and if her husband were alive there, they would find him. Although she believed they would look, she detected some skepticism, too, a reluctance to believe her story: the SOS, accurate in distance and heading, had been well over a hundred kilometers away.

"Demain, il ne sera pas là," she said quietly.

"Pardon?"

She shook her head and did not reply. He had left the marker and kept moving, she knew. Already, by now, he could be anywhere.

Below them, the landscape scrolled by, featureless and unending.

# Twenty

Of course Dan understood, had been realizing for a long time on a level gradually approaching consciousness, that his elaborate flash-forward might not ever come to pass, not just in his impossibly projected level of detail but at all, in any way that would bring the three of them out of this alive and together. With no means of going back and retooling now, though, he returned to that unlikely construct, the same depleted coping mechanism. Grown-Susan's edges were wearing thin, in her implausible blind, but he cast her forward again anyway:

She makes lists, weighs things she can quantify against everything she can't. Racing comes easily for her, but she knows intellectually how that ends, betting everything on the body. Instead of committing to the training camp now, she could spend the summer banding tanagers in the Andes, and work toward a career tracking the migrations and short bright lives of winged things. She could study their fragile beauty for her lifetime, or she could be weightless herself, and burn bright now.

Below her, one of the avocets hurries busily along the line where the water meets the sand, totally unaware of its own tiny beating heart, the handful of warmth it cups against the cold wet air. The little bird could be literally anywhere, but is here.

"Either one of us would have died to keep you safe," Deb will tell her later, when she comes down from the blind. Dan sees them sitting together in a car, something large and black and square and indifferent to any kind of terrain. Deb rests both her hands on the wheel, a fine pull to the lines around her eyes, the only way she's visibly aged against a thousand lonely gravities. "You can't understand what that's like," she says to Susan, and tells her that's another reason she can't throw herself away.

"Don't worry, ma," Susan will breathe. She's decided, she'll say, telling a lie as true and old as time. Everyone only does what they have to do, after all; there's never really such a thing as letting go.

Here is where Dan wants Deb's tired eyes to warm, and for her to say, "He wanted to come back to you more than anything, you know," and for Susan to say, she knows.

The scene shudders and flashes with light, a filmstrip slipping off its reel.

## Twenty-one

Tilting his head back, Dan smiled a little, causing his upper lip to split. It didn't hurt at all, it was only a pulling apart and then a warm wetness, a taste of salt and iron. Reflexively his tongue reached toward the moisture, and his eyes opened on the sky, and on bare trees, and on this cruel, unending, impossibility of a road. And across the road, one other thing, a horizontal barrier that was not a downed tree, not when the muzzy sunlight shone off it like metal.

From somewhere, out of the depths of his numbness, echoed up one more emotion: despair, that he would have to investigate this final hallucination. For a second he believed he was capable of not doing it. Unwilled, though, crazily, he found himself a prisoner inside a body stumbling forward. Inwardly, with the part of him that could still laugh, he laughed, without making a sound apart from his rasping breath. Patience, the virtue that had always most eluded him, was his penance now. He'd learn it biologically, if no other way. His flaw was partly a lack of confidence, and partly a self-destructive impulse, and he'd inherited it honestly, from his father, from Longer, from all kinds of botched models. At least it would stop with him now, breaking the cycle before he could pass the trait on.

He walked slowly, limping, no longer in a hurry. Presently the structure ahead of him revealed itself as a gate, even though it felt like he was making no progress toward it. After a very long time he stood a matter of steps from it, and the angle of the daylight above seemed to have changed not at all.

It was a simple gate, a metal arm hinged at one post and chained at the other. Beyond it, the road continued unchanged around a bend. A metal plate was mounted to the center of the gate, blank on his side. Resigned, he trudged around to see what it read. In reflective paint, like a highway sign, was lettered a single word: "Fermé." Brilliant, he thought, magnificent: closed. Everything he'd been working for, his whole life, had all been fermé.

In the middle of this, though, impossibly, he thought he heard voices. He shook his head and cuffed his ears like a dog with fleas. The auditory hallucinations were the most unnerving. The sound came again, though, and was not inside his head. It had a direction.

Grumbling, shuffling, he hurried toward the bend in the road. He saw himself as if from outside, and what he would look like to someone else now. A dirty man lurching toward them as if detaching from a painted landscape, unshaven, crying hoarsely, his clothes stained with mud and sweat and filth, his shins black and bumpy with clotted blood.

He imagined a hiker turning from him and running, or a startled hunter shouldering his rifle and mercifully, almost lovingly, placing a bullet between his eyes. He felt dehumanized, deserving no better than to be humanely dispatched, put down like an animal.

The voices ahead grew more distinct and waned again, like a scene glimpsed through filtering leaves. And between the thin trunks of trees, he thought he saw a glint of metal. He didn't imagine a search party, surely he had come too far from the crash site for anyone to look for him here, but still—people. Human beings. Not a quarter mile away.

Just a thin stretch of trees separated him from the shape of a big SUV, and movement, human movement, but he would take the slightly longer way around, and not risk leaving the trail now, in his weakened state. This was the most dangerous time. He thought of shipwreck survivors who gave up too soon, thinking they were saved, drowning within sight of rescue. A wrong choice could still make him one of those victims. He had time. He had time.

Clearing the trees, though he was still two hundred yards away, he saw a family, two adults and a child, no, two kids. And what kind of sense did that make? He'd been expecting hunters, wildlife management, maybe workers for the power company—not a family, with children, tourists picnicking at the end of the world. He thought he recognized the car; it seemed likely they were not real. He caught scraps of speech, though, that sounded like French, and the vision in front of him did not shimmer like a mirage or evaporate. He thought: "Aidez"? Deb, he thought—oh, Deb would know. Trying to call out, his throat only wheezed. He would have to go to them, just a little closer.

Then his tortured heart jumped at the slam of a car door. They could be going. His vision faded and he blinked, and saw one door opening again. A child, a little girl, getting out, he imagined to pick up a missed piece of trash. He could not be hallucinating this now; he had to believe it, and move faster.

The father and the mother came partly around the side of the car then, and the father said something to the girl. The woman was turned away, and he didn't know if it looked like Deb or some other woman, and the kids were only motion and voices, but Dan felt strongly that the guy he saw was him, and that the family on this stage before him represented a future he had to claim or give up on. And, they were leaving. As he shuffled and waved one arm in the air, the woman was leaning into the back seat, buckling a child in.

Here it was, all to be determined by whether he could cover this last small distance, a hundred yards of smooth gravel road after everything else, in time or too slowly. And he was too far off, he had no movement left, he was simply depleted. He couldn't go another inch. Maybe another man, in better shape, could do it. Or, himself when he was younger, and stronger. A hundred yards, a hundred miles. He stood still, swayed, and decided to sit down.

Then, hating it, he thought: an inch. A step. Another one. The only way left for it to never always get worse. Here was the singularity, the overlap of *never* and *always*. What he required was impossible, but still, nothing was going to happen for him just because he needed it to.

And unbelievably then, he felt it, the same stupid old miracle firing up again, the one foot in front of the other, the muscles' familiar consecutive lift and stretch and lock and contract and release and repeat, and because this thing was still there when all else had deserted him he almost cried with relief, even though it was killing him, literally killing him with every step.

The SUV's engine turned over. If the family in it was not real but only an idea, it was one Dan wanted as much as life itself.

Even as he broke into a run again, he felt every cell of muscle that it cannibalized, the full price it cost as his body mercilessly ate itself for fuel. It was a sublimation, a chemical transubstantiation, matter into energy, self into motion. Abstract thoughts of immolating monks in Asia. A calmness, a happiness that, momentarily, all would finally be decided.

Every day, he thought, our bodies make decisions that our minds cannot. The mind gives up, when the flesh has so much left. He felt an unlocking, a permission slip handed finally over from the deep primal part of his brain. Every muscle, use everything, reach and pull with every knuckle of every toe. He had forgotten this, the adrenaline rush flailing abandon of a final sprint to the finish. The sheer velocity, running with no other purpose attached. The feeling of being used up, absolute, was virtuous its own way, freeing.

Just a little faster, and he would feel uncatchable, and he saw suddenly, he understood, why Deb did it: if she could only make herself strong enough, she would be immune, body and soul impervious. Being fastest meant never needing anyone or anything again. As if she could become undisappointable.

While she'd been building unassailable walls, all along he'd been working to obliterate himself, because an absence, an erasure, could not be abandoned. He wanted to tell her it didn't matter, and he understood, and it was neither of their faults, they weren't the ones who'd made each other this way. He wanted to tell her, and his father too, he forgave them. His mother. Damage fell like rain on everyone, from simply living in the world. Sure, we all failed each other, and would keep doing it, but wasn't that what it came to? A negotiated contract, an agreement to accept someone's failures, and entrust them with your own? The most terrifying thing was allowing yourself to be someone else's problem. To stop swimming and trust the thrown rope.

Ahead of Dan, the SUV's exhaust coughed as it backed up, toward him. There was no reason for the driver to check his mirror. The vehicle stopped backing and shifted gently into forward gear. The shifting sun shone on its taillights, but no brakes were tapped.

His injury grated, sending him out of his mind with pain on steady pressure, but in motion, when load passed through it and did not stop, it was not so bad. A transient pain, it was worse in anticipation. During each step, the pain only flashed through an instant. True, that instant was like flashbulbs exploding behind his eye sockets, a filmstrip burning to white—but then it passed. It was only an instant, and he could concentrate on the instants in between, burrowing into them and finding a way to live in each one that was pain-free. Each moment in between was large enough to hold a life, and there was no before and after, only a succession of moments.

He imagined a future, some part of him living on without him. If it couldn't be a future of him and Deb with the time they needed for coming back together, he'd settle for Susy grown and smart and strong and into that rarest of things, a child with too many choices. Even if it hadn't happened yet, it was as real as anything else he'd made, and it was beautiful, and he'd clung to it for a time.

He felt light, rising up on his toes and going fast now, the weight of his body falling away. Part of him still wanted to think ahead, of surviving this, but that didn't matter anymore. He might be imagining the family ahead of him, the receding black square of their SUV nothing but an addled dream, flickering in and out of focus as his vision clouded with purple—but that didn't matter either.

It was funny, he thought, all the work and effort he'd put into dying more slowly, while missing so much of life, every day. Running though, right now, he wasn't dead yet—or now, or in the next second, or the next. The lid lifted off his world to one beautiful moment: a flash of a second, a frozen snapshot of a stride.

# Special Thanks

Thanks to: coaches Lisa Klingshirn and Marc Arce at the University of Findlay, for filling in the research gaps in my own running career; Marianna Hofer and all of my colleagues in the English Department and College of Liberal Arts at UF; Brian Whitaker for signing off on the science-y bits, and my cousin Joel Schmid for consultation on the biochem; Mark Carroll for more medical and PT advice; Leanne Lindelof, Allison Lyman, and Amy Drees for help with the French; Walter Muma for research on the James Bay Region, and the nice guards at the Canadian border who wanted to make sure I had adequate survival gear; Ron and Allan Ekstrom for the light aircraft expertise; Sue Angell and Amber Partin and John & Linda Nelson for the advance reads; my mother, Cathy Essinger, for encouraging the writing and believing I could do it, and my wife, Alice, for putting up with me while I actually wrote it; Jim McManus and Carol Anshaw and the faculty at SAIC for showing me how to actually be a writer; Carol Anshaw and Mark Brazaitis and John Morelock for their gracious words for the cover; and every aid station volunteer who's ever given me a cup of warm buggy water at some godforsaken outpost out in the middle of some pitch-black forest.